# Counterpoint

## LAUREN E. RICO

Harmony House Productions

# The Music of Counterpoint

*The musical selections mentioned, both in passing and in detail
throughout this book were carefully selected to complement the
mood of each character and to reflect the tone of the of the story
at that point in time. If you have the opportunity to listen to
some of the selections as you read, I think you'll find the music
adds an entirely new emotional depth and dimension.
Happy reading and happy listening!
-Lauren*

**GRIEG:** PIANO CONCERTO IN A MINOR, OP. 16

**BEETHOVEN:** PIANO SONATA NO. 14 IN C♯ MINOR
OP. 27 *MOONLIGHT*

**DEBUSSY:** PETITE SUITE

**SAINT-SAENS:** DANSE MACABRE (PIANO FOUR-HANDS
ARRANGEMENT)

# CHAPTER 1

# Alexandria

I'm wearing *the* dress. The perfect black dress with the lacy hem that swishes around my ankles as I glide across the well-worn planks of the stage. The rich fabric is dusted with tiny little crystals that catch the overhead lights at every angle, making me shimmer and twinkle like the night sky. The effect is dazzling. I know this because my mother has told me a dozen times, trying to convince me that this really was a better choice than the deep crimson gown I had my heart set on. But that dress wasn't perfect. And anything short of perfection simply will not be tolerated tonight. The night of my Carnegie Hall debut.

I register a swell of applause as the audience greets me. Just as we've rehearsed, I turn my head slightly and acknowledge their welcome with my best smile. My *perfect* smile. It's the smile I've been working on in the mirror for months...not big and cheesy, not small and tight. It's a warm and welcoming smile that conveys confidence, friendliness and professionalism. The smile that goes perfectly with the perfect dress.

I shake hands with the concertmaster, a kindly gentleman old enough to be my grandfather. His hand is warm and soft in mine and he gives it an extra squeeze as he winks at me. An "Atta girl!" from someone who has seen countless others like me come and go over the decades. It's the perfect sentiment, meant to put me at ease. Unfortunately, it doesn't.

When I've reached the Steinway concert grand, I turn to face the house, my left hand resting gently on the smooth black enameled lid of the instrument and I bow. One Mississippi. Two Mississippi. Three Mississippi. There. The perfect amount of time to stay in the downward position before straightening up again. I don't allow my eyes to sharpen focus on the people who fill the rows in front of me. My parents' reputations have ensured that this is a sold-out show. But if I can trick my mind into seeing them as a faceless blob, then I can pretend they're not real. That this is just another no-pressure rehearsal. Unfortunately, it's not.

Once the applause subsides, I slip onto the black tufted bench and face forward. There is no music in front of me because a perfect performance is one that is memorized—unmarred by the presence of a pesky page-turner to distract from my presence. I glance at the podium, where Maestro Bello is facing the orchestra, his head tilted just far enough to the side so that he will see the signal when I give it.

*Well, here goes nothing...*

I take a deep breath and give the slightest of nods. His hands go up briefly as his glance shifts from me to the timpanist poised to play in the back row of the orchestra. Satisfied that the time is right, the Maestro drops his strong hands into the pattern that sets Edward Grieg's *Piano Concerto* into motion.

The sound of the timpani roll is a whisper so soft and subtle that it seems to emerge out of thin air. It builds to an impossibly intense peak in an impossibly brief time, reaching its zenith at the same moment that the piano makes its grand entrance.

My two hands, separated by half an octave, move in tandem as a single, solid unit. They slam down, forming a powerful chord that rings out across the concert hall. It's as if it just hangs there for a second, teetering on the edge of some invisible precipice. And then it tips, tumbling into a cascade of chunky chords, each one as fiery as the first. It is dramatic in its presentation but by no means showy—because this isn't about flourishes and fripperies. Nor will this be one of those concertos where the piano and the orchestra have a genteel dialogue. This is the piano staking its claim right off the bat, controlling the melody and taking the lead. Once I've hit the bottom of the keyboard it's as if the two "unified" hands shatter apart and split up into ten distinct fingers. They start the mad rush, scurrying back up the intervals to the top.

Now, the thing about a downward spiral is that there are a couple of ways it can happen. The first is very, very slowly over a substantial period of time. In this scenario, your divergence from the plan is so subtle as to be nearly undetectable. Little by little you drift off course, totally unaware of the seconds ticking by as they bring you closer and closer to imminent distress. This kind of spiral is survivable, depending on your ability to identify and correct the problem before it's too late.

There's a lot less wiggle room in the second scenario. What often transpires in this instance is that a relatively minor event occurs. Under any other circumstances you would simply recognize the problem, take corrective action and resume without further difficulties. But these aren't just any circumstances. This "minor" event is only one in a chain of minor events that, when threaded together, become a major meltdown. Before you realize it, you've pitched forward at a terrifying angle, picking up speed with each passing moment. It is so violent and so unexpected that all you can do is hang on for dear life, frantically trying to figure out how things could've gone so wrong so fast as alerts shriek around you and the earth rushes up to meet you head-on. This kind of spiral almost always ensures a terminal outcome.

My spiral starts off as a single little bobble. One of my fingers misses a key on the rippling intervals that run back upward. That, in and of itself, isn't an insurmountable error. I can still adjust and correct course, making the error nothing but a little hint of turbulence in an otherwise perfect journey. The problem is that perfection, by its very definition, must be devoid of any errors—no matter how miniscule they may be. So, in that respect, I am already doomed.

As an entire cluster of wrong notes unfurls from my fingers, I will myself to make it to the orchestra's entrance. It's only a few more bars away. If I can just hang on, I can take a deep breath and reset. But I can't. It's too late. I've already slipped, headlong, into the spiral, banking too far to pull up out of the nosedive.

The orchestra peters out as the Maestro brings them all to a halt. He's looking at me with clear disgust and barely-contained rage. I hear a quiet buzz humming throughout the house and flash upon an image of my father in his suit, hands gripping the armrests until his knuckles turn white and his face warms to a deep crimson color.

"Shall we begin again?" I hear the conductor whisper loudly from the podium, breaking me free of the picture in my head.

I force a smile at him and nod, knowing full well that I'm not ready to go again.

Maybe if I'd requested a few minutes backstage and a glass of water. Maybe if I'd taken a few deep breaths. But the déjà vus of the rising timpani roll tells me that it's already too
late for either of the above.

I repeat the same phrases as earlier—with a bit more trepi-dation—only this time I don't even get to the bass range of the piano before my traitorous hands falter and fumble. By the time I'm moving upward again, my wayward fingers are doing whatever the hell they please. I try to continue, but there's just no way. I can see the ground rushing up to meet me as I hurtle towards it, head-on. The orchestra stops again and this time the buzz in the audience is more like the excited murmurings and horrified gasps of people who have just witnessed a terrible tragedy. Probably because they have.

Before the conductor can even turn in my direction I've pushed back from the piano and am bolting for the safety of the stage left wings. Though, right now, safety is a relative term. I barely blow past a flummoxed stage manager when I run headlong into my father, nearly sending us both tumbling to the floor. Somehow, he manages to grab me by the forearms and stabilize us. And then I'm looking up into the hardest, steeliest gray eyes I've ever seen. It occurs to me that he must have left his seat to come back here before I even made the second attempt at the Grieg. He was waiting for me.

I hear a horrible raspy wheezing sound and it takes me a few seconds to realize it's coming from me.

"Alexandria? Baby? Are you okay?" my mother asks, pushing her way around my father and extricating me from his grip. She puts her hands on my slumped shoulders.

My chest feels unbearably heavy.

*Oh my God, I'm suffocating. I'm going to die right here, backstage at Carnegie Hall.*

"Jesus Christ!" my father hisses, interrupting my macabre reverie. "All that work. All that time. All that goddamned money and we're exactly where we were a year ago!"

"Hugh, stop it!" my mother demands in an uncharacteristically sharp tone. "Can't you see she's in trouble here?"

"Oh, she's in trouble all right..." my father mutters viciously.

"Can't you see that our daughter is suffering from—"

Before my mother can even finish her sentence, my father has redirected his scorching fury to her.

"You," he spits, the single word an accusation and threat rolled into one. "You did this, Madeleine! You and your incessant coddling."

She replies, but I can't pay attention to either of them for a moment longer. I'm too busy concentrating on getting oxygen into my lungs.

"Alexandria..." My mother is hovering too close to me. I wave her away even as I plant my palms on my thighs and hunch over.

"They're calling for an early intermission," I hear the stage manager say.

Oh, Jesus—are my parents and I going to be on the hook for lost ticket revenue if people walk out now and demand refunds? Suddenly I'm on the floor, diving for a trash can.

"Alexandria, sweetheart..." I feel my mother's hands pulling my hair back and away from my face as I retch.

"Ohhhhhhh..." I groan.

"I think maybe we should call an ambulance," the stage manager suggests.

"No. Ambulance!" my father hisses at the suggestion. "In fact, let's get her out of here before someone else wanders backstage. I don't want anyone to see her like this or, God forbid, get a picture of her in this...this *state*."

I get to my feet slowly, noting the swaths of dust that now decorate my dress. The perfect dress.

"Come on, baby," my mother whispers as she takes my arm and guides me down the back hallway and into my dressing room.

My father stomps along behind us. Once we're inside, he slams and locks the door so we won't be disturbed. I go right to the long couch and get myself horizontal before the urge to hurl can return. Mom sits down, gently pulling my feet into her lap. She removes my shoes and rubs my stockinged feet.

"It's all right, Alexandria," she soothes. "It's going to be all right."

I so want to believe her, but I can't. The way my father is glaring at me right now tells me, without a doubt, that it is most certainly *not* going to be all right.

"I'm so sorry, Daddy," I whisper. My vision blurs from the tears brimming just under my eyelids. "I'm so, so, sorry."

Hugh Fitch, violinist, Tchaikovsky Competition gold medalist, Grammy award-winning recording artist and one half of the renowned Mickelson-Fitch Piano and Violin Duo, regards my apology with clear disdain and open hostility. I'm in some serious trouble here. Not even my mother—the ultimate diplomat—is going to be able to assuage the kind of ire that's rolling off of him in waves. He paces for a few very long moments before nodding to himself and informing us of his plans.

"All right. Here's what we're going to do. We'll say that Alexandria was overcome by food poisoning and couldn't continue the concert. Then we're going to reschedule a recital for the fall."

"Daddy, I don't think I can do this again..." I protest weakly and am met with a withering stare and punishing tone.

"Don't you dare even *think* about saying no to me, Alexandria! You have embarrassed us for the last time. I will not let your childish insecurities impact my career."

"Hugh!" His name is a strangled gasp on my mother's lips. "Stop this right now!"

He continues outlining my new future as if she hasn't spoken.

"No more apartment, young lady. You will pack up and move home for the summer. You will practice six hours a day at a minimum. Your mother and I will give up our vacation so we can oversee every aspect of your preparation..."

I can hardly believe what I'm hearing. This is a nightmare —moving back home? My parents supervising my practicing? No, no, no...

"And I think we can safely say that the therapist isn't worth the paper her degree is written on. No, I think we're done with the airy-fairy, kumbaya approach here. You'll see my physician, Dr. Steadman. He can prescribe you a beta-blocker and perhaps a sedative..."

With great effort, I manage to sit upright, nearly kicking my mother off the couch as I do. By the time I'm right-side-up again, I'm already shaking my head.

"No. I'm not going to take any medications, Daddy. I won't do it," I say as fiercely as I can muster. He greets my exclamation with a snide, thin-lipped smile as he takes a few steps towards me, not stopping until we're face to face, barely a foot apart.

"Oh, you will, Alexandria. You'll do exactly as I tell you to do and you'll do it without question."

I gulp reflexively. Having been in this position before, I know it doesn't end well for me. And he knows that I know it.

"Do we understand one another, Alexandria?" he presses.

I take a long shaky breath, my eyes never leaving his. There's nothing I can do. There's never anything I can do.

"Yes," I say in barely a whisper, my two-second mutiny squashed just like that.

"I can't hear you," he says, the smile turning to a sneer now.

"Yes, Daddy, I understand," I say louder this time.

He harrumphs and turns his back on me, walking to the dressing room door.

"Don't you so much as stick your head out of this room

until I tell you," he instructs me, not even bothering to turn back around.

Once he's slipped out into the hallway, I turn to my mother, who's still sitting on the couch, her face damp with tear tracks.

"It'll be okay, sweetheart," she assures me once again.

Perfect.

# CHAPTER 2

# Nate

The day I didn't die was bright and sunny. A Tuesday in mid-October. I wasn't thinking about dying—or not dying, for that matter. Not that I was thinking about baseball or videogames or any of the other things that a normal twelve-year-old thinks about. But then, I was never a "normal" kid.

My mother used to say that I crawled onto the piano bench at the age of two and never got off. I was reading music before I could spell my own name, playing Chopin before I could "See Spot run." The pediatrician called me precocious. My neighborhood piano teacher next door called me a wunderkind. Several people seemed to think I was some kind of a circus freak. And who could blame them? I looked ridiculous in my micro-tux, playing chords that my hands weren't wide enough to span while working pedals that my legs weren't long enough to reach. It was insane. But it didn't stop me. By the time I was seven, I was performing with some of the top orchestras in the country. At eight, I went on my first European tour. At nine, I was scouted by the Juilliard School

—an offer which my mother staunchly refused, saying it would leach the last ounces of childhood from my life.

So, there I was at last, after years and years of lessons; hours and hours of practicing. Countless recitals and endless guest performances around the globe before I was even in the double digits had finally culminated in a high point that ninety-nine-percent of professional pianists will never know. I was the first American in nearly two decades to take gold at the Rossi International Piano Competition—the Olympics of piano. I beat out competitors from a dozen different countries, not one of them under the age of seventeen.

The airline bumped my parents, my younger sister, Annika, and me up to First Class and announced my victory to the plane full of cheering passengers en route from Munich to New York City. I was even permitted to sip a little celebratory champagne once we'd reached our cruising altitude. And yet, when I think back to that time and its life-changing implications, it's not that heavy, gold medal in my carry-on bag that had the biggest impact on my future—it was the fact that the first class lavatory was occupied at the exact same moment I really had to pee. Talk about a twist of fucking fate.

* * *

When Wyatt finally picks up his cell—after nearly three hours of being relegated to his voicemail—he sounds as if he's running a marathon. In the rain.

"Wyatt...where the hell are you?"

"I'm out, Nate," he manages to rasp between heavy breaths. "Why? What's wrong?"

"I wanted to ask you something... Hey, is that...rain? Are you out in the *rain?*"

Considering the fact that I'm standing in Austin—where

it hasn't rained for nearly three months—I'm guessing he's no longer in the great state of Texas.

"Nate, just tell me what you need."

"Where are you? When will you be back?" I ask, feeling more agitated by the second.

"You realize I don't need to report to you, right? I'm the teacher. You're the student. I'm thinking maybe you don't quite appreciate that dynamic."

"You're my teacher because I allow you to be," I point out with a sense of entitlement that I don't possess.

"No, actually, Nate, you're my student because *I* allow *you* to be. Now, if you're done debating the semantics of our relationship, I'm a little busy at the moment."

"Doing what?" I press, trying my best not to sound quite as needy as I know I am.

"Trying to help someone."

"Who?"

"Hanging up now, Nate."

"Wait, Wyatt..."

"Nate—"

"I'm sorry. I just... Something happened and I got a little freaked."

There's a long pause, filled only by the sound of the rain in whatever state he's in. Finally, he takes a deep breath and softens his tone considerably.

"Okay. Tell me about it. What's going on?"

"I was practicing tonight. And I thought... No, I was certain someone was there, in the concert hall, watching me play. Listening to me."

"Okay. And was there? Someone there, I mean—listening to you?"

"No."

"You looked."

My turn to pause. It takes a full five seconds for me to fess-up, finally. "Yeah. I couldn't keep playing until I'd walked through every row of seats in the house and the balcony. And checked backstage. And in the audio booth. And the coat closet. But there wasn't anyone."

"No one knows you're in Texas. Unless of course you told someone..."

"I didn't," I confirm quickly. "I didn't tell a soul." I leave out the part about how there's really no one *to* tell.

My parents have been gone for nearly a decade-and-a-half. In that period of time, it was my mother's sister, my Aunt Jennie, who kept watch over me. She ensured I had everything I needed. She safeguarded my health, protected my privacy and saw to it that I had all the physical and emotional support a kid could ever require. She did an exceptional job of keeping me as close to happy as someone like me is cable of being— quite a feat, all things considered. But, in yet another cruel twist of fate, breast cancer claimed her before she turned fifty. And then, I was alone.

"Nate?" I've missed whatever it was that Wyatt just said.

"Sorry, what was that?"

He can't conceal the sigh of irritation from his end of the line.

"I said, you know I would never tell anyone, right?"

When I hesitate just a second too long, he reiterates the question.

"Nate, you know that, don't you?"

Do I?

"Yes," I say softly into the phone.

He sighs heavily.

"If I know you, you haven't been anywhere but the music building and your apartment. Am I right?"

I see where he's going with this and he's not wrong.

"Yes," I mutter grudgingly.

"Right. So, unless someone recognized you waiting in the drive-through line at Jack-in-the-Box, it's not likely anyone is sneaking into the concert hall to secretly videotape you practicing. Make sense?"

"I suppose. But, do you think it's possible that—"

"No."

"You don't even know what I was about to say!" I protest.

"No, Nate. I don't. I'm really sorry, but there's something I have to do right now. I want you to go back to your apartment and watch something stupid on TV. Have a beer. Try to get a little sleep. Just get the hell away from the piano for a few hours. You need a break."

"I don't."

"You do," he replies flatly, all empathy evaporating with his annoyance. Clearly, I've pressed my luck a little too far. "And I don't give a rat's ass what you think you know. You came to me because of what *I* know. So, either you trust me to help you, or you don't. It's that simple. And if you don't trust me, then maybe you'd better pack up your things and go back home to Minnesota."

I want to tell him to piss off, that what I do is my own business. But then I remember that he's right. The simple fact is that I didn't come looking for Wyatt McFadden, he came looking for me. At a time when the only people interested in me were nosy journalists and ghoulish Lookie-loos—he was genuinely concerned about my wellbeing. And genuinely interested in seeing me play the piano again. He made a point of stopping by anytime he was anywhere in the Midwest and, to my amazement, Aunt Jennie took a liking to the blond-haired, blue-eyed, boot-wearing, hat-tipping music professor from Texas. It might have been those rugged good looks...or it might have been the fact that he wanted nothing more than to help. Not to pry. Not to poke and prod.

We'd been doing this dance for several years when he showed up at my aunt's funeral. He even insisted on sticking around long enough to help me sort out her house so I could get it on the market. That's when I finally agreed to play for him. There, in the kitschy country living room, surrounded by needlepoint pillows and angel figurines, I poured myself into the music as he sat on the couch behind me, so quiet that I forgot he was there. I pounded my anger out in Beethoven, fretted about my future in Bach and, finally, threw every ounce of grief and sorrow I had into Chopin. By the time I slumped over the keyboard, my body convulsing with each anguished cry and sob, he was there, next to me on the bench. Wyatt held me, shushed me, soothed me and, finally, helped me stagger to my bed where I slipped into the blissful oblivion of sleep.

When I awoke many hours later, I found he'd gone—leaving behind a full fridge, a realtor's business card, and a note telling me that he'd be waiting for me in Austin as soon as I was ready to go. At first, I dismissed the idea. But then, as the house grew more silent and still with each passing day, I knew that I had to leave. And I knew that I had nowhere to go. No one to be with.

Except for Austin.

Except for Wyatt.

So, right now, I take a deep breath, close my eyes and somehow, manage to get my emotions under control.

"I...I'm sorry, Wyatt," I start in a whisper. "I just—you know how I get..."

"I do," he agrees, his tone noticeably softer now. "Nate, I'm a man of my word. I told you I can help you, and I will. But only if you let me. So, please, take the rest of tonight and tomorrow off. I promise we'll talk about this when I get back. Okay?"

"Yeah. Okay."

"Trust me, Nate," he urges me quietly from someplace far away.

Like it or not, it's my only choice. And my only chance at finding my way back.

# CHAPTER 3

# Alexandria

I promised my mother I'd call an Uber. I lied. I just needed the time to walk and to think. Time to work out how it is, exactly, that everything went to hell so damn fast. And time to work out where it is that I go from here. Though, if my father has his way, I won't need to worry about that because he'll be the one making those decisions. I should be used to that by now. Hugh Fitch has been calling the shots for all twenty-four years of my life.

It was misty when I left the concert hall. At two blocks the mist turned into a light drizzle. At six it was a steady shower. Now it's pouring down, the jeans and hoodie I changed into soaked through. But, on the plus side, the rain conceals my tears and I can cry openly as I walk the city streets toward home. I'm on a side street, just a few blocks from my building when I have to stop and tie one of the sodden shoelaces on my sneakers. That's when I hear it. There's someone walking behind me. This, in and of itself, isn't unusual for New York City—especially on a Saturday night. Still, it's a little less likely on this side street at this hour. In the rain. But what I find most alarming is the fact that when I stop, the footsteps stop.

I get up slowly and start walking again, picking up the pace and mentally mapping out the next turn that will take me back to Broadway. The footsteps match my new pace. I can feel the accelerated pounding of my heart in my chest and my ears and neck. My breath has become shallower and faster as well. I'm about to break out into a full-on sprint when he calls out to me.

"Alexandria? Alexandria Mickelson-Fitch?"

I stop but I don't turn.

*No, you idiot! Run! Run, run, run!*

"Please don't be scared—I'm just a pianist like you..."

He knows my name and that I'm a pianist, so not likely this is a random abduction and murder. Though, it could be an un-random abduction and murder... I turn around hoping to get a good look at his appearance. Information that will come in handy later on when I relay it to police. He's backlit against a streetlamp and that, combined with the rain, makes it hard to see any other distinguishing features. What I can see from twenty feet away is a tall, masculine figure. He's long-legged and lean, wearing some kind of hat. Fedora, maybe?

"Who are you?" I call out to him over the sound of the rain. I must look ridiculous, my fancy up-do all drippy and hairspray-encrusted.

He holds up his hands to the sides, like he's trying to show me he's not armed.

*Holy shit! Maybe he's armed!*

Before I can let this terrifying thought grow legs, he answers me.

"My name is Wyatt. Wyatt McFadden. I teach at Austin University. In Texas."

"And why are you following me, Wyatt McFadden?" I call back, trying to slow my still-pounding pulse.

"I wanted to speak to you after the concert so I waited around out back of Carnegie Hall. But then you seemed upset and I didn't want to bother you…but I wasn't comfortable with you walking home alone at this hour, so I thought I'd just make sure you got there okay."

"Or you're stalking me to find out where I live so you can cut me into a hundred tiny pieces and feed me to your freaky cat named Precious," I offer alternatively.

I don't know where the asinine accusation comes from, but it just flies out of my mouth. We consider each other for a long moment before he doubles over, his hands on his knees as he roars with laughter.

*Hey! No fair laughing at my potential murder and subsequent dismemberment!*

"Oh," he gasps, trying to straighten up and regain his composure. "Oh, Good Lord, you are something else, Alexandria!"

I stomp the distance between us and take a good look at my would-be killer/stalker. He *is* wearing a hat, though now I see that it isn't a fedora at all, it's a cowboy hat. It pairs well with the large belt buckle and the cowboy boots on his feet. Well, he certainly looks Texas enough. And I should know, my grandmother lived in Austin until she died a few years back. Okay, yes, this guy passes the Texas Test.

"What do you want?" I ask again, this time with less fear and more annoyance. I mean, how dare this Long Horn interrupt my internal angst and misery!

He looks down on me with kind eyes and an amused smile. "Can I buy you a cup of coffee? You pick the spot. Anyplace. I just want to talk to you about something."

Texan or not, pianist or not, I'm not going anywhere with a strange man who has just followed me for fifteen city blocks. I shake my head. "No, I don't think so."

"Look, look, look," he says, pulling his wallet out of his back pocket and shoving his driver's license at me. The picture matches the soaked man in front of me and the name is, indeed, Wyatt McFadden. Okay, he passes the I.D. test, too. Then he pulls a small white card from the interior of the wallet and hands that to me as he takes the license back. "Listen, I'm sure you just want to go home and crawl under the covers right about now—and I don't blame you. You've had one helluva night, for sure..."

"I was sick. I had food poisoning," I say defensively, repeating my father's lie verbatim.

Wyatt McWhats-his-face tries, unsuccessfully, to suppress a smile.

"Uh-huh." His clear disbelief of my excellent fibbing pisses me off. But before I can open my mouth, he reaches out and puts a heavy hand on my left shoulder, leaning forward slightly so I can take a good look into his eyes. They're blue, I think. "I can help you, Alexandria."

"With what?"

"With your problem."

"I don't have a problem," I say, pulling my shoulder out from under his grasp.

"You do. You know it, I know it, your parents know it. And if you have another public meltdown like the one you had tonight, everyone will know it...and your career will be over before it ever began."

He's right, I do know it. He's verbalizing my worst fear and the only thing I can think to do is turn and run.

"Alexandria!" he calls out after me. "Call me! I swear, I can help you!"

It takes another three blocks for me to get up the nerve to stop and look behind me, but he's nowhere to be seen so I take a second to catch my breath before resuming at a calmer pace. The rain has subsided when I finally arrive at my apartment building but I'm absolutely drenched. By the time Arthur, the night doorman, rushes to usher me into the lobby, my teeth are chattering and there's a river of moisture dripping off of me and onto the marble floor.

"Oh, my goodness, Miss Alexandria! Why, you're soaked right through. I was expecting you to come home in a Town Car…"

"No, I needed a little time," I explain. "I wanted to walk."

"Of course, of course. You must've been very wound up after your performance. How was your big night?"

I could lie and tell him it went fine…but I'm sure he can see for himself the answer to that. And even if he can't, he'll know soon enough when the story turns up in the Arts section of the *Times* tomorrow morning.

"Well, not so great, Arthur," I admit quietly and try to muster a smile for him. But I can't. I just can't do it and before I can stop it, I'm crumbling. I hug myself, crossing my arms and holding my elbows as I pitch forward in a torrent of tears.

"Oh, Miss, I'm so sorry to hear that," he says. I'm vaguely aware that he's digging around in the pockets of his jacket. "Here, take this."

He's holding a crisp white handkerchief. I take it gratefully and use it to swab my sodden face. When I pull it away I'm horrified to see that it's covered in my makeup.

"Oh, Arthur, I'm so sorry—I'll get you another one…"

"No need, no need. Now, come over here by the desk."

I sniff and follow him, my sneakers making an obnoxious squishing noise with every step across the posh lobby. He reaches over the counter and produces a big silver thermos. "Here, this is my wife's homemade chicken soup. You get some of that into you and you'll be right as rain."

"What? No, Arthur, I can't take your supper—" I start to protest but he waves a dismissive hand at me.

"No, it's fine. She always packs more food than I can possibly eat—if you can imagine that," he chuckles as he pats his paunch. "Take it, please."

"Okay, well...if you're sure. Thank you, Arthur. I suppose I should be getting upstairs."

"Yes, Miss," he agrees, leading me to the elevator and hitting the call button. "Get into some dry clothing, have the soup and get some sleep. I'm sure everything will look much better in the morning."

I smile and nod politely, well aware of the fact that no amount of chicken soup is going to make what happened tonight look any better. Upstairs in my apartment, I shuck my soaked clothing in the entryway, leaving it in a wet heap on the tiled floor. Once I'm in the shower, I crank the temperature as hot as it will go and sink down into the tub, pulling my knees up to my chest. Finally, I can cry the way I need to. Loud, ugly, hiccupping wails shake my entire body, uninterrupted by cowboy pianists, disapproving parents and curious onlookers. I don't even notice that my skin has turned an angry shade of red or that the tips of my fingers are already starting to pucker and prune. I just let the water cascade down my head and back, creating a thick mist all around me.

I'm not sure how long I stay like that but when I finally manage to drag myself up and out, the clouds of steam billow outward into my bedroom, instantly fogging the mirror and dampening everything in its path. The room is a shambles—it looks as if my closet exploded, spewing its contents far and wide. The bed, the dresser, the floor...nearly every square inch of space is covered with clothes, makeup and accessories which I considered and discarded while getting ready for the concert. It's like the "before" of the "before and after" of my tragic fall from grace. I can't sleep in the before. Not tonight, at least, so I throw on an oversized Juilliard t-shirt and curl up on the couch under my grandmother's afghan. Maybe Arthur is right. Maybe, somehow, I'll wake in the morning to find that this was all a dream.

* * *

Oh, I'm dreaming all right. Dreaming about people with pitchforks and torches setting my piano on fire and chasing me through the streets of Manhattan—all of them wearing cowboy boots. It's such a nightmare that I'm actually grateful when my mother's insistent ringtone wrenches me out of slumber on Sunday morning.

"Your father's on his way over," she informs me quickly, before I can even croak out a greeting. I'm cocooned under the blanket, on the couch. In fact, I haven't moved since landing in this spot last night. Or was it this morning? Same difference, I suppose.

"What? Why?" I groan.

There's a long sigh on her end. "Alexandria, you know your father loves you. And he just wants to see you succeed..."

"What he wants is for me to *not* embarrass him. The way I did last night," I correct.

"Honey—"

"No, Mom. I screwed up in front of all his friends and colleagues—in front of the *Times* critic for God's sake!" And that's when I remember. "Oh, my God. The *Times*. What did the *Times* write about it, Mom?" I ask, my voice suddenly shaking with the fear I've managed to quash. Until now. There's a long, uncomfortable pause, which tells me pretty much all I need to know.

"Honey..." she begins at last, but I don't let her finish.

"All right, well, thanks for warning me. I'd better clean up before he gets here. Love you," I say, disconnecting before she can tell me how he only wants what's best for me, blah, blah, blah.

I sit up straight and swing my bare feet onto the carpeted floor, hoisting myself up with an involuntary groan. Within ten minutes, I've thrown on some clothes, pulled my hair up into a ponytail and started gathering the clothing I ditched at the door last night. I'm about to toss it into the laundry pile when I reach into the pockets to make sure I didn't leave a rogue lipstick or twenty-dollar-bill in one of them. Instead, I pull out a white business card, damp and crinkled.

*"I can help you."*

That's what he'd said. Before I can help myself, I've got my laptop and I'm Googling Wyatt McFadden. Page after page comes up, highlighting a very respectable career as a performer and a stellar reputation as an educator. So why haven't I ever heard of this guy? Near as I can tell he's about my mother's age and I wonder if she ever came across him when she was living in Austin, before she met my father.

I pick up my phone and start to text her but then something makes me backspace and clear the message. On impulse, I type in the number on the card.

**I'll be at the Grind Café across from Lincoln Center in twenty-minutes.**

And before I can change my mind, I hit send.

# CHAPTER 4

# Nate

I don't remember much about those first few weeks in the hospital. By then I'd undergone four surgeries. Both of my legs and one of my arms were in casts and I wore an unyielding metal brace that supported my midsection up to the base of my skull. There was no talk of whether or not I would walk again. Actually, there was no talk at all. Not from me, at least. At this point the doctors were just trying to get me from one day to the next, fighting off infections and monitoring my internal injuries. I found myself drifting in and out of consciousness for days on end—long bouts of drug-induced slumber punctuated by the faces of kindly doctors and nurses.

I'm not certain at what point my Aunt Jennie was among the floating apparitions in my semi-consciousness, but once I caught sight of her, she was never far away. Her dark eyes and sweet smile were so reminiscent of my mother's features that it was comforting to wake to them, even if only for a few minutes before lapsing back into the darkness.

Most days I was only marginally aware of what was happening around me, catching bits and pieces of conversations with the doctors, hearing the soothing voice of a nurse as she took my vitals and examined my dressings. Unfortunately, the first time I was really able to process the words being spoken around me, they weren't the most encouraging.

"What a waste," the doctor was saying. "Such a talent and he'll probably never walk again, let alone play the piano."

"And what kind of a life can he possibly have? All those people dead around him. His parents, his sister…"

I couldn't speak. I could barely open my eyes. But I could hear every single word. And I could cry.

* * *

Her name was Lindsay, and she was a dental hygienist. We met when I was in the office for a cleaning and she happened to spot my face on an old copy of *People* in the waiting room. She spoke with the flat vowels of the Minnesota dialect and peppered her speech with localisms such as "You betcha!" and "Oofta!" Her hands were actually inside my mouth when I asked if she wanted to go out sometime—but she got the idea and I could tell she was smiling behind that hygienic facemask by the way her green eyes crinkled at the corners.

I don't know where I got the courage to ask—I was twenty and had never been on date in my life. I don't know where she got the courage to accept—she was a few years older than me and drop-dead gorgeous with close-cropped blond hair and legs that went on for days. And she probably had guys hitting on her all day as they drooled onto their paper bibs. But, once again, I bucked the odds and took the lovely Lindsay out for dinner. We talked until the place was deserted and the waiters had started to vacuum. I took her out again the next night. And the next.

I had my first sexual experience with her. From there, I quickly became fascinated—not to mention totally immersed —in my study of the female form and psyche. She was kind and patient, never commenting on my scars. Never making me feel insecure in my reassembled body. After three weeks of this, she moved into my St. Paul apartment. It wasn't anything fancy, but it was more than most young men my age had the means for. Then again, most young men my age didn't have multi-million-dollar settlements with an airline, either. Not that she ever asked about the money. Or my family. Or the accident itself. Lindsay allowed me to unravel my complicated story in bits and pieces in my own time, always listening without pitying. She changed my world. And then she ended it.

I don't believe that she intentionally set out to destroy me. In fact, she was also fairly decimated by the end of our relationship. It began the evening she came home full of tales about Rhonda, the new receptionist at the dental office. The two hit it off almost immediately—enjoying drinks after work and a "chick flick" date every week or two. She was happy and that made me happy, but I was reluctant to meet this woman who was quickly becoming a third person in our relationship. When it couldn't be avoided any longer, I finally gave in and agreed we could host her for dinner.

I knew almost immediately that something was off—clues that Lindsay never would have picked up on because she never needed to be concerned that people weren't who they told her they were. But I needed to be concerned. And I knew the signs. This Rhonda woman was a little too curious. She looked around the apartment a little too closely and visited the bathroom a little too frequently—claiming she had a tiny bladder or some bullshit like that. I suspected something more insidious.

When she asked me to play the piano for her, I politely declined. She pressed. I resisted, more firmly. Lindsay grew more agitated and uncomfortable. Finally, I excused myself to the bedroom with a headache. Several minutes later, Lindsay came in and sat on the edge of the bed, apologizing for her friend and explaining that she'd never seen that side of her. I asked how much she really knew about Rhonda. She bristled at the accusation and called me paranoid.

We did what you're never supposed to do—we went to bed angry. While she was at work the next day, I somehow managed to convince myself that she was right—that I was overreacting. I was about to say so when a befuddled Lindsay returned home, saying that Rhonda had quit with no notice and no excuse. Her cell number was now out of service. On some level, I knew the truth then—I just didn't want to admit it. Or, maybe, I wanted us to have one last night together before I admitted it. In the end, we did have our last night and I didn't have to admit a damn thing.

An ashen-faced Lindsay came into the bedroom, clutching a newspaper in her trembling grip. I simply extended my hand and waited for her to give it to me.

"I didn't..." she began, her voice shaking as badly as her hands.

"I know."

"I mean— Oh, Jesus, I didn't mean to..."

"Let me see it, Lindsay."

"Nate..."

"Give me the paper, Lindsay."

When she finally managed to relinquish her hold on it, I unfolded the crisp, inky pages to see a picture of myself staring back at me. On the front page. Above the fold. The headline read:

*MIRACULOUS NO MORE.*
*THE SAD LIFE OF NATHANIEL CALLOWAY.*

The byline read "Rhonda Whittier."

Clearly our little Rhonda was not a dental administrative assistant. She was an investigative reporter who had put a lot of thought and time into pulling this off. And I could have lived with Lindsay's carelessness and naivety had they not been accompanied by my biggest bugaboo, indiscretion. The story chronicled what I'd been doing in the years since the accident — how I'd been living off of the settlement money and rarely, if ever, played the piano. And, when I did, it apparently wasn't very good. At least, not by my girlfriend's standards.

In all fairness, Lindsay wasn't the only source cited. Rhonda had apparently gotten in touch with some of the family members of the crash victims. They painted me as a surly, reclusive individual who clearly felt he was "above it all" and who couldn't be bothered with attending the reunions. One man whose son was only a few years older than me when he perished on the flight, came out with a humdinger of a quote about what a waste of a life mine was and how his boy was so much more deserving of the miracle that I had squandered.

She knew it was over then. It had to be. There was just no walking this back. Even though it had never been her intention to hurt me. Even though she had been groomed and cultivated as an unwitting accomplice. Even though I still loved her more than I'd ever loved anyone else. I made a reservation for her at the Marriot near the dental office, helped her pack the things she'd need for the immediate future and cut her a check to cover the cost of hiring a mover and getting her set up in a new place.

She cried. I cried. We cried together. We kissed. And then I closed the door to my apartment—and my heart—locking them both up tight behind her.

# CHAPTER 5

# Alexandria

There are people lined up out the door when I arrive at the little breakfast spot in the Upper Westside. Three times I almost chickened out but in the end curiosity—and fear of facing my father—propel me inside to the hostess station. I'm about to tell her I'm meeting someone when I hear my name across the dining room. My eyes follow the sound to a tall, lean man with sandy blond hair and matching scruff. His smile is broad and easy. And genuine. He's much less scary in the broad light of day, amidst the eggs benedict and pancakes. I offer a small, uncertain nod of acknowledgment in return, my feet leading me through the tight tables to a booth in the back corner—a private oasis in a sea of chattering brunchers.

"Mister McFadden."

"Please, call me Wyatt. And you're Alexandria."

"I am," I confirm, sliding into the booth opposite him.

"Well, I'm really glad you got in touch," he says.

"It occurred to me you might have gone back home already."

He shakes his head. "No, ma'am. I'm on a flight out of

town later this afternoon. If all goes well, I'll be sidling up to the bar at the Prickly Pear for a cold beer and some pulled pork tacos by seven."

Before I can reply, a grumpy-looking waitress stomps up to our table and glares down at me.

"What'll you have?" she asks curtly.

"I don't think my companion has had a chance to look at the menu," Wyatt informs her in a quiet but firm tone.

"Mister, we've got a line a mile long out there. You mind hurrying it up a little?"

I think he's going to tell her off, like any New Yorker would. But then, Wyatt McFadden is no New Yorker. He just smiles up at her, his face a study in empathy and understanding.

"Ma'am, I don't know how you do it! I've been watching you tend to at least five other tables without missing a beat. Where on God's green earth do you find your energy?"

The woman, whose nametag reads Angela, blinks hard and stares down at him as if he's just spoken in Portuguese.

"I...uh...well, I don't know..."

"Well, I wish my students were half as efficient and energetic as you." When he flashes a perfect white smile, I actually see Angela melt a little. Oh, this guy is good.

"You know what? I actually am ready to order," I pipe up. "May I please have the turkey avocado scramble with fruit—no toast or potatoes. And some decaf tea would be great."

"Well doesn't that sound healthy," my companion proclaims. "Let's just make that two—except I'll have a cup of the high test, please."

A markedly nicer Angela offers a shy smile as she jots down our order and rushes away.

"Why are you here?" I ask before we can be sucked into pleasantries. "In New York, I mean. Are you...are you stalking me or something?"

"What? No! No, no, no. I've been in town visiting an old friend."

"And you just decided to come hear my debut?"

He shrugs.

"Sure, why not? I'm always on the lookout for up-and-comers who I can poach for my program in Texas."

"Are you saying you were scouting me?"

"In a sense."

"You don't even know me."

"Well, I don't...and I do. We've never met before, but this is a very small community we work in, you and I, and word gets around pretty far, pretty fast."

"You mean because of who my parents are," I deduce.

The cowboy leans across the table and locks his eyes on mine.

"Alexandria, is that what you think? That people are only interested in you because your last name is Mickelson-Fitch?"

I'm taken aback by his question. No one has ever asked me that before.

"Yes. No. Wait...I don't know..." I flounder.

My confusion makes him smile and if I didn't find that so irritating, I might actually find that Wyatt McFadden is an attractive guy. I was right last night—his eyes are blue. A deep blue that sets off his blond hair. Then there's the slightly darker blond stubble around his jawline. It gives him that rugged look and helps to perpetuate the whole cowboy thing. But it's his broad, bright, easy smile that's the show-stopper.

Suddenly alarm bells are going off in my brain.

*Whoa, whoa, whoa, Alexandria. This guy is definitely too old for you. Plus, he's a would-be stalker/murderer/dismemberer, remember?*

"Look," he continues, oblivious to my ridiculous internal dialogue, "I work with students who have, shall we say, difficulties. Performance anxiety chief among them. And I've had tremendous success. I know I can help you get past this."

And just like that, all the warm fuzzies about his appearance and the concerns about his motives evaporate. They are instantly replaced by horror—served up with a heaping helping of irritation on the side.

"What exactly are you trying to say to me? That I'm broken, so you'd like to 'fix me' with your magic piano?"

My voice has crept up in volume and intensity and a few people turn to see what the fuss is about. But the cowboy pianist remains completely unfazed.

"In a sense, though, the voodoo thing is not for me. I'm more like the Piano Whisperer."

"Oh, yeah, that makes me feel better," I mutter under my breath. "Like the guy on TV with the dogs. You got a special collar for me to wear or something?"

"Okay, I get that you're skeptical but I haven't got a lot of time here. So, I'm just going to lay it all out for you," he informs me, losing the smile. "I'm damned good at what I do. And what I do is help pianists overcome issues that keep them from realizing their full potential. I've worked with some of the top names in the business—not that I'd ever disclose their identities. Musicians come to me for my help *and* for my discretion, so you never have to worry about anyone knowing we've worked together. I only take two students at a time, and only over the summer break, when I don't teach, and when the music department is closed for three months. No one will ask any questions."

I open my mouth to interject but he holds up a hand to stop me.

"Hold on one more sec now and then you can ask me whatever you like. Just to be clear here, what I'm offering you is a chance to be one of my summer students. I know it's last minute, but I just had another student drop out. You could slip right into that place—that lesson slot, that practice room...the whole shebang. I've even got free housing lined up."

He sits back now and crosses his arms over his chest, watching my reaction closely. What is my reaction? I'm not sure. I don't know this guy. And yet, there's something about him that makes me want to trust him. Of course, that could just be my inner desperation getting the best of me. That and the appeal of not spending the summer living at home with my parents. Oh, God, my parents...

"Look, Mr. McFadden—Wyatt—I really appreciate your...offer...but my parents would never allow me to study with you. And certainly not so far away from home..."

His blond brows draw together in confusion. "I'm sorry, Alexandria... I just assumed because you've got your Master's degree that you're over twenty-one. Was I mistaken about that? Are you younger than I was led to believe?"

"Well, no," I reply, not sure what he's getting at. "I mean, I don't know how old you *thought* I was, but I'm twenty-four."

Now he looks totally perplexed.

"So, why would you need your parents' permission to do anything?"

I suppose it's a fair question. It's just not one that anyone's ever asked before. Probably because pretty much everyone I come into contact with knows my father—either personally or by reputation. And if you know Hugh Fitch, you don't have to ask why I need his permission. You already know why.

"Well, I just do. That's the way it works. They paid for college and they're supporting me while I get on my feet as a concert pianist. It's only right that I follow their advice and honor their wishes..."

He snorts. The man actually snorts at me. I feel my face growing warm, which means it's growing red. Which means I'm getting pissed off.

"And what did your daddy say about last night? I'll bet he was not a happy camper, was he?"

"That's none of your—"

"Oooo! I'll bet ol' Hugh was just *hopping* mad about what went down!" Wyatt howls, slapping the table for effect. "And I'll just bet he was embarrassed, too. What all did he say to you, Alexandria?"

"I don't... What do you mean?"

He leans toward me again and lowers his voice.

"He announced from the stage of Carnegie Hall that you were taken ill and that the debut would be rescheduled for the fall. We both know you weren't sick, Alexandria. What's the rest of your father's plan?"

I find myself staring down at my perfectly manicured hands, folded neatly on the table.

"He...he wants me to move back home for the summer so he can oversee my preparations for another performance in the fall." I don't know why I tell him. The words just come out. Jesus, maybe he does have some special power over pianists. That's not really a thing, though. Is it?

"At the age of twenty-four, he wants you to move out of your apartment and back home so he can supervise you as if you're a naughty child."

"Well, when you say it like that it sounds so...so..." I search for the right word.

"Controlling? Manipulative? Obsessive? Yes, that's exactly what it sounds like."

"Hey, wait a minute, he's my father..."

"And you, Alexandria Mickelson-Fitch, are a Grown. Ass. Woman."

I gasp. Shocked not by the words, but by the fact that he's actually spoken them aloud. I've only ever heard them in my head before and now, out here in the open, they just take my breath away.

I don't even notice when our plates hit the table. Wyatt McFadden spends the next half-hour regaling me with stories of his own performance malfunctions. I smile and laugh politely, my head still swimming with his spot-on assessment of my life and my relationship with my parents.

As appealing as this insane fantasy is, it's just not realistic. And, while I promise Wyatt McFadden that I'll give his offer serious thought, I know it'll never happen. It's just not feasible. Or responsible. I can't just pack a bag and take off for Texas. Can I?

*No! You cannot, Alexandria. Just let the cowboy ride off into the sunset. Without you.*

As I walk back to my apartment, I find this realization to be a little bit disappointing and I'm not even sure why. It's not like I was seriously considering this. It was just fun to...entertain the option for a little while. To entertain *any* option for a little while, actually.

"And just where, exactly, have you been?" my father demands the second I walk in the door. The day doorman already warned me he was up here. Since the lease is in my father's name, he gets to come and go as he pleases. Lucky me.

"Out," I pronounce, hanging my jacket on a hook and kicking off my shoes.

"Out where?"

"Having breakfast. With a friend."

He walks over to my tiny dining table and picks up a copy of the Sunday arts section.

"Were you now? Out to breakfast with a friend? Because I'd have thought you'd be here, lying low in light of this." He smacks the paper back down for emphasis.

I walk past him, and it, resisting the urge to snatch it up as I head into the living room.

"Questionable illness," he says. "That's what that idiot, Abner Beckett, wrote. He implied that you weren't really sick.

That you got cold feet and that perhaps you're not cut out for public performance."

I stop and stare at my father, incredulous about his outrage.

"Are you kidding me? Daddy, he's right. That's *exactly* what happened. I had a panic attack."

I wouldn't have thought it possible, but his face burns an even deeper shade of crimson than it did last night. "Don't you *ever* say that!" he spits. "No daughter of mine is going to have a reputation for some...some psychosis! There is nothing wrong with you that can't be hammered out with a little discipline, Alexandria."

"Daddy, I don't think—"

"I don't care what you think. It's not your job to think. It's your job to play. And to do as I tell you."

Holy shit. We've just reached a whole new level of dysfunction. I think about Wyatt McFadden's reaction when I told him that I've essentially turned over my life and my career to my parents in exchange for their financial support. It's the only dynamic I've ever known. But now, as I consider what it must look like from the outside, I realize how *unnatural* it is.

"Dad," I begin, trying to keep my voice calm and even. If I approach him like a reasonable adult, maybe he'll treat me like one. "I really am so sorry about last night. I can only imagine how embarrassed you must be." He harrumphs but doesn't cut me off, so I continue. "And I know you've only ever had my best interests at heart. I love you so much—you and Mom. But...I've been giving it a lot of thought and I believe I'd be better off spending the summer here in my apartment. I could come and play for you every week, maybe double up on lessons and..."

The cold hard set of his mouth—almost a sneer—stops me in my tracks. So much for reasonable.

"You seem to be under the impression that this is up for

debate, Alexandria. Let me assure you that it is not. I've offered your apartment to a visiting cellist with the Chamber Music Society. He'll be moving in on Wednesday, so I suggest you pack up the things you'll need for the next eight weeks, because you won't have access to this place until sometime in August."

"What?" The single word explodes out of my lungs. So much for calm. "You—you gave away my home? Are you insane?"

"Quite the opposite. I just wanted a little extra insurance policy that you wouldn't be sneaking back here every chance you got. If all goes well and you perform as expected, you should be back here in no time."

I can only stare at him, mouth open, hands balled into fists at my sides. Maybe I would have hit my limit even if I hadn't spent the morning with Wyatt McFadden. Maybe I would have just hung my head a little lower and shoved my self-esteem a little further down inside myself. Either way it's a moot point, because I'm about to seriously lose my shit.

"Okay. You need to get out. Like now," I demand, pointing toward the door. He looks not so much threatened as amused. "Did you hear me? I said I want you out of my apartment. Now."

Hugh Fitch walks toward me rather than away from me, stepping closer and closer until he's very much within my personal space. When he finally stops, we're separated by just a few inches.

"I won't tell you again, Alexandria." His breath is warm on my face. It smells of coffee. And cigarettes. I wonder if my mother knows he's smoking again.

"What will you do, Dad? What will you do if I disobey you? If I don't move out? If I don't spend the summer at home with you and mom?"

His thin lips curl up in the corners into a snarl. "I can tell you what I won't do. I won't pay a dime of your rent or utilities. I won't pay for your groceries or your lessons with Madame Fourquet. You'll have to get a job and support yourself. And with no marketable skills, I suspect you'll be flipping burgers somewhere for minimum wage. And you know what? After last night's performance, I'm not convinced you even have the skill set for that."

Looking back, if I had it to do again, I might have taken a beat. I might have filtered, or paused, or done something—anything—instead of what I ended up doing. Because there are some things you can't take back. And slapping your father is one of them.

# CHAPTER 6

# Nate

Wyatt McFadden doesn't so much as bat an eyelash when he pulls his faded red pick-up into the driveway and finds me waiting on the front porch. He gets out, wearing his faded jeans with the brass buckle and his well-worn hat and boots. It's like looking at a life-size Ken doll. Cowboy Ken. He's old enough to be my father but you'd never know that to look at him. It might be the white-blond hair. Or maybe that crooked smile. Or his "boyish" charm—whatever the hell that is.

"Nate." He utters the single word greeting with a nod as he walks past me, opens the front door and strides into his house.

I follow silently, closing the door behind me before I trail in the direction of his bedroom. When I catch up with my teacher, he's already sitting on the edge of his bed, rubbing his now-bootless feet.

"So, where'd you go?"

"New York City. And, let me tell you, I will not make that trip without tennis shoes again. My poor aching dogs have been bitchin' for hours now. Dress boots are not meant for urban hiking."

"New York City? That's where you were?" I ask, taking a step towards him.

"Yup."

"Why?"

"I told you on the phone last night. I was visiting an old friend."

"I'm sorry I bothered you like that." My voice comes out softer than I'd planned, making me sound more contrite than I actually am.

He shakes his now-hatless head. "It's fine, Nate. You know you can call me anytime. How are you feeling today?"

I shrug.

"A little better, I suppose. I got a couple hours sleep but not much more."

"Nightmares?"

What he really means is "*nightmare.*" There's only one and it's a real motherfucker. I just nod.

"Well, we'll start up again tomorrow afternoon. I'd like to hear what you've done with the Grieg..."

"I was hoping we could start early. Just do a marathon day, if that's okay with you. I'd really like to see if we can accelerate my progress."

He gives me that stupid, lopsided smile of his. "Afraid I can't. I need to leave the morning slot open for a potential new student."

I feel my body extend and tighten into a defensive posture, like a gazelle poised to flee a predator on the Serengeti. I make a concerted effort to sound normal when I speak again. And I fail miserably.

"Oh?" The single word comes out like some cross between a question, a fearful gulp, and an accusation.

"Yup. I don't know for sure if this person is coming, but I

have to keep the time free just in case. So, in the meantime, you'd probably do best to go back to the schedule you had before that other student I had left."

Back when we first started planning my little summer excursion, Wyatt was very open about the fact that there would be two of us working with him. I wasn't thrilled about the prospect but he assured me that so long as all parties adhered to his strict protocol, everyone would remain anonymous. That was a crucial point for me. But when, two weeks in, the second guy—or girl—decided to bail, I suddenly had the freedom to come and go as I pleased and the luxury of commanding all of Wyatt's teaching time. It was a situation I'd grown accustomed to and now, the idea of having my movements restricted again is galling.

"I...uh...I thought it would just be me. You know, at this point, I mean. It's a bit late to take on someone new, isn't it?"

He stands up and leaves the room, headed for the kitchen.

"Beer?" he asks over his shoulder. I shake my head no. "Truth be told," he continues, sticking his head into the fridge, "I'd not planned on another student. But then an opportunity presented itself while I was in New York and, well, I just couldn't resist."

He's upright now, twisting the top off the long-necked amber bottle and tipping it to his lips with a long, slow gulp.

"Damn, that's good," he mutters and presses the cold bottle to his sweaty forehead. "It must be a hundred and ten out there. I swear it was like hitting a wall when I stepped outside the airconditioned airport."

"I'm sure. Especially after all that rain in New York," I mutter with just a hint of snark. He smiles.

"Nate, if I didn't know any better, I'd swear you were jealous." I open my mouth to contradict him, but he holds up a hand to stop me. "Listen, it's been really nice being able to work with you so intensely this last month. And you're right

—normally I wouldn't take on someone three weeks in. But this is a special situation. If this person decides to make the trip—and there's an excellent chance they won't—I'm going to do everything in my power to help them."

"So why is this situation so special?" I ask, surprised that I actually get an answer out of him.

"It's a rare thing, my friend, when you're there to watch someone's undoing. I mean being right there, with a front row seat. It's even more rare when you're in a position to do something to help that person put their life back together. It's an obligation—and a privilege."

I'm tempted to ask him if that's the way he feels about teaching me, but I'm fairly certain it isn't. Wyatt McFadden has been courting me like some nature enthusiast trying to earn the trust of a woodland creature. Over the course of the last five years he's gotten gradually closer and closer—making contact, getting me accustomed to his presence and finally holding out his hand for me in hopes that I'll eat the seeds right out of it. Whatever it was that he was party to this weekend, it was clearly extraordinary.

"Must've been something pretty catastrophic," I venture.

A sad smile crosses his face. "You could say that. But all is not lost. Not for them, not for you, not for any of us. So, you have tonight at the hall if you want it, and then I'll make out a new schedule tomorrow."

"If this person shows."

He nods. "Right. If this person shows. Now, if you'll excuse me, Nathaniel, I need to be someplace in a few hours and I'd really like to catch what's left of the Astros game before I head out again."

"Hot date?" I ask with a sly grin.

He quirks a mischievous brow. "You got that right. Me, a prickly pear margarita and a plate of tacos with plenty of jalapeños. About as hot as it gets around here."

Well that's a shame, I think, then realize it's a damn sight better than the plans I've got tonight. "Want some company?"

"Not this time. Besides, you've got homework to do. I want you at your lesson tomorrow with a list of eight potential pieces for your recital."

I suck in a breath involuntarily. "You think...you think we're that close? That I need to be picking a program?"

He shrugs. "You'll have to do it sometime, Nate. So, give it some thought and I'll see you in my studio after lunch. Sound like a plan?"

It does sound like a plan. Just not *my* plan.

# CHAPTER 7

# *Alexandria*

Wyatt McFadden doesn't so much as bat an eyelash when he sees me walk into the Prickly Pear dragging a roller bag and duffle behind me.

"Is this seat taken?" I ask, nodding with my chin toward the empty barstool next to him.

"Nope. Been holding it for you," he replies, taking a long pull from his beer bottle. "Took you long enough."

"How did you know I'd come?"

He shrugs. "I have a knack for things like this."

"How did you know I'd come *here*? Tonight?"

He shoots me a lopsided grin that makes him look about ten years younger.

*Too. Old. Alexandria.*

"Well I left you enough breadcrumbs, didn't I?"

My turn to shrug. "I'm starving."

He holds up his hand slightly and a woman in jeans and a cactus t-shirt approaches from behind the bar. "Molly, my friend here would like to order some food."

"'Course," she agrees with a smile. "Whatcha having, honey?"

"I hear the pulled pork tacos are something special."

Another smile. "Yes'm. That they are. And to drink?"

"She'll have the prickly pear margarita," Wyatt orders on my behalf.

Molly looks to me for confirmation. "Uh... Sure, why not..." I don't drink much but today wouldn't be a bad day to change that.

When we're alone once again, I let out the sigh that's been pressing on my chest for hours now. It's long and low and it feels so damned good that I wish I had another one in me.

"Did you tell your folks you were coming?"

I shake my head.

"But something happened," he guesses correctly.

I nod this time.

"Okay, fair enough. We'll start lessons tomorrow."

I sit up straight on the stool and look at him incredulously.

"Tomorrow? Like as in the day after today?"

"The very same."

Holy crap. This is really happening! Like the ticket I bought and the flight I took weren't any indication of that. Well, I suppose this is as good a time to come clean as any.

"I have to tell you something," I begin quietly. He raises a curious eyebrow—my signal to continue. "I don't have any money. I mean, I pulled out what was in my bank account...and I have credit cards, but it's not going to be enough to pay your fees and support myself. Maybe I could pay you off a little at a time? And if you can suggest a few places I might look for a part time job..."

He looks at me for a long moment. "Alexandria, I don't want you to worry about the money right now. And a job is out of the question. I need you to be one-hundred-percent committed to your playing while you're with me. There won't be time for a job. And, unless you want your daddy coming down here to drag you home, I'd stay away from the credit cards. And the cellphone, too. Pull the SIM card out of that baby and get yourself a disposable one on campus."

He's right. I can't believe I didn't think of that myself. My credit cards are just copies of my parents'. Well, if my father doesn't know I purchased a plane ticket yet, he will soon enough. Hopefully he won't be able to strong-arm the airline into telling him where that ticket was to.

"I uh...I just feel kind of stupid, you know?" I admit. "Embarrassed..." I huff in exasperation. "Look, this is insane. I don't even know why I came here..."

"I do. You came here because, more than anything, you want to spend your life playing the piano. Also, because the fear and intimidation method of teaching hasn't worked for you so far. And now you're to the point where you're desperate enough to try just about anything—including pissing off your parents and coming hundreds of miles to study with a guy you've known for less than twenty-four-hours. Sound about right?"

It does, but I'm too shocked by his candidness to speak, so I just nod.

"Alexandria, I'm not doing this for the money. I make plenty during the regular school year and from solo gigs. As long as I make enough to keep me in beer and tacos, I'm happy. So, as far as my fees go, there are none."

"Oh, no, I couldn't possibly—"

"You can. And you will," he says firmly then stops himself, something occurring to him. "I'm sorry. I must've sounded like your father just then. Let's start over... Hey, can I call you Alex?"

I'm taken aback by the question. I've never been called anything other than my full name. Ever. Though I have to admit I'm liking the idea of a nickname at the moment. It makes this all a little easier to swallow—like I'm my own evil twin or something. Like Alexandria isn't responsible for all of this insanity, Alex is.

"Umm, yeah, sure. Alex is fine..."

He extends both his smile and his hand. We shake.

"Hello Alex, I'm Wyatt. Pleased to meet you."

"Pleased to meet you, Wyatt," I parrot him.

"Alex, it would be my great pleasure to teach a fine pianist such as yourself. I hope you'll do me the honor of being my student for the next two months."

Why do I feel like I've just been proposed to?

"I'd like that," I agree softly. "I'd like that very much."

"Fantastic!" His enthusiasm is accentuated by a slap on the bar top. "I've arranged for you to stay with a lady colleague of mine, Ellie Dominguez. She's got a spare room and lives just a few blocks from campus. You can walk from there. It's also on a bus line. And if you need to go someplace further out, just let me know and either I'll take you or you can borrow my truck."

As I listen to all of these plans he's made, I realize that this man had absolutely no doubt he could convince me to come here. And it prompts me to ask the one question I haven't asked yet. Perhaps the most important question of all.

"Why?"

He doesn't need for me to clarify, he knows exactly what I'm asking him.

"Because what I heard last night at Carnegie Hall was nothing short of perfection. Before it all went to shit, that is." He snorts briefly and then straightens his features again. "But seriously, Alex, if you're even a fraction as good as I suspect you are, you're poised to become one of the greatest musicians of your generation."

"What?" I gasp. Shit. Maybe he's crazy after all.

He tilts his head slightly, as if he's trying to work something out. "Why do you seem so surprised by that? Surely, your parents have said the same thing. I mean, why else would they be pushing so hard for your Carnegie debut?"

"I—I don't know... No, not really. I mean, my mom tells me I play beautifully, but it's never good enough for my father. So, no, Wyatt. No one's ever thought I was *that* good. I certainly don't think I am." This last sentence comes out as a whisper I'm not sure he was meant to hear. But he does.

"Well then, Miss Alex, we've got more to work on than just your scales and arpeggios."

Before I can reply, Molly comes by and sets my drink down in front of me. It's a frozen concoction in a bright fuchsia.

"What is it?" I ask Wyatt, turning it around so I can see it from all angles.

"I told you. It's a prickly pear margarita. Try it."

I put the straw to my lips and draw in a sip. It's sweet. Very sweet. The flavor is some cross between watermelon, bubblegum and cotton candy. And it's heavenly.

"Wow. That's good," I murmur appreciatively, getting ready for my next sip. "What is a prickly pear, exactly? I don't think I've ever come across one in New York."

"Probably not," he agrees. "It's a cactus."

I choke, struggling not to spew the pretty prickly punch in his face.

"Whoa, whoa, there! Easy..."

Wyatt pats my back and hands me his glass of water to sip.

"Sorry," I rasp when I can breathe again.

"I guess I should've warned you. Not everyone takes to drinking cactus juice. But you'll get used to it. Austin is a strange and magical place, Alex."

When I take a second to consider where I was twenty-four-hours-ago and the whirlwind of events that have brought me to this barstool since then, I have to admit that I'm inclined to believe him.

* * *

"And this will be your room," Ellie Dominguez says as she opens the door for me. I'm so tired that a bed of nails would've looked good to me right now. But, as it turns out, my accommodations are much nicer. A queen size bed sits in the middle of the room, flanked by long windows. An over-stuffed chair and reading lamp occupy one of the corners and a small desk and chair sit against the wall opposite the door. It's light and bright and airy, a stark contrast to my somber apartment in Manhattan.

"I really can't thank you enough," I murmur for the tenth time in five minutes.

"Please, Alex, I do this every summer," she assures me, using the name by which Wyatt introduced me. "Honestly, it works out well for me, too, because I spend a couple of nights a week and some weekends in San Antonio with my boyfriend, Sam and I hate to leave the cat alone."

I don't know why I'm surprised that Ellie has a boyfriend. Maybe because she's my mother's age and "boyfriend" just seems so...young. Not that Ellie even remotely resembles the frazzled, exhausted shell of my mother. She's petite—five-two or three—and trim. She likes her jeans tight and her neckline low and a long thick rope of hair falls down her back in a braid. She's wearing the obligatory cowboy boots.

"That door is your closet and the other one is a bathroom. Now, you should get settled in. Wyatt told me you have a lesson in the morning. I have to be up at the campus anyway so I'll give you a lift and show you the best way to walk to the music building. Can you be ready to go at nine?" she asks.

"Absolutely," I agree. Ellie leans in and gives me a big hug.

"I'm so happy you're here," she says, then pushes me away from her just a little so she can look into my face. "I knew your mother, you know."

"What?" I gasp. "No, I didn't know! How?"

"It's kind of a long story, but we were undergrads together."

"Oh, at Pearson Conservatory, then."

She shakes her head. "No, that was later. She started out here at Austin U. It wasn't until she met your dad that she transferred to conservatory. We lost touch after that, but it's been a thrill to watch her career take off. And now yours!"

"Yeah, well, that remains to be seen..."

"You don't know this yet, but you've met the one man who can help you to change everything. Wyatt could have been a major concert pianist—he was well on his way, in fact. But he had some personal issues that derailed his career and when he was ready to come back, he wanted to do it on his terms. So, he started teaching. And, somehow, he always managed to find the students who needed him most. Not the college students that he teaches in the fall and spring, but his special summer students. He's turned around more careers than anyone will ever know because he won't talk about it. He's committed to your privacy."

"That's—that's pretty amazing. But I still can't figure out why he does it. I mean, if not for the money..."

Her bright red lips tip up into a lovely, warm smile that makes her entire face soften. "He does it because he lost someone close. Someone who needed his help. Now he's made it his mission to work with the students who need him most. Some are beginners with extraordinary promise. Some are musical celebrities who are suffering a setback. But most of them are like you, students poised on the verge of success. The world of professional classical music can be an unforgiving one, Alex. Wyatt knows, as do I, that if you don't pull out of this tailspin soon, there's a good chance you never will."

I'm struck by her words. This woman is on exactly the same page I am. Is it possible that she gets it? Here I was thinking I was in this all by myself—that no one could possibly understand how I was feeling. But here this stranger has hit the nail right on the head.

"Tailspin. That's exactly how it felt when everything went south at the debut concert..."

She nods her understanding. "I'll just bet. Well, I've been in that position and I remember that horrible feeling as my stomach dropped and I felt like I was headed toward terminal velocity. So maybe that experience is the same for all of us."

I'm wondering how this incredibly put-together woman could ever make so much as a flub, let alone a total crash and burn when she puts the subject—and me—to bed.

"Okay, enough about death and destruction," she says with a grin. "You'll find extra blankets and pillows in the closet. Goodnight, Alex."

I wish her the same and watch as the door closes. And then I'm alone.

I pull out my iPhone. Wyatt's right, it needs to go, but my parents won't have realized I'm gone yet so I should be safe for now as I check my messages. There are ten voicemails from my mother. When I failed to return any of those, she sent me fifteen texts. The most recent came in about ten minutes ago. I take a deep breath, close my eyes and hit call.

"Alexandria! Where have you been?" my mother whispers into the phone with an urgency that tells me my father is close by. "I've been trying to reach you for hours! Is it true? Did you really slap your father? Or is he just exaggerating? Please, baby, please tell me he's exaggerating..."

"Mom," I answer loudly, trying to break into her frantic one-sided conversation. "Mom! Mom, will you please just listen for a minute?"

She takes a loud breath to calm herself before speaking again.

"Okay. Go ahead, I'm listening..."

"Yes. I slapped Daddy. I'm sorry I did it, but he still deserved it." I hear her suck in a breath on the other end but I continue. "I just...I need a little space, Mom. I've gone away for a bit, but I'm okay. I'm fine. And I'm somewhere where I can play and get myself into a better headspace. I think if I do this—and if Daddy and I take a break—everything will be much better when I come back."

"Come back? Come back from where? Where *are* you, Alexandria?"

Suddenly my full name sounds wrong in my ears. It's too long. Too formal. It's not the person I want to be anymore. I marvel, once more, at how much can change in a single day.

"I can't say right now, Mom, but please don't look for me. I swear to you I'll check in every week and I'll keep an eye on my email account. But I'm disconnecting this phone and the texting. I'll be fine, Mom. I promise. I love you."

"Wait! Alexandria, don't you hang up that phone!"

But she's too late.

"Bye, Mom," I whisper to the dead line. And then I pull out the SIM card and crush it under the heel of my shoe.

# CHAPTER 8

# Nate

At first, I didn't mind all the attention. In fact, it was a welcome distraction from the grueling pressures of surgery, recovery and physical therapy. Aunt Jennie would read to me from the growing heap of letters and cards sent by well-wishers from around the globe. And then, more than a year after I'd arrived, I bucked the odds—once again—by taking my first halting, tentative steps. Shortly thereafter I was finally able to leave the confines of the hospital and head home. I was practically blinded by the explosion of flashbulbs and TV lighting. People were shouting questions at me from all directions. It was surprising, overwhelming...and kinda cool to the then thirteen-year-old me. That impression changed substantially by the time I turned fourteen.

Losing someone in a plane crash is, thankfully, an extremely rare occurrence. And as such, the number of people who have had this experience is incredibly small. So, finding someone who can relate—really, truly comprehend the kind of loss you have suffered—is very unlikely. Still, there are enough of these people out there that they're able to form support groups and networks, and to reunite annually in memory of their loved ones. The first time I met the group associated with my particular crash was October eleventh. The second October eleventh since I was still laid up in the hospital for the one-year anniversary.

It was a child psychiatrist who recommended my aunt take me—back on an airplane—to the site I had absolutely no recollection of, to meet people who were complete strangers to me. I know the doctor meant well. He thought that it might bring some closure, some peace. Some healing beyond my flesh and bones. But here's the thing that none of us considered at the time—surviving a plane crash is *not* the same thing as surviving the *death* of someone in a plane crash.

I was immediately struck by the number of them. Hundreds of fathers and mothers, brothers and sisters, husbands, wives, children, and friends gathered around a bronze sculpture in the middle of the Canadian meadow. The names of the dead, engraved on a large bronze plaque alongside the sculpture, were read and a prayer was offered. They knew each other—first from those terrible, endless days and nights spent huddled together in the nearby village waiting for confirmation of the worst in the immediate aftermath. Later, they reunited at the site for the dedication of the memorial. So, when I arrived on the scene for the second anniversary I was an outsider walking into their already close-knit group and I regretted making the trip the moment I arrived, walking with a cane and clutching my aunt's arm.

First came the silence. The crowd went absolutely still as I made my way slowly to the plaque where my father, mother, and sister's names were all engraved. I ran my fingers over the smooth, cold surface for a few seconds and then turned to find them all staring at me. That's when they started to applaud. At first, it was a few random people. But the gesture caught on and before I knew it they were all clapping and cheering and whistling for me.

Suddenly all my anxiety was replaced by a swell of relief so great that a weight was lifted from me. A weight I didn't even realize I'd been carrying all those months. I realized that, in my mind, I feared these people would hate me for living when their loved ones had died. They didn't. As it turned out, what they felt for me was something far more complicated...and onerous.

"Nathaniel?"

A petite redheaded woman stepped forward out of the crowd to approach my Aunt Jennie and me. I nodded that I was, indeed, him and she grabbed my hand, clasping in between both of hers.

"Nathaniel, my name is Peggy Moody and I'm the wife of Glenn Moody. The pilot. I just want to tell you how happy we are that you could be here."

"Uh...thank you," I replied in my embarrassed, awkward teenaged manner.

"God has blessed you, child," Peggy continued. "Amongst all of this tragedy, you have been given a second chance. Now you must live up to that responsibility and lead a life that reflects how fortunate and grateful you are. Go out into the world and show us that you deserved to be the one. The miracle."

I wasn't quite sure how to respond to that because I didn't quite understand the magnitude of her statement. I was about to nod when my aunt took a step closer to the woman, her voice so soft that only the three of us could hear her words.

"How dare you!" she hissed at the woman, who gawked back at her, perplexed. "How dare you put that responsibility on this boy! He's lost both of his parents and his sister—just like you lost your husband and all these other people lost *their* loved ones. It's not his job to prove himself worthy of surviving. And it's no one's goddam business what he does or does not do with his life."

That was the first and last time I ever met with any of the people associated with flight 7079...which was really just as well. Because I realized then that I wasn't one of them—could never be one of them. Could never share in their grief or revel in their mutual comfort. I was on my own in my misery, my guilt and my suffering.

That was the day I finally understood that surviving could be just as much of a curse as it was a blessing.

* * *

There are more than three-thousand emails in my inbox. Some are offers for walk-in tubs and erectile dysfunction medication. Some are queries from various outlets requesting a comment or interview in light of the approaching fifteenth anniversary. I hit delete again, and again, and again, and again, barely putting a dent in the mass of cyber spam.

It's not until I'm several hundred emails in that I spot the familiar address. I have to take a deep breath, close my eyes and count to ten. Only then am I able to open the message from Peggy Moody.

*Dearest Nathaniel,*

*I hope you can forgive me for not reaching out sooner. Did you receive the flowers I sent after your Aunt Jennie's passing? I know what she meant to you and I was so very sorry to hear about your loss.*

*As you know, this year will mark the fifteenth anniversary of that terrible day. I know you've been reluctant to attend the annual memorial services, but I am hoping that this year you might make an exception. Please know that you are welcome there. In fact, several people have contacted me wondering if you might come this year. It's been a long time, Nate. You were just a little boy when we first met. I hope you will consider joining us. After all, you are a very special member of our very unique family...and you are missed. I know that one day soon I will read of your renewed success and happiness—perhaps even a family of your own. But whatever your future holds, know that your other family will be waiting for you patiently, with open arms.*

*Sincerely,*
   *Peggy*

Holy hell. How am I supposed to respond to that? I think I liked it better when they were all angry at me for being alive. But over the years the whole lot of them appears to have gained some perspective—and now, all of a sudden, I'm "one of them." Well, thanks, but no thanks. I had a family. And now they're gone. These people will just have to find some other way to drum up press coverage, because that's what this is really about.

If I go to the stupid reunion, it becomes a news story. And then what? Pictures of me on CNN, tossing white roses into the ocean or setting free a cage full of doves? Maybe there would be photo on the front page of the *Times* with me holding a candle, looking forlorn as I sing some tragic song. But I have no intention of being "The Musical Miracle" or any other kind of miracle ever again.

I drag Peggy's message to the trashcan on my computer desktop and enjoy the satisfying crunching noise it makes. Now, if I could only drag actual people there, my life would be so much easier.

# *Alex*

Unlike its vast, sprawling counterpart—the University of Texas—Austin University is a small, liberal arts college. It sits in a quiet corner on the outskirts of the city, backing up to a nature preserve that's bisected by the Colorado River. It's reminiscent of a small Ivy League school with its perfectly matched brick buildings and grassy quads. That is, except for the heat. The ivy would be wilting, burning to a crisp and plummeting from any building sitting in one-hundred-and-three-degree temperatures.

My once-wavy hair is drooping before I even make it to Ellie's car in the driveway. She's right—it takes only a few minutes to get from her house to the smallish two-story brick building where the music department is housed. It will be an easy walk for me. Right now, the parking lot is empty save for the red truck that I recognize to be Wyatt's from last night.

"I don't understand. Don't any of the other music students want to use the practice rooms over the summer? Doesn't the university lose money by not offering summer classes? It seems so strange to me that they'd just shut down the building for three months."

Ellie's carrying her to-go cup as we follow the front walk to a set of double glass doors. "Would you please hold this for a sec?" she asks, passing it to me so she can fish out an entry key card from her purse. There's a click as the latch releases and she pulls the door open. "You know, Wyatt is a big draw for students. He brings in a good bit of revenue for the college and the administration seems happy enough to honor his request to have the place to himself all summer long. And there are a lot of grateful summer students of his who write very large checks to show their appreciation for his work with them."

"Crap. I hope he doesn't expect that from me," I mutter. "I'd be surprised if my father hasn't already closed out my bank account."

"I can assure you that no gratuities are expected from Wyatt or the University of Austin." She gives me a sweet, reassuring smile. "All right then. You think you can find your way back home later?" she asks me as I follow her up a flight of stairs.

"Yeah, I think so."

"Good, good. Now, those are the practice rooms over there," she informs me with a point of her index finger. We keep walking. "Wyatt will assign you one and give you a key. See those double doors over there? That's the concert hall. There's a concert grand piano set up on stage there for you all summer."

"For me? Specifically?"

She glances at me and we keep walking. "Well, you and any other students Wyatt has here for the moment. I'm not sure if you're the only one or not. He's so protective of their privacy that he doesn't give out many details. Not even to me. The only reason I know you're here is because he needed a place for you to stay while you're in town."

"Oh," I mutter, trying to process what this might mean.

Are there more of us running around here on Wyatt McFadden's Island of Misfit Pianists? If there are, I suppose I'll run into one of them sooner or later.

"Anyway," Ellie continues as she leads me down a long corridor, "this is where the professors' studios are. This one is mine," she explains, tapping a closed door that has her name plate attached to it as we pass by. When we arrive at the very last door along the narrow hallway, she raps on it with the back of her knuckles.

"Come in!" Wyatt's muffled voice calls out.

When Ellie opens the door, I suck in my breath. The space I'm looking at is huge. And it would have to be, considering there's a concert grand piano sitting in the middle of it. There's a rug on the floor that looks to be of Mexican origin with dark red-browns woven against a cream background. Floor lamps with amber shades are set up in the corners, giving the space a warm glow. Southwestern art fills the walls, complemented by small accent pieces—sculptures, figurines and the like—scattered on Wyatt's enormous desk and bookcases.

"Well, if it isn't Alexandria Mickelson-Fitch! And in my studio, no less! Welcome, welcome," he exclaims, jumping out of his chair to give me a friendly shoulder pat as Ellie sees herself out.

Where Wyatt looked wildly out of context sitting in a Manhattan café with me just one day ago, he couldn't be more perfect in this setting. Without his hat on, I'm struck by just how blond his hair is. He's wearing a simple black button-down shirt and well-worn jeans, accompanied by his signature cowboy boots. This time they're black. My God, he's a good-looking man. If he weren't my mother's age I'd be doing some serious crushing on teacher right now. While I'm having this ridiculous little discussion in my head, I realize he's asked me a question.

"I'm sorry, I missed that…"

"I was just wondering if you'd like to play for me? Or would you prefer to sit and talk for a bit?"

I shrug. "You tell me, you're the whisperer, aren't you? How do these things usually go?"

"Any way you want them to go," he says as he spreads his palms out wide. "I've had musicians through here who didn't play a note for the first week. Others couldn't wait to get to it. This is really about figuring out what the nature of your particular challenges are."

"Is that what you'd call it? Freaking out, melting down and running off stage in front of hundreds of people, I mean. A challenge?" I didn't intend to sound snarky but that's exactly how it comes off when I hear myself. I'm certain he must catch it, too, but he doesn't seem to be bothered by it.

"I would call it a challenge. Any problem that has an eventual solution is a challenge. You can't see it yet because you're too close to it, but believe me, there's an end to this road for you. I can see it in the distance. Now that you've made the decision to be here, with me and this process, I have no doubt you're going to leave here ready to start your career."

I sigh and find myself looking down at my shoes. "I'm sorry. I don't know why… I just feel so out of sorts."

He smiles and nods knowingly. "I'll just bet you do. And that answers the first question. If in doubt, sit at the piano." He gestures toward the giant black beast and I walk to it tentatively, as one might approach some exotic creature. I'm slow and gentle as I slip onto the tufted leather bench with great care. Wyatt pulls his big rolling office chair to my side and back a little, presumably so he can observe the way I play from behind.

"What would you like to hear?" I ask. "The Grieg concerto again?"

"No, not yet. Too much baggage there right now, don't

you think?" I do, actually, and nod my agreement with his assessment. "How's about the Moonlight Sonata?" He swivels around and starts to reach for the music, which he must keep in the bookcase. But I'm playing it before he can even reach for the volume on the shelf.

It begins as an exhalation—my body expelling, through my fingertips, the continuous motion of churning water under a moonlit sky. The fingers on my right hand spell out a rolling triplet, punctuated by the high and the low—the octave—in the left hand. Those periodic utterances stretch out into a full-fledged lament. It is a story that unravels under my fingers against that incessant churning. As the melody on the left shifts higher in pitch, it becomes more desperate, more insistent and intense before it begins to unfurl, note by note, finger by finger.

It builds once more, the constant undercurrent of the right hand pushing the left until they are both underpinned by the chords in the bass. Then, by degrees, the entire thing climbs back up the keyboard only to experience a slow free fall down the keys once more. When the melody comes back for a reprise, it does so in the right hand—the bass. In the lower range these same notes take on a dark, fatalistic tinge before eventually fading away into nothingness.

It's not until the very last hum of the very last note has died away that I lift my hands from the keyboard. I look over my shoulder for some indication that I should continue on to the next movement. Wyatt just stares at me for a few long seconds.

"Was that...okay?" I ask him, not sure what to make of his impassive expression.

After a moment his blond brows go up over the impossibly blue eyes and that wide, easy smile appears to fill his entire face.

"Why, yes ma'am. I think that'll do just fine."

CHAPTER 10

*Nate*

The heavy metal door slams closed behind me, sending my heart right out of my chest and up into my throat.

*Shit!*

Here I am, trying to be all stealth, and I go and pull a bonehead maneuver like that. I stand stock still for several seconds, holding my breath until I'm sure no one has heard me. When no one appears to investigate, I exhale and continue on my quest, creeping from one area of the building to the next. I come up empty. No one in the practice rooms. Or the concert hall. Or the studios. No one in the lounge where the vending machines are located. I even make a quick pass around the second floor to see if maybe someone is making use of a piano in one of the classrooms.

Nothing. Nada. No one. There isn't another soul here. Just me. Which means even though it's not my turn to be here, I could have been here practicing all evening instead of sitting in my apartment, counting the minutes until it would be my turn. Whoever this guy is—this other pianist—I'm going to track him down and teach him some manners. But that'll have to wait because right now I'm going to take advantage of his absence to work on my Grieg.

I grumpily stomp through the backstage area of the concert hall, flip the light switches and claim my place on the piano bench. The Steinway is a behemoth. At more than five feet wide and nearly ten feet long, it is an intimidating presence, even in a performance space of this size. I run some scales, lifting and lowering my body as I make my way first down and then up. In the days *before* playing was as easy as sitting on the bench and putting hands to keys. I could just close my eyes, take a deep breath, and go. But this is not *before*. This is *after*, and everything is different now. My limbs don't extend as far as they used to, so at times, I have to physically shift my entire body to reach the fringe keys on either end.

I've been told more times than I can count that the fact I can walk is nothing short of miraculous. Personally, I loathe the very word "miracle" and all its derivatives. I was present for every excruciating second of every excruciating step those first years and the fact that I can walk is nothing less than a testament to the strength of my will power. No God here. No universe, or angels, or fairy fucking godmothers. If any one of those entities existed—if there were an iota of justice or empathy or mercy in this world, I would be dead now. I wouldn't have had to live through the pain of death only to endure the pain of life. Because the very thing that I love more than anything—playing the piano—has become a balancing act between the pleasure of making the music and the excruciating pain that always accompanies that pleasure.

It's been a very long time since I've performed publicly, so I've had the luxury of stopping and starting when it suits me —standing up when my muscles cramp, sitting down when the pain and fatigue are too much. I've gotten out of the habit of playing pieces of music in their entirety—and it's for that reason that Wyatt is understandably concerned about my ability to play for any extended period of time. So, before I settle into the Grieg *Piano Concerto*, I take a deep breath, roll my head on my neck from side to side and take one last opportunity to stretch. No matter what, I am not going to stop. First note to last. No do-overs. No resets. No getting up and having a stretch and a glass of water between movements. The roof could cave in, a SWAT team could surround me, some guy could show up with a million-dollar check that has my name on it. I will not stop playing.

No. Matter. What.

I hear the timpani roll in my head and wait until the absolute last second to slam my hands down—until it's almost too late. Only it's not. Countless pianists play these same notes every day and if I'm going to stand out among them—if I'm going to be better than they are—I have to do things in my own unique way. The Nate Calloway way. So, I ride the edge of every chord, *just* laying it down in time to move on to the next—knowing that I'm a hair off of a split second from being behind the beat. Only I'm not. And the effect is, quite frankly, thrilling. Like hanging on by the seat of your pants. Only you're not.

The Grieg *Piano Concerto* drips off of my fingers, my touch melting into the keyboard. If I close my eyes, I can hear the orchestra and I can see the conductor. I can sense the audience packed into their red velvet seats in the concert hall, leaning forward as they listen with bated breath. By the time I make it to the third and final movement, I'm feeling the drag of fatigue, but I keep pushing—fingers flying up and down the keys in what promises to be a scale, only breaking away in the middle of the run to double down into a chord or become entangled in the snare of a spiraling trill.

In the notes of Grieg, carefree moments are book ended by demanding, percussive exclamations—always threatening to swallow the melody whole. For the orchestra's part, the brass echoes the harsher moments, set against the flute, dainty as a bluebird on a sunny morning. These opposing factions usher the piano into a long, stretching, contemplative section that builds in intensity...only to wind back down again. Out of the ether, the piano spins an ethereal melody set against the backdrop of a twinkling blanket of strings. I can take my time here, the flying flourishes of only a few moments ago now slowly deconstructing under my fingers.

What was once furious and death-defying, has become a languid exploitation of every interval, every note, every phrase. Like a maddeningly slow seduction—it is ecstasy hanging onto the razor's edge of sanity. It echoes and echoes and echoes before returning to the energetic and frenetic beginning. My hands are a blur of falling waves broken up by the chunky chords that send them splintering. My fingers are moving a hair faster than my brain can command them, leaving me feeling out of control. And terrified. And exhilarated all at the same time.

I can feel the sweat-soaked shirt clinging to me as I make one last solo run up and down and up again—take a pass through the lively dance figures under my fingers and then it all starts to spin down. It's as if we're all playing in slow motion all of a sudden. In my mind's ear, the orchestra echoes me as we build to what I can only describe as a "Hollywood" ending, complete with a romantic underpinning of strings, fiery brass up top and always the rolling timpani—all building to the desperate, frenzied crescendo of passion at last released. It's the cowboy riding off into the sunset. It's the guy sweeping the girl into his arms. It's the moment when you know everything will be alright and everyone will be happily-ever-after. Or, at least, happily for now.

When I finally withdraw my hands from the keys, they are warm and slick. The sounds of my own heavy breathing fill my ears. I don't even realize I've been playing with my eyes closed until I open them. That's when I see her. I think I must be imagining it for a moment, but I'm not. Up in the balcony, she turns and flees, a veil of long, dark waves billowing out behind her as she runs up the aisle and out the back door.

Two things cross my mind in that moment—she's the most beautiful woman I've ever laid eyes on...and she's come to do me harm and therefore, must be stopped.

# CHAPTER 11

# *Alex*

At first, I think I'm imagining it. I'm just back from a quick dinner break and headed toward my practice room when I hear it. But then, of course, I've been hearing it non-stop since that shit show of a recital I gave, so it takes a few seconds for me to realize that the Grieg *Piano Concerto* floating down the hallway is not in my head. It's in my ears. And it's under someone else's fingers. Someone who is really, really good.

I glance down at my watch. I know there's another pianist studying with Wyatt, but we're on a strict timetable so that we don't run into one another. So, unless I've misread Wyatt's schedule, I should still have the place to myself for a while yet. I can't help myself—I have to investigate. There's just a little light cast by the illuminated exit signs scattered here and there above stairwells. I follow the Grieg around the second floor until I'm standing outside of a door marked "Rear Balcony" along with red-lettered admonitions about being quiet at all times. This must be the back of the concert hall, which has its entrance outside of the building on the lower level.

I try the door handle and am surprised when it turns easily

and I'm able to push right in. The steel door is heavier than I thought and it slips from my fingers. I dive, catching it just in time to keep it from slamming, but not soon enough to keep from closing loudly. I freeze where I am, my heart feeling as if it's going to pound right out of my chest. But, after a few long seconds, I realize the Grieg has continued without interruption. I catch my breath and work up the nerve to slip further inside, keeping to the shadows as I inch along the back row, not quite close enough to glimpse the stage. Finally, I drop silently into a plush red seat at the end of a row that's sitting in partial darkness. Now I'm close enough to get a good look at the stage. And at *him*.

I don't have the best view, but I can tell that the pianist is a young man, probably about my age—maybe a little older. He has a shock of messy dark brown hair and he's wearing shorts and a t-shirt. I can't tell how tall he is while he's seated, but those are definitely some long legs. The way the piano is placed on the stage, I can only see him in profile—his strong jawline accentuated at this angle.

*Nice.*

But his appearance isn't the show-stopper here, it's his playing. He doesn't do any of that distracting swaying that so many concert pianists do in an attempt to appear enraptured by the music. When his hands fly down the entirety of the eighty-eight keys, he actually lifts himself off the bench, hovers for the time it takes him to make his way down the scale and then he slams back down again, like the momentum will somehow translate to his hands. It's as if he's able to draw energy and power from every quadrant of his body.

I'm mesmerized as I watch him move with an ease and effortlessness that I've never had a day in my life. He exhales and the music swells. He inhales and it becomes the barest shadow of sound. When his fingers fly down the keyboard, I can almost see it ripple under his hands. I cannot take my eyes off of this man who makes my entire body hum with the sound he's producing.

I play well. Exceptionally well, in fact. But this is something on a whole other level. What I'm witnessing at this moment isn't some pianist simply interpreting the notes and hammering them out on the keyboard. This is someone who makes the wood and metal and strings of the Steinway grand come to life. Literally. When he plays, I hear the beating heart of the piano. The music is the lifeblood that flows through it. It creaks and cracks and groans and sings under the weight of his hands on the keys, his feet on the pedals and his body on the bench.

By the time he gets to the final bars of the final movement of the concerto, I'm leaning forward, holding my breath as his ten fingers move in one last rippling wave from lowest bass to highest treble before slamming down in the defiant final chords. He's the only one on the stage and yet, somehow, I can still hear the swell of the orchestra behind him and the return of the timpani that began the journey with the piano at the very top of the piece.

It takes me a second to remember that I'm supposed to be in stealth mode up here in the balcony, but I'm so blown away that it's all I can do to keep myself from jumping to my feet and applauding. Without warning, the pianist goes from having his head bowed down over the keyboard to sitting bolt upright and looking up and out into the empty rows of seats. I duck down as fast as I can and quickly half-crawl, half-run to the door where I entered, praying the whole time that he didn't catch sight of me. The truth is that he should be the one hiding—we're still in my time slot here. Still, my heart feels as if it's going to pound out of my chest as I run through the music department hallway and bolt to the staircase as if I'm being chased by the Phantom of the Opera, himself. The creepy one. Not the hot one pretending to be creepy.

When I get to the glass double doors that exit out onto the sidewalk, I stick my head out and glance around. But the only thing I see is the empty parking lot, illuminated from high above by rows of tall lampposts. The only sounds I hear are the hum from those lights and a chorus of bugs coming from the grassy fringes of the lot. Still irrationally afraid that he might come looking for me, I take off at a jog, not stopping until I'm safely behind the locked front door of Ellie's dark and silent house. She's already gone for the weekend so I don't worry about disturbing her as I make my way back to my bedroom and collapse on the bed, my pulse still racing as I stare up at the ceiling trying to figure what the hell just happened.

* * *

"Come on, come on, Alex. Get your head in the game," Wyatt says as I miss the same note for the third time in a row. "It's only your first week and we've got a lot of ground to cover. It's important that we keep moving forward."

I look down at my hands in my lap, waiting for the berating that always follows when I make stupid mistakes like this. But none comes. Confused, I glance up at my teacher through the curtain of my long, dark hair. I find him looking at me, his face filled with concern. Not frustration. Not anger. Not disgust.

"What is it?" he asks softly, "What's wrong?"

"I—uh—I'm just waiting for you to finish."

"Finish what?"

I shrug. "Talking. Telling me what a crap job I'm doing."

Wyatt's blond brows rise high in surprise. He reaches up and runs his left hand through his matching blond hair as he seems to consider me closely. Finally, he leans forward.

"Look at me, Alex."

I sit up straight and meet his gaze.

"No one here is going to belittle you. You're safe with me —you'll learn to trust that at some point. But my job right now isn't to teach you to play piano. You already know how to do that—and quite well, I might add. My job is to figure out what it is that's keeping you from playing to the best of your ability. So, tell me, what's going on in that head of yours?"

"I'm sorry..."

"Don't be sorry. You have nothing to apologize for. Just tell me why you're having trouble concentrating today when you did such a bang-up job yesterday. Is it your parents? Are you worried about them?"

"No," I say, shaking my head quickly and then stopping. "I mean, yes, I'm worried about them but that's not what's distracting me."

"Okay, then what?"

I consider telling him the truth—that I witnessed the most amazing performance last night. That I laid in bed half the night playing it over and over in my head. That I got almost no sleep and I still can't stop thinking about the guy with the dark hair—and the glimpse into his eyes that I had. Because I did...or, at least, I'm pretty sure that I did. Over the last twelve hours I've become convinced that not only did he see me up there, watching him from the shadows, but that we actually locked eyes for the briefest of instants. Maybe it happened. Maybe it didn't. Either way, I'm not about to try and explain to Wyatt McFadden that I can't stop thinking about this guy.

"I just... I stayed up too late practicing and then I had trouble getting to sleep..."

He nods his understanding. "Fair enough. You're sleeping in a strange bed and playing on a strange piano. And I threw you into the deep end of the pool pretty quick, too. Why don't you take the rest of the afternoon off and go explore

Austin a bit? The bus line will take you all over downtown. That's a great place to start."

"Oh, I actually know Austin a little bit."

For the first time it appears I've surprised him. "You do?"

"Sure. My mother's from here. I used to spend summers with my grandmother. Until she died..."

"Right, right. I seem to remember reading that somewhere —that your mom is from Texas."

I'm about to ask him if they ever met when there's a rap on the door. It swings open before Wyatt can even invite the knocker in. A tall, lean man just sort of spills in from the hallway, all tousled brown hair and gray-blue eyes.

"Hey, Wyatt, there was this girl hanging around the concert hall last night..."

It's him. It's the guy from last night. Only now he's here, in Wyatt's studio, standing not five feet away from me. And, now that I'm looking into his eyes, I know for a fact that he saw me. The recognition on his face is unmistakable.

"You." The single word is an accusation, proclamation, and judgment all rolled into one.

*Well,* now *it's starting to feel like a lesson.*

Wyatt looks from the guy to me and back again. I remain perfectly still.

"Okay, let's just settle down for a second—"

But Piano Guy over here isn't interested in settling down.

"Who are you?" he demands as he stomps toward me. "And what the hell were you doing spying on me last night? Are you a reporter?"

"What?" I ask, totally perplexed. "No, I'm not a reporter..."

"You promised me, man," he says, pointing a finger in Wyatt's direction "You said it'd be totally anonymous here, that I'd be safe from prying eyes. And now I've got this chick stalking me—"

"Hey! Wait just a second there, you pompous ass!" I cut him off as I jump to my feet. "Stalking you? *Stalking* you? Dude, I don't even know who you are. I'm a pianist, too, idiot—just in case me sitting here—at the piano—isn't a big enough clue for you. And, unless you have some sort of inability to read a schedule, then you know that it was *my* night to practice late."

"Oh, yeah?" he counters indignantly. "Then why weren't you here? I checked and there wasn't any once else anywhere in the building. That's just wasting resources."

He glares at me with a "Take that!" expression on his face.

"I took a forty-five-minute break to get a sandwich and a cup of coffee over at the student union. Did I give up squatter's rights or something? Do I need to remain on the premises at all times or I forfeit them?"

I don't miss the fact that Wyatt sits back in his chair, taking this all in. He quirks an eyebrow at my assailant, indicating that the ball's in his court now. The guy runs a hand through his hair, not unlike the way my teacher did not five minutes ago. I can tell by his expression that he's feeling a little less confident now that I've stood my ground.

"No, I didn't say that—don't twist my words," he says petulantly. "And you shouldn't be sneaking around in the balcony in the middle of the night. I almost called the cops on you, you know!"

"For listening to you play? Oh, so sorry, Your Highness! I didn't realize I had to be cleared through security before I'm permitted to listen to you do Grieg. And, like I said, it was my night. I should've called the police on you!" I add indignantly.

"I... You just can't... I mean, really, you shouldn't..." He's visibly flustered by my switch from defense to offense.

"Okay. Enough," Wyatt intercedes at last, putting the poor guy out of his misery. "No one is calling the police." He makes a waving gesture between us as we stare at him. "Alex, this is

Nate. Nate, Alex. You're both working with me this summer and, while I usually manage to keep my students far enough apart that they don't run into one another, that, clearly, has not worked this year."

I consider everything that Wyatt has said about protecting our privacy. Even now he's only using our first names. I eyeball this Nate guy with renewed interest. Whoever he is, he's a kickass pianist. Good enough that I should know his name, even if I don't know him. But, while he looks vaguely familiar, I really can't place him anywhere. So...what's *his* story? I see him staring back at me and I'm certain he's wondering the same thing about me.

"I'm sorry if this is upsetting for you—for both of you. And it's for exactly this reason that I insist on the adherence to the schedule. *Nate.*" He adds this last word pointedly. "That being said, if you do speak with one another or if you happen to recognize one another, I expect nothing but total discretion. No one is to ever know that either of you was here. No. One. Do I make myself clear?"

This is the harshest tone I've ever heard from Wyatt. He's serious. I nod my head solemnly because I have absolutely no intention of getting on his bad side. A glance at this Nate guy's expression tells me he's thinking the same thing.

"Alrighty then," Wyatt declares, satisfied that we won't do anything to piss him off in future. "Now, Nate, Alex and I have about an hour's worth of work to get through yet, so why don't you go get yourself one of those latte things you like so much and come back in a bit. We need to have a little discussion about your..." He seems to search for the right word.

"Paranoia level?" I offer.

Wyatt snorts. Nate glares.

"Not how I was going to put it," our professor says, "but, essentially, yes."

Shaking his head and mumbling something under his

breath, the puffed-up pianist heads back the way he entered. He's about to open the door when Wyatt asks him to hold on a second before turning to me. "Alex, since you did happen to hear Nate play the Grieg last night—and since I know that's a piece you're intimately acquainted with—what did you think of the way he played it?"

Nate doesn't turn around to hear my comments. He just continues to stand there, hand on the knob, facing forward with his back to us.

I clear my throat. "I...uh...I thought it was...fine," I say. It's the understatement of the year—I thought he was brilliant. But I just can't bring myself to say it to this arrogant jerk.

Nate snorts, shakes his head and leaves, closing the door a little too hard as he does. Suddenly, I'm quite sure I'm going to be on the receiving end of more of those.

# CHAPTER 12

# *Nate*

"*Fine!*" I mutter under my breath, mimicking her tepid response to Wyatt's question. "Fine. It was *fine.*"

Maybe if she hadn't been up there, lurking around in the goddamn shadows, I might've been able to concentrate on what I was doing. How long had she been there? Had she taken any pictures or video? I didn't see her with anything— not even a phone.

It's not like I don't have good reason to be paranoid. I've been burned before. Big time. People who wormed their way into my life—to differing degrees—just to get a look at me up close and personal, as if I were some sideshow act or an exotic animal at the zoo. And, at first, I didn't mind it so much. I mean, seriously, what average, horny, teenage boy is going to walk away from the attentions of the head cheerleader? *Even* if the only thing she wants to talk about between make-out sessions are the gory details that I didn't remember.

But there have been a few—mainly teachers and the occasional professional musician I'd come into contact with—who wanted to hear me play. They'd ask nicely at first. I'd decline with equal politeness. They'd cajole. I'd laugh it off. They'd push a little too hard. I'd shut down. The press, on the other hand, was not so easily deterred. They thought I owed them something. It was as if my story—my pain, and loss, and devastation were available for public consumption. As if I were some A-list celebrity who had given up his privacy in exchange for fame and fortune.

Thank god for my tough-as-nails Aunt Jennie. She sat me down at a very young age and explained the pitfalls of being a "special" person such as myself. How most people would be mildly curious about what I was like. What *it* had been like. Others, she accurately predicted, would have less-innocent motives. Some might go so far as to mock me and call me names like "freak."

Over the years, with the help of my aunt and an exceptional therapist, I learned how to assess and handle these situations. The unfortunate side-effect of this was a lifetime of second-guessing peoples' motives. Always assume the worst. If the person turned out to have some ulterior motive, it was apparent soon enough. If they didn't, I might just have a friend for a time. If they didn't get sick of all the attention I got. Or teased for hanging out with me. If they didn't eventually get pissed that I wouldn't confide in them, or show them my scars. Unfortunately, nine times out of ten, he or she was nothing but a rubbernecker, slowing down as they passed me by, hoping to get a glimpse of my grisly, tortured soul.

Yeah, well, fuck them. I had every right to be suspicious of this Alex chick. Maybe I still should be! Maybe she's got Wyatt fooled too. Maybe... Maybe I don't know jack shit about her. Except that she's really pretty...

*What. The. Actual. Fuck?*

I huff in frustration, rolling my eyes and shaking my head as I continue on my trek toward the student union with a bit more stomping than usual. The name Alex doesn't ring any bells and I know most of the players on the professional concert circuit. Maybe she's a newby? Who knows. I don't care. Not really. Do I? Clearly, I must because once I've got my grande latte—extra shot, extra foam, extra hot—I sit at a small table and start searching with the browser on my phone.

Alex. Piano. Texas. Wyatt McFadden. Concert Pianist.

One by one I plug the keywords in and come up short. I can't find anything or anyone resembling the girl with the long dark hair. The hair that hangs down past her shoulders. It wasn't a dark, flat brown...more like brown with gold mixed in it. Is that a thing? Do women do that?

*Stop it, Nate. This is* so *not a road you want to go down. Not with her. Not with anyone. Not right now.*

And those big, rich brown eyes! I could get lost in those eyes...

"Stop. It!"

I don't realize I've spoken the words aloud until the guy at the table next to me turns my way.

"Dude, what's your problem?" he asks with irritation.

"A girl."

His face morphs from anger to empathy. He nods. "Yeah, I've been there. Good luck, man."

"Thanks," I reply, getting up with my coffee. "Thanks a lot."

* * *

The mysterious and infuriating Alex is gone by the time I return to the studio. Wyatt's sitting at his desk when I come in —this time waiting to be invited, lest he have any other strange piano-playing stalkers with him.

"Have a seat, Nate," he says with a nod toward the sitting area in the corner of his office. He follows me over, sinking into a distressed leather armchair that must've cost him a fortune.

"I'm sorry I barged in like that," I jump in before he can scold me like a naughty child.

He nods his acceptance of the apology. "No worries. I don't know why, but I suspect you two would have met eventually. It was just a matter of time."

"So, her name is Alex?" I'm hoping he'll give me a few more details—which is insane, because I'd be pissed as hell if he was giving her my info.

"It is," he says, not offering any additional data. "And you were quite rude to her."

"Yeah. I know…"

"But, what concerns me more than that is this overriding fear that you have. This idea that there are people lying in wait, ready to ambush you."

This gets my hackles up. "And, what? Do you think I'm overreacting? Or that I'm making it up?"

"Nate, I seriously doubt anyone's trying to track you down still…"

"You have no idea," I inform him coolly. "Not a week goes by without someone sneaking around, looking for a quote or a picture. Wanting to do a 'follow-up' or to tell my side of the story. And now—with the fifteenth anniversary coming up? I'm getting hit from all sides."

Confusion crosses his face for a moment. "What do you mean by that?"

I shake my head dismissively. "No, forget about it."

But Wyatt's like a dog with a bone sometimes. "Come on. What's going on that you haven't told me about?" he coaxes.

"I'm getting a ton of press requests. And now the survivor's group—"

"Wait, wait, wait… I thought you… I mean, I didn't think there were any other survivors…"

I shake my head and clarify.

"No, that's just what they call themselves—the survivors of flight 7079. They mean the surviving family members of the passengers on the plane. Well, the other passengers..."

Wyatt raises his palm and I stop.

"Say no more. I apologize, Nate, I didn't realize there was so much pressure on you from these outside sources. You did the right thing, you know, coming here to tell me about your concerns."

"Yeah, well, turned out I was wrong. I should've known after you said there'd be another pianist here. It didn't occur to me..."

He smirks. "Of course, it did. I may not know you well, but I know you well enough. You were here on her night, hoping to get a glimpse."

I shake my head in a vehement objection. "No. That's not it at all!"

"Uh-huh." The smirk turns into a grin. "And what'd you think? She gave you a pretty sound ass-whooping, don't you think?"

"I don't know about that—"

"And she is a very beautiful young woman. Not that I'm supposed to notice such things—I'm old enough to be her daddy. But you, on the other hand..."

Oh, he is *not* suggesting what I think he's suggesting!

"Jesus, Wyatt, when did you become a matchmaker?"

He shrugs and looks sheepish. "Just observable fact, my friend. Regardless, Alex is no one for you to worry about. Believe me, she's got her own demons to deal with." He starts to say something but stops himself.

"What? What is it?"

He shrugs again. "I was just going to say you two should get to know one another. She's a fascinating young woman and I think your..." he pauses, looking for the right word. "I think your particular brand of independence would be a real inspiration to her."

"Yeah, well, I'm not looking to be anyone's inspiration," I reply sharply. "I just want to get my life and my career back on track. I don't have time to be distracted."

"Understood," Wyatt says with a nod. "I won't go there again." And yet, somehow, I know he will. But before I can comment, he's getting to his feet and rubbing his hands together.

"Okay, seeing as you're here and all, why don't we take a little field trip over to the concert hall? I'd like to hear the Grieg the way Alex heard it. Up in the balcony."

I mutter my agreement and follow him toward the door of his studio.

"Is she good?" I ask on impulse. I don't have to tell him who the "she" is.

"Exceptional. Someday—very soon—she's going to give you a run for your money, Nate."

Great. That's just what I need. And, now that I have the answer to that burning question, I have a feeling I'm not going to be able to get her out of my head.

# Alex

By the end of my first week, I've fallen into a comfortable routine, walking to campus each morning, stopping for a coffee at the student union along the way. Then I go to my practice room and run some scales and warm-ups so that I'm good to go when I meet Wyatt for my lesson. We work whatever piece he throws at me. Some of them I know from memory. A couple I've never heard before. All along he prods me with questions like "Why did you play that phrase like that?" and "What, exactly was going through your mind just before you missed that octave in the Chopin?"

I know what he's doing. He's training me to be more self-aware while I'm playing. Not just aware of my body, but of my thoughts as well. Then he tries to show me how the two are connected. And it's working. Where I was a little shy to play for him after my repeated bumbling in Tuesday's lesson, today I recognized the tightening in my hand that led to the problem in the first place. That, in turn, led to the realization that I tighten my muscles in anticipation of a tricky fingering—the stiffness making it impossible for me to move as fluidly as I need to. I'm just amazed by this man's talent. In a matter of days, I'm already so much more relaxed and confident than I've ever been in my life. At this rate, I'll be able to play my best for anyone, anytime, anywhere. That's what I hope, anyway.

Ellie is with the boyfriend in San Antonio, so it's just me and the cat when I return to her house. As much as I like my new friend/landlady, it feels good to be alone. I kick off my shoes and curl up in bed with a bowl of Cherries Garcia and a tablet—both of which Ellie left for me. And I'm so grateful. For the ice cream *and* for the contact with the outside world. I've felt so lost without my smartphone. The first thing I do is log into the online email server that I use.

"Holy. Shit," I murmur as I count the sheer volume of messages. The first few are from my mother, all of them pleading with me to come back before my father notices I'm gone. It's obvious that horse is out of the barn when I see the spate of messages with his email address in the "From" column. I move my index finger down the line, counting. Five, ten, fifteen... I stop counting when I hit thirty, randomly clicking here and there to get the gist of some of the messages. But the gist is all the same.

*"Come home. Now."*

*"I will not tolerate this behavior."*

*"Don't make me come and find you."*

*"You are the most ungrateful child parents could ever have."*

Wow. That last one kinda hurt. I've never thought of myself as an ingrate. But maybe I am. God, to read these, you'd never know I was his flesh and blood. I log out of the mail account and find my way back to the web browser. There, I type in the keywords "Nate" and "Piano." It returns exactly twelve-million-three-hundred-thousand hits. Who knew so many guys named Nate like to play the piano? Okay, way too many to wade through, so I decide to see if I have better luck with keywords "Nathaniel" and "Piano."

Five-hundred-thousand this time. Considerably better, though still substantial. But I have one more trick up my sleeve. I click on the button that isolates the search results to only those featured in news items. If, like me, this guy is *just* well known enough, then somebody has likely written about him. In the time it takes me to blink the webpage refreshes with the new data and I'm looking at a picture of Nate. Nathaniel Calloway, to be precise. And suddenly I know exactly how I know him.

* * *

At the age of twelve, Nathaniel Calloway was on a winning streak the likes of which had never been seen in the world of competitive piano performance. He placed in the top three at a half-dozen high-profile competitions and there was a strong buzz starting to build around the young man. Things came to a head when he won the gold medal at the prestigious Rossi International Piano Competition. Nate was the youngest winner in the event's history—and the first American to take gold in decades.

After the competition and obligatory press junkets and celebrations, the entire Calloway family boarded the plane home. Several hours into the flight the plane began to lose altitude at an alarming rate. One after the other, the engines flamed out as the pilots scrambled to make an emergency landing. Five minutes later, two-hundred-and-forty-eight passengers and crew hit the ground in a field just outside of a small village in the Canadian countryside outside of Quebec. It was a horrific crash that killed all souls on board—all save for one.

Nate Calloway was in the aft lavatory when the plane went down. And, while the tail of the aircraft suffered tremendous damage on impact, it had separated from the fuselage and was spared the engulfing flames that took the lives of every other passenger aboard—including his parents and his eight-year-old sister. In the days and weeks immediately following the crash, Nate would be dubbed "The Musical Miracle." His pre-crash pictures were plastered across every newspaper in the country and he became a symbol of hope in the midst of tragedy—a real life phoenix rising up from the ashes.

Of course, he didn't survive unscathed. Nate broke both of his legs and one of his arms. He also suffered severe damage to his spine that left doctors wondering if the young man would ever walk again. I remember being transfixed by the images on the news. I remember my mother crying for the young boy—not much older than her own daughter—who had lost so much in an instant. I remember my father grumbling that they'd probably give the gold medal to the second place Russian now.

As I pore over the pages of archived articles and interviews and news clips, I'm starting to get a picture of who this guy is…or rather, who he was. Nate Calloway was a kid with an extraordinary gift—standing on the precipice of an extraordinary adventure. Poised to reap all of the accolades and opportunities that came along with his newly-minted status of classical music celebrity. And then he lost everything. Literally everything. And his life would never be the same again. Then, to have people wanting to know every detail about his progress —and his setbacks—must have been maddening. No wonder he was freaked out that I might be a reporter.

At some point, the press coverage starts to turn. Nate as a reclusive twenty-two-year-old doesn't play as well in the media as the frail child he'd been a decade before. Snide comments start to appear from reporters and readers, wondering what he's done to live up to this incredible gift he was given? Some articles turn downright hostile at Nate's refusal to be interviewed or even comment on the occasion of the tenth anniversary. Particularly disturbing is a picture of Nate's life painted by a reporter who clearly had an inside track. She knew him—or someone close to him. The woman, Rhonda somebody, is almost gleeful as she details the life of a broken man trying to hold it together.

What. A. Bitch.

The thing about all of this is that I can't find so much as a single mention of Nate playing. No public performances. No recordings or competitions. Near as I can tell, no one has heard him play publicly since that night he won the Rossi competition. Maybe he's afraid. Maybe he doesn't want to share that part of his life with the world anymore. Maybe it's just too painful to try again. There are a million different reasons why Nathaniel Calloway could be holed up at a tiny college in Austin, Texas, studying with a wacky cowboy pianist. But, knowing what I know about the cowboy and having heard the Miracle with my own two ears, I'd put my money on them staging a comeback.

Suddenly I find the tall man with the messy dark hair and the blue eyes a whole lot less irritating. What he thinks about me...well...that's a whole other question. As is why I should even care.

# CHAPTER 14

# Nate

She knows. There's absolutely no doubt in my mind because I can see it in her eyes. It's a very distinct mix of pity, curiosity, and awe. And it makes me sick to my stomach every time I see it on the face of someone who has just made the connection. I wonder if it just came to her? Maybe from the cover of a *People* magazine she saw way back. Or one of those air disaster recreation shows. Who knows—maybe she just got lucky with the Googling. It's been known to happen before. I'd rather she hated me than look at me like that. Right now, we're both standing in the hallway outside of Wyatt's studio, side by side as we lean against the cinderblock wall waiting for him to come back from lunch.

"Stop it," I say quietly.

She looks startled. "Stop what? I'm not doing anything."

"You know what you're doing." Of course, she doesn't.

She turns toward me, her face incredulous. Incredulous, but definitely not pissed, like she was yesterday. Oh, yeah. This chick knows it all.

"How'd you find me?" I ask and watch as her expression

eases. She was thinking I couldn't possibly be talking about what she thought I was. But I was. I am.

"Web search," she says, leaning back on the wall and facing forward again so she's looking straight at Wyatt's door. "It wasn't very hard. I was kind of young when it happened so I don't really remember all the details. You look different. I never would've recognized you." I don't reply. There's a long, awkward pause between us, the only sound the ticking of the big wall clock at the end of the hall. "I'm sorry," she says at last.

I assume this is a general statement—a platitude expressing her regret that this terrible thing has happened to me. I assume wrong.

"No wonder I spooked you the other night. If I'd known, I never would have gone in there without checking with you first. It's just that you were so... Your playing was really..."

"*Fine*?" I offer up with my best snark.

She snorts and dares a quick glance my way. She's actually kind of cute when she's kidding around. "Yeah, well, I thought you had a bit of an ego problem and I didn't want to give you any more fuel for that particular fire."

I nod thoughtfully. "So, then, you thought my playing was...better than fine?"

"Yes. I thought it was...extraordinary."

My head swings toward her. I have to see if she's lying to me—blowing smoke because she feels bad for me. But that's not what I see in her dark, chocolate-colored eyes. This woman is either dead serious or she's an exceptional liar.

"Well, thanks," I say finally. "What did Wyatt mean when he said you have a personal relationship with that piece?"

She sighs deeply and I notice she's spinning the ring on her right hand nervously.

"I don't think I can talk about it."

"Oh, come on now, fair is fair. The least you can do is tell me what skeletons are hanging out in your closet," I coax as I poke her gently with my elbow.

Another quick glance my way. I could tell her to forget it, that I don't need to know and that she doesn't need to tell me. But I don't. I just wait.

"I messed it up while I was performing it," she says quietly.

"Well, that's not so bad. It happens."

"The orchestra had to start over."

"Not great but—"

"Twice. They had to start over twice. And then I ran off the stage."

Holy. Shit. I know this story. I read about it in the *Times* and it's been all over those stupid online piano chat rooms I'm always lurking in. So *that's* what Wyatt was doing in New York City last week!

"*You're* the one? Last weekend at Carnegie? That was *you*?"

Her eyes are closed now and her head tipped back and up toward the ceiling.

"That was me," she concedes ruefully.

I give a long, slow whistle. "So, Alex is short for…"

"Alexandria."

"And your parents are…"

"The Mickelson-Fitch Duo."

"Huh."

"What's that supposed to mean?" she asks, sounding defensive all of a sudden.

"Nothing. 'Huh.' It means…you know…huh. Why? What do you think it means?"

"I think it means you have something else to say. Something that you're not saying."

"Paranoid much?" I mutter.

"You want to talk paranoid? How about accusing me of being a reporter?"

*Touché.*

"Look—honestly, I was just thinking that you're lucky to be who you are. That'll go a long way to getting you a second chance."

She's facing me again, hands on hips, head tilted slightly to the left. Oh, yeah, *this* is the woman I met yesterday in Wyatt's office. And She. Is. Pissed.

"Is *that* what you think? That my parents can just buy me out of whatever problem I have? That they can throw their weight around and everyone will just look the other way while I put on a shit show at Carnegie Hall? You seriously think they have that kind of money? That kind of power?"

"Well, yeah. Kinda. I mean, now that you mention it..."

Bad idea. Now she's huffing and her face has become an alarming shade of red. Oh, hell. I'd better sort this out before Wyatt gets back and kicks my ass for upsetting one of his delicate little flowers.

"What I think, *Alexandria*, is that you're classical music royalty. And yes, that counts for something. Do you know why I haven't performed publicly since..." I can't seem to get the words out. So, I don't. "Since it happened? Because I only get one shot and a lot of people will be watching. I won't get a second chance. Not like you. I'll bet you've already got another Carnegie Hall date set, don't you? To give you a little time down here with Wyatt? Is that it?"

She steps forward and pokes me in the chest with her index finger.

"You don't know anything about me, Miracle Boy, so you should just shut up before I say something I'll regret."

"You mean you're not regretting the fact that you just

mocked me for being the sole survivor of a fucking plane crash? Really? '*Miracle Boy?*' Pretty low, Alexandria."

She's tall for a woman, but I've still got a good six inches on her and when I stand up straight she has to look up at me. That's when I see them—the tiny flecks of gold that are embedded against the velvety brown of her eyes. The eyes that are glittering now as they fill with tears.

*Oh, hell. This is so not fair.*

"What? Why are you crying?" I ask incredulously. "*I* should be the one who's crying, don't you think?"

And then she does something totally unexpected. She nods her agreement.

"I do," she whispers. "I'm sorry. You're right. I'm an entitled brat and I don't deserve a second chance."

Before I have a chance to reply, she's running down the hall. Wyatt comes strolling through the corridor just in time to see her fly by. In tears. He looks at her over his shoulder, then back at me.

"Something you want to tell me there, Nathaniel?" he asks in a tone that does not bode well for me at all.

* * *

"This is another reason why I prefer to keep my summer students apart," he's saying as I follow him into his studio. He flips on the lights and sinks into his leather armchair, gesturing for me to join him on the loveseat opposite.

"Look, man, I'm not the one who went digging around in *her* past."

"I know, I know. But this shouldn't come as any surprise to you, Nate. She comes across one of the best pianists she's ever heard and has no idea who he is. It's only natural for her to wonder why she hasn't heard of you before."

I glare at him. Now he's just pissing me off.

"This isn't about me, okay? This is about her. I'm sorry I upset her, but she had no business coming at me all 'pity, pity, big brown eyes, boohoo.' You know?"

He's staring at me. "Uh...not really," he says, his brows drawn together in puzzlement. Then they arch up in surprise. "Oh!"

"Oh? Oh what?"

A sly smile creeps across my teacher's face. "Big brown eyes, huh? If I didn't know any better, Nathaniel, I'd say you've got yourself a little crush on Miss Alexandria Mickelson-Fitch."

I huff and wave a dismissive hand at him. "Please."

"That's not a denial."

He's right, it's not. So, I'm about to issue one when the office door creeps open and the woman of whom we're speaking sticks her head in.

"Excuse me, Wyatt, may I come in for just a moment?"

"Of course, of course," he replies a little too jovially. He's enjoying this.

Alex comes in and stands in front of me, looking considerably less upset than the last time I saw her.

"Nate, I apologize. I can't believe I said that to you. I was just...I'm still trying to sort out this whole mess with my parents and I took it out on you. For what it's worth, I think you're an amazing pianist."

I shift in my seat a little uncomfortably. "Uhh, yeah, of course. Apology accepted. And I'm sorry if I upset you. Maybe we both should try to steer clear of the past. Deal?"

When she smiles, her entire face transforms—her eyes get all soft and crinkly and I realize she has dimples in her cheeks.

"Deal," she agrees. "Okay, I'm going to leave you two alone now..."

Wyatt stands up and holds up a hand to stop her retreat.

Then he looks from her to me and back again, his other hand rubbing the scruff on his chin thoughtfully.

I don't like this expression. One. Bit. And the words that follow don't do anything to put me at ease.

"I have an idea."

# CHAPTER 15

## *Alex*

"Oh, come on now, you can get closer together than that," Wyatt coaxes from behind. He's got his arms wrapped around both of us from the back —as if the three of us are posing for a selfie in a big group hug. And it's weird.

"Uh, Wyatt..." I begin to object as my thigh touches Nate's.

"Shush now, Alex. I'll find you a bigger piano bench later. But for right now the two of you need to share. I know it's a little tight, but it's not like either of you has the cooties."

"Well, I don't know about her..." Nate mutters from next to me. My response to that comment comes in the form of a kick under the bench.

"Ouch!" he cries out, looking like a wounded puppy. His hair is back to being tousled again, I can't help but notice. It's a look that's starting to grow on me. I give him a smile and a shrug.

"Now," Wyatt continues, ignoring our shenanigans, "let's just give this a whirl."

He's set up some sheet music for us. It's a beginner's piece for piano four-hands. In other words, one piece of music, one piano, two players. In my mind, that's one player and two hands too many. I get the distinct impression that my bench partner over here is even less thrilled about this than I am. I look back over my shoulder with a pleading expression, hoping Wyatt will take pity on me. He doesn't. He just winks and grins as if he knows some juicy little secret that I'm not privy to.

"Okay, so, Alex, you play the upper line. Nate, you've got the lower line. Let's go in three...two...one!"

Once he's counted us down, I start the melody in my left hand tentatively. It's not a difficult piece at all so I don't have any trouble sight-reading it. The sweet little tune is reminiscent of a lullaby or maybe a nursery rhyme. My right hand joins the left and before I've finished my second run at the melody, Nate comes in on the bass line. His fingers ripple up from the bottom of the keyboard and then take a place directly next to mine. His right hand follows my left, like he's my shadow. Then, we move in tandem—both of us playing our respective chords, picking up our wrists and relocating a few keys lower. We are in perfect unison.

In the middle of the piece our parts crossover. Literally. He raises his right hand up and over, slipping it in between my two hands. The warm, soft flesh of his wrist and forearm brushes against mine in the process. My pinky, his thumb. Our upper arms touch as we lean together—first one way, then another. Suddenly having our thighs abut one another isn't such a bad thing. In fact, I rather like the press of his flesh.

Wait. Did I really just think that? *Press of his flesh?*

"Come on, Alex, concentrate," Wyatt says when my mental detour causes me to miss a note.

I nod and pay closer attention to what's happening on the page in front of me, rather than with the person next to me. Now it's my turn to go roaming as one of my hands comes off the keyboard altogether, the other one sneaking in and under both of his. I feel a bit of a chill when I pull away, returning to my own end of the piano. But then we start a game of tag and telephone and ring-around-the-rosy all rolled into one. I start the phrase, he finishes it. It feels sort of like finishing one another's sentences...only you have to end in the same voice and tone and volume that your partner started. After that, the melody is all mine, only he has to imitate and echo it a moment later and an octave below me.

"Here we go," Wyatt calls out over our rising volume. "It's about to get tricky so pay close attention."

He's right. In a matter of just a few measures, we're both going full bore. Those four hands—those twenty fingers—are pounding and rippling and flying from one end of the keyboard to the other. The effect is stunning and I feel the goose bumps rising on my arms. When he builds from the bass up, I feel it in my chest. We're on what could be a collision course. But it's not. Our hands intertwine effortlessly. By now we've worked out any awkwardness in the physical machinations of this little exercise. We're beyond learning one another's timing and pacing. We breathe together, we move together, we anticipate one another's movements before they happen. As our hands slam down in the final chords, we are one pianist.

I've never experienced anything like this in my life. For the first time, I know what it's like to feel complete when I play. Nothing lacking. No worries or fears that I was going to make a mistake along the way. He carried me. And I carried him. It was...spiritual, in a sense. To me, anyway. I'm not quite sure what to make of Nate Calloway as we remain, side-by-side, on the too-small piano bench, breathing hard and staring straight ahead at the music we've just finished playing.

"Well," Wyatt begins softly. He walks around to the other side of the piano so that he's facing us. "Well, well, well. I think we might just have stumbled onto something really big, you two." We stare at him, waiting for him to enlighten us as to what the hell that was. And what the hell it means. "Did you feel it?" he asks.

I glance over at Nate who looks perplexed. Ah. Well, I guess that's my answer then. Because I *did* feel it. But I'm not going to be the one to admit it if he didn't. So, we all sit there silently for what feels like a long time. Finally, Wyatt sighs in frustration and rolls his eyes.

"Enough with the posturing. When you have a partner, you have to be equals. Otherwise it will never work. One of you can't be tougher, or stronger, or cooler than the other. It causes problems mentally and they can manifest physically when you're performing. So, Alex, how did you feel while you were playing with Nate?"

*Oh, God. Really? He had to ask me first?*

"I... I, uhh, I felt safe." I can't say where the word came from, or where I found the courage to just throw it out there, but I did. And our teacher looks thrilled. His brows go up and he nods slightly, encouraging me to elaborate. "I wasn't afraid of screwing up."

"Why?" Wyatt asks.

I glance nervously at Nate, whose eyes are focused firmly on the keyboard.

"Because I knew he had my back. I knew I wasn't in this alone." I'm on a roll now and the more I speak, the more attention he seems to be paying. I clear my throat. "Once we hit our groove, it all felt so...natural. Like I've always wanted playing the piano to feel like."

Wyatt looks as if he's about to burst with pride. "Yes! Yes, exactly, Alex. Because that *is* how playing the piano is supposed to feel. And you, Nate?"

My performance partner shifts uncomfortably next to me. "Yeah, it was okay."

"That's it? Come on, you can do better than that," Wyatt insists.

"What do you want from me, man?" Nate snaps. "It was okay."

Wyatt seems to consider pursuing this, but thinks better of it.

"All right, then. I think you both did a kickass job. Now, take the rest of the day off. Alex, you come see me tomorrow morning, but we'll just do an hour. Nate, you should join us at eleven and you can work together. Then Alex can go and I'll work with Nate. Sound like a plan?"

I nod and smile weakly, not at all sure of what's going on here. Is this our new paradigm? Are we going to be taught in tandem from here on out? Nate just grunts and heads for the door as quickly as possible, leaving me alone with Wyatt.

"That really was something..." I say to him.

"I know. And let me tell you, Alex, 'something' doesn't come around every day. In fact, you're lucky if 'something' comes around once in a lifetime."

* * *

He's waiting for me when I cross the quad, headed toward the student union.

"What the fuck *was* that?" Nate asks as he jumps up from a concrete bench.

"What was what?" I ask, continuing my pace so he has to scramble to catch me and follow.

"You just went along with that bullshit and now...now he's going to make us pair up like that all the time!"

"And, so what?" I counter, stopping to turn to him. I put my hands on my hips. He's not the only one who can be indignant here.

"I don't know about you, but I'm a *solo* act. I don't need someone else hanging off my coattails."

I suck in a harsh breath as my blood pressure spikes.

"Wow. Just...just wow," I spit, shaking my head in disbelief. "You are really something. You felt it. I know you did. So, don't you dare pretend that was just another little exercise. There was chemistry there, jackass!"

"Chemistry!" He snorts. "Oh, that's classic. Chem-is-try." He savors the word, a cruel smile curving his lips. "What you had there was nothing more than a couple of pianists who happen to be good at sight-reading. Nothing more, nothing less."

"Yeah, right, you keep telling yourself that," I mutter, turning my back on him and resuming my walk.

"Hey! Don't you walk away from me!"

Now that hits a little too close to home. I mean, I can practically hear my father's voice in that demand. Still, I decide to keep stomping toward my destination, even as I hear him hustle to catch up again. That's when I feel his hand on my forearm. It stops me dead in my tracks, pulls me back a foot and then spins me around.

"Are you insane?" I screech at him. "What makes you think—"

I forget what I was about to say when he grabs both my arms just under the shoulders, leans down and puts his lips to mine. At first, I'm so shocked that I just stand there stiffly. But that kiss...his lips are so soft and tender on mine. I instinctively close my eyes and open my mouth, my arms snaking up and around his neck. He groans deep in his throat and smashes us together as if he can somehow make us connected. Like he can recreate the way it felt when we played together.

And then, it ends as abruptly as it began. When I open my eyes again, Nate Calloway looks as if he's just been caught with his hand in the cookie jar. As he inches back away from me, his eyes are big, his hand across his mouth.

"What?" I ask. "What is it?"

"I'm sorry..." he begins, shaking his head as if in disbelief over his own actions. "I shouldn't have... I just couldn't... But you're just so..."

He's afraid he's gone too far. He doesn't know me—not really—and he's just grabbed me and kissed me. Not very politically correct these days.

Well, to hell with politically correct. I haven't been kissed like that since...honestly, I've *never* been kissed like that. And I'm not about to miss the opportunity to experience it again. So, before he can turn and bolt for the safety of the practice room or god-only-knows where he goes to hide, I step towards him. Once. Twice. The third step brings us toe to toe and I tip my face up towards his.

"It's okay," I murmur. "You don't have to be sor—"

Before I can even finish the sentence, he's pulled me up against him, his lips finding mine again. I turn my head to the side slightly and suddenly he's kissing my ear. "Oh. Oh, my god," I moan.

"Hey, get a room!" a guy on a skateboard hollers as he whizzes past us.

An excellent suggestion if I ever heard one.

# CHAPTER 16

# *Nate*

"Come home with me," she whispers in my ear.

I lift my head just enough to get a look at her face.

"What?"

A kiss is one thing. But...

She closes her eyes for a long moment and then opens them again, changed. There's something resolute in her expression now.

"Look, Nate, I haven't been in control of my life in a very long time. Probably never, if I'm honest. But—right here, right now—it's all me. And all of me...wants all of you." Now something different shifts her features. Something uncomfortable and raw. "Unless of course you don't want to..."

Insecurity. Yeah, I know that one well.

"Alex, I can't think of anything I want more at this second. But we don't know each other... Hell, I'm not even sure we like each other."

I can't believe I'm cockblocking myself. But I can't risk screwing things up here. What happens in the next few minutes might have an impact on much more than my summer.

"Isn't this what people do now? Hook-up? It doesn't have to be anything more than that, okay? I'm not expecting some grand gesture like a proposal on stage at Carnegie or anything like that. I'm just saying that I think we should take Wyatt's advice."

"Funny, I don't recall Wyatt saying that we should go back to your place," I point out, feeling less concerned and more amused by the second.

She gives me a coy grin and a playful slap on the chest. "No, he didn't. But what he did say is that we need to stop thinking and start doing."

My God, this woman is beautiful. I could spend all day counting the tiny little specks of gold that dot the velvety brown of her irises. I don't know what it is but suddenly, everything she says makes perfect sense.

"Oh, well, since you put it that way, this sounds like something he'd give his cowboy seal of approval on."

She screws up her face.

"He doesn't actually have one of those, does he? A cowboy seal, I mean?" she asks, only half kidding.

I chuckle—something I haven't done in more months than I can recall. It is both strange and liberating at the same time.

"More like a branding iron," I mutter.

"Tell you what, I'm staying at Ellie Dominguez's place. It's just a few blocks from here. I can make us some lunch and we can just see where things go from there. How does that sound for a plan?"

Before I can think of a reason to beg off, she's got my big, beefy hand in her dainty, elegant one and she's pulling me across the quad. To wherever it is we're going. And whatever it is we're doing. Because, right now, I'm not really sure of either.

* * *

"Nice place," I say, looking around at the simple southwestern décor and the huge piano sitting in the middle of the living room.

"Right?" she calls out from the kitchen. She returns momentarily with two glasses of iced tea. I take one from her and enjoy a long sip. The temperature hasn't dipped under a hundred degrees all week and the walk over here from campus was like pushing through a very long sauna.

"Would you like a tour?" she asks me before taking a sip of her own tea.

"Umm, it's not a very big house. Is there much more to see?" I ask, glancing around doubtfully. There's no second floor and we appear to be standing in the center of the house.

"Just my room," she replies casually.

"Do you—do you think Ellie will mind me being here?" I ask.

Her eyebrow quirks.

"I don't know. But, if it'd make you feel better, I'll call her in San Antonio and ask her."

"She's in San Antonio?"

"Yup. All weekend. With her boyfriend."

"Oh."

"What's that supposed to mean?"

"Really? We're doing this again? Last time we discussed the origins of my 'huh' you ran away crying and I got a lecture on consideration from Wyatt."

She snorts into her glass. "Did you now?"

I nod with half a smirk on my face. "Yeah, I did. Then I complained about your big brown eyes."

Alex sets her glass on the coffee table and closes the distance between us.

"Huh," she says thoughtfully.

Okay, I'll play along.

"What's that supposed to mean?"

She shrugs. "I don't know. Huh. What do you think it means?"

"I think it means that you have something to say but you're not saying it."

"I see."

She reaches down and takes my glass from my grasp, setting it down next to hers. Then she bends down and slowly pulls the sandals from her feet before returning to her post directly in front of me. She's really something this one, the way she looks up at me all wide-eyed and innocent. Her little pink tongue flicks out and she licks her lips.

"Well, do you?" I ask as she looks up at me expectantly.

"Do I what?"

Oh, God, she is so good.

"Do you have something to say to me that you're not saying?"

"I do. I have something to say and I'm not saying it."

"And what's that?" I ask her softly. "What is it that you're not saying, Alexandria?"

"What I'm not saying, Nathaniel, is that I've wanted to touch you since I saw you playing that night in the concert hall."

She reaches out and casually slips her hands under my t-shirt. They're cold and wet from the iced tea and they feel incredible against my skin. I start to say something, but she puts a long, slim finger to my lips.

"I'm not done yet."

I nod my understanding. Now she has one hand resting on my chest and the other gently outlining the shape of my mouth. I shift as I start to feel some stirrings in the vicinity of my lower quadrant. If this isn't headed where I think it's headed, I'm going to be mighty embarrassed. And mighty uncomfortable.

"And this afternoon, when we were playing together, it was..." she pauses and seems to search for the right word, "Electric. Every time our hands brushed or our thighs touched I had to try to keep myself from gasping. I felt more from you in those two hours than I have from anyone else in the last two years."

I smile as she switches out her index finger on my lips to her thumb rubbing against my jawline. Her touch is soft and gentle, like little butterflies are dancing on my skin.

*Wait...where the hell did that come from? Butterflies? I am so* not a butterfly kinda guy...

Before I can evaluate those thoughts too closely, she pulls her left hand from my face and it joins her right at the bottom of my t-shirt and before I know it, it's over my head and on the floor.

Holy. Shit.

"I don't know if this is a one-off, or a summer fling, or what. I just know that I'm game to find out if you are."

It's not necessary for me to answer that question with words because I do it with my actions. I grab her around the waist and hoist her up so that she has to wrap her legs around me—sort of like a forward-facing piggyback ride. She giggles and loops her hands around my neck.

"Which way?" I ask hoarsely.

"What?"

I quirk an eyebrow at her. She gets it.

"Oh! Down that hallway. The room at the very end."

My shirt is a distant memory as she leans forward and brushes her lips against mine. I have one eye open so I don't careen into the wall and impale her on a longhorn or some other funky piece of art. When I get us to the door unscathed, I'm relieved to see it's slightly ajar so I can just kick it open.

From there, it's only six steps across and three feet down onto the bed, where I lower her gently.

"I hate to spoil the mood," she begins tentatively, "but do you happen to have a condom?"

*Shit! Shit, shit, shit, shit!*

Clearly the horror must be plastered all across my face because she jumps up and rushes past me down the hallway, calling back to me over her shoulder.

"Hold that thought!"

I hear doors opening and drawers slamming shut. She returns less than ninety seconds later, triumphantly holding the necessary item, which she tosses to me.

"Ellie has a stash in her bedside table," she explains, hopping back up on the bed in exactly the same position she was just in.

I examine the label of the Trojan.

"Wow, extra-large. Good for you, Ellie," I mutter as I hurriedly unzip my jeans, pulling them and my briefs down together. If there was any doubt as to how much I wanted her before, there's absolutely no hiding it now. It's right there, in the flesh—so to speak.

"Oh, I think that'll fit you just fine," Alex says with a naughty grin. It makes me want to jump on her. But I've got other plans. So, on goes the condom and up goes the skirt of her sundress.

Alex sighs when my palms find their way along the outside of her long legs. I run them down from just below her panty line to just above her knee and then back up again. And down. And up. She lifts herself up enough to place her mouth against the shell of my ear.

"Higher," she whispers.

It's not a request, it's an order. And I am *not* one to disobey orders from a woman in bed. Ever. *"Yes." "No." "Maybe." "Hell no!" "God, yes!"* What she says goes. Always.

And I'm not about to change that policy now, so my index fingers find the elastic band of Alex's lacy nether-garments and they tug. And tug. Until they're sliding down those long legs and right off. Once they're in my hand, I toss them to the other side of the room and she throws her head back in a laugh that sounds like wind chimes on a breezy afternoon. If there was such a thing as a breeze in Austin, Texas. I could listen to her laugh like that all night long, although, I think there are a few other noises I'd like to hear her make before we get there.

I pull away from her and she supports herself on her elbows, watching as I move to a kneeling position at the foot of the bed—and the foot of her body. From there, I start kissing my way up her body. Her ankles to her calves. Her calves to her knees. Her knees to her thighs. I slow down there, my lips caressing first the inside of her left leg, then the inside of her right. I move up, shifting back and forth from side to side as I do, until her skirt is bunched up around her waist and I'm eyelevel with the smooth rise at the apex of her thighs.

Without hesitation—or warning—I lean down and kiss her, my mouth barely grazing her soft skin in a series of light, glancing brushes. I work my way around and down so that I'm just at the top of her inner thigh. What do you call that? I suppose it's tantamount to the armpit. A "legpit" maybe? The thought makes me expel a tiny snort of air.

"Something funny down there?" she asks from above me. I glance up and she's watching my every move with keen interest.

"I'll tell you later. Don't want to spoil the mood. Why don't you sit back and relax? That can't be comfortable, sitting up on your elbows like that."

She looks a little distrustful. "I just want to keep an eye on things, make sure you're not some pervy guy wanting to do something bizarre."

"Like what? I didn't exactly bring any props with me down here. No clamps or plugs or—"

"Okay, okay! I'm lying down. Just don't mention...clamps again."

I suppress a smile, lower my head, and get to work.

# CHAPTER 17

## *Alex*

O*h my God, oh my God, oh my God!*

I can't believe I'm about to do this...and with a guy I couldn't stand maybe five minutes ago. Suddenly I'm grateful that my mother insisted on that full-body waxing as part of my pre-debut spa day. I never would've let him—or any other guy for that matter—within a hundred yards of my dark, stubbly legs—or anything else for that matter. I mean, I've had sex before. Not that it ever turned into anything other than a short-lived fling. My father told me, in not so many words, to enjoy the company of a man if I needed to—he actually used that word, "need" as if I were scratching an itch. He made it quite clear that while casual sex was fine, a serious relationship with anyone was out of the question at this juncture of my career. I opted not to point out that he and my mom were my age when they got married.

*Ugh! Talk about a mood killer.*

*Note to self: Do not think about your father just before you're about to receive oral sex for the first time.*

It turns out to be a moot note because the second I feel Nate's tongue at the very top of my slit all thoughts of anyone and anything but him evaporate. Him and the exquisite tension I feel when he ventures lower, tracing along the outside of my sex. I'm holding my breath, waiting for him to—

Holy. Sweet. Jesus.

I gasp at the same moment my hands fly down to his head, running through that perpetually messy hair. It's about to get a whole lot messier because now he's circling my clit and I've just lost all control of my body's responses.

"Oh! Oh, God!" I cry out, gripping his hair a little too tightly, I'm sure. But I don't care. I have never felt anything this amazing in my life. Is this what it's supposed to be like? Pleasure, I mean? I've had "pleasant enough" but never, never anything like this.

And then he takes me in his mouth and begins a gentle, rhythmic tugging that causes my hips to fly up off the bed. It's almost too much and I'm fighting the sensations by closing my legs around him. But he's not having it. Nate puts a strong hand on each of my knees and pushes me open roughly. I'm writhing against the unbearable tightening in my core. It snakes all the way up from where he is feasting on me to my breasts and back down to the tip of my toes.

"Nate," I whimper pathetically. "Nate, please..."

I don't even know what I'm begging for. Until I do.

With a garbled, unintelligible cry I feel everything tighten —my entire body straightens at once, as if someone has pulled it taut from either end. Just as quickly, it releases and, somewhere, an invisible dam crumbles, sending a wave of pleasure so big that it catches me up in the pull of its tide and washes over me until I'm soaked and panting and begging for mercy. Which I don't get.

I've no sooner experienced the most amazing orgasm of my life than he's making his way back up my body—scaling it, until his hips are resting between my splayed thighs and his face is hovering over mine. Somewhere in there he's managed to find and don the condom though, for the life of me, I have no idea how I could've missed it. I'll have to ask him later.

"Sounded like you enjoyed that," he says, a little too smugly for my taste but I can't bring myself to comment. I can only nod and smile stupidly.

The smug disappears immediately, replaced by desire. His blue eyes are soft and unfocused as he lowers the side of his head to the side of mine, stroking my smooth cheek with the rough stubble of his. It's not sexy so much as...comforting.

"You are the most beautiful woman I have ever seen in my life," he murmurs against my ear.

Still mired in the haze of afterglow, I can't respond to that other than to wrap myself around him. My arms slip under his and slide up his back until I have my hands on his shoulders. I use the leverage to both push and pull him closer. He's all lean muscle as his hard, flat chest presses down on the soft, pliable flesh of my breasts. At the same time, I wrap my legs around his waist.

I know what he wants. I know what I want. He doesn't need any further encouragement as he aligns himself and thrusts into me in a single motion that robs the breath from my lungs. He lets out a sigh of relief so deep that I wonder how long it's been inside of him, waiting for the chance to escape.

"Christ," he whispers, still not moving from where he's lodged in me. "You feel... I can't even..."

Rather than leave him floundering for the words that aren't there, I wrap my arms around his neck and pull his mouth to mine. I can taste myself on him—which I'd have thought would've been a turn off. But it's the opposite, actually. The tang of my body on his lips drives me wild.

"Fuck me," I murmur.

Nate smirks down at me and then manages to capture both of my slim wrists in one of his big hands.

"Is that what you want?" he asks casually as his other hand thumbs one of my nipples.

Bastard wants to make me beg for it. But I don't mind. One. Bit.

"Please," I utter on a breathy exhalation. "Now."

I don't have to ask again. We're a little off for a few seconds, but then everything clicks into place and I'm writhing under the weight of him. He sets a steady pace, driving into me in firm, confident strokes that push me further and further on my way to a second peak. I hear moaning and it takes a moment to realize that it's coming from me. I pull against the restraint of his hold over my head, but he doesn't budge. Just kisses me, moving a little faster as he does.

I'm so close and yet, at the same time, I want this to go on forever. But it's like trying to hold back the tide. I'm panting and suddenly he's spearing in and out of me. Just the idea that I'm trapped under him, helpless, makes me moan loader, spurring him on. The bed creaks noisily beneath us and all I can think about is how much time I wasted sleeping with anyone else. This is the only man who's made me into a desperate, pleading, wanton participant in my own pleasure.

His thrusts are coming faster and harder, making me pant in anticipation of the thrill I feel coming. It starts in the extremities of my toes and my fingers, which instinctively curl inward. I can't seem to stop my head from rolling side to side and suddenly I'm raising and lowering my pelvis to meet his every reentry into my body.

Nate feels it, too. He's abandoned his control in favor of pure, instinctual pleasure. His deep, throaty grunts—so primordially *male*—are coming closer and louder. When I can't stand it another second, my body gives itself over to the arresting pleasure, allowing me to be pulled over the edge of the abyss. My mouth is wide open in a scream I can't even produce and my eyes are squeezed shut, brows drawn in intense concentration. It's as if I'm just tumbling—the bottom falling out of my stomach, while I clutch him tightly inside me. When I hear him give a hoarse shout of satisfaction, I know he's right there with me, freefalling. He loosens his grasp on my wrists and my hands fly to his hips, helping him drive us both through to the other side.

When we've finally stopped moving, he lets himself drop, catching himself on his elbows before the sheer weight of him can crush me. Lying like this, chest to chest, I can feel his heart from the inside out and wonder if he can feel mine, too. It's racing. We're both covered in sweat, our rasping breath the only sound in the room. Nate lowers his forehead so that it's touching mine.

"Holy shit," he whispers in dazed amazement.

"Holy shit," I echo.

At last he rolls off me and up from the bed, making his way to the bathroom, presumably to dispose of the extra large evidence. As he does, I take in his rear view. His well-cut muscles ripple right up through his calves and thighs, buttocks and back. He is really quite spectacular this man—in more ways than one.

I hear the flush and then the water running in the bathroom. He sticks his head out.

"Come have a shower with me."

As much as I'd like to just lie here, boneless and spent from the sex we've just had, I can't pass up the opportunity help him lather up. I get up and stroll across the bedroom, the air conditioner chilling the sweat on my body. It gives me a shiver.

"Me, too," he says, noticing my goose bumps. "It's nice and steamy in here."

I follow him into the glass shower stall—which is more than adequate for the both of us—and we stand there facing one another, a cloud of warm mist rising around us. As the water beats down my back I flash back to the night of my catastrophic performance. The hour I spent crying in the shower with only the clouds of steam for comfort.

Nate leans down and gives me a long, sweet, slow kiss that makes my knees go weak. Again. I pull him closer and closer until my breasts are pressed up against the hard plane of his chest, the water sluices between our two bodies.

"Hi." He smiles down at me when our faces finally separate.

I return the smile. "Hi."

"That was pretty fucking amazing, Alex."

"I know, right?" I agree a little too enthusiastically.

He throws his head back with a deep, throaty laugh.

My smile tips up into a full-on grin and then I'm laughing, too. He grabs me around the waist, lifting and spinning me in a tight circle, barely missing the soap dish. When he sets me down again, I hurl myself against him so hard that he nearly topples over, taking me with him. My head is to his chest, my arms wrapped around his midsection and my hands are mapping the geography of his back. Every ridge and line and... I stop cold and push away from him slightly.

"What?" he asks. "What is it?"

"Turn around."

He looks confused for the briefest of moments. And then he doesn't.

"No, Alex, don't—"

"Turn around," I repeat more firmly this time.

With a sigh of resignation, he does as I ask and suddenly I'm there, face to face with the very literal scars of Nathanial Calloway's past.

# CHAPTER 18

# Nate

Thirty-six, thirty-seven, thirty-eight...

I count the tiles in the shower stall. Eighty-two up, forty-eight across—give or take a few that are cut to fit against the floor and the ceiling. It's a habit I got into years ago. A way to take me out of myself—distract my mind from whatever horrific procedure my body was undergoing. Not that this is horrific, exactly. It's more like extreme discomfort.

"Breathe," she coaxes me softly from behind. I hadn't even realized I'd been holding my breath, and now it comes rushing out of me in one long gust.

Her hands are gentle as they trace the lines of the zipper scars running up and down my spine and back. I nearly jump out of my skin when I feel her brush across the back of my right arm. That's a bad one. I needed four surgeries on that arm. The other is a little less gruesome. Wait till she gets a good look at my chest and legs from the front.

One, two, three, four, five, six, seven...

I stop counting when her arms wrap around me from behind and her cheek presses up against my back.

"Do you still have pain?" she asks me.

I shrug. "Sometimes. It's not like it used to be. My back can become a problem when I'm playing something long. I have to change my position all the time and it looks really weird…"

"Oh! Like when I saw you playing the Grieg the other night. You kept lifting yourself off the bench while you were playing."

I nod. "Yup."

"Funny, you didn't do that today when we were playing together, and we were at it for a while."

She's right, the searing nerve pain was strangely absent as we shared that piano bench this afternoon.

"Yeah, I noticed that, too. I think it might have something to do with me not having to work quite so hard when there are two of us. You've got one end of the keyboard covered and I've got the other. I'm not having to lean quite so far one way or the other to compensate."

"That makes sense." She pauses for what must be a full minute, just holding me to her tightly, as if I might levitate up and away if she doesn't anchor me with her body. "Was it horrible?"

She doesn't mean the aftermath of the crash. She means the crash itself.

"I don't know," I admit. "I don't remember it really. I mean, I remember a loud cracking noise and then I was tumbling, hitting the walls and floor and the ceiling of the lav. I had that sensation of being in free fall, but I couldn't see anything."

"My God," I hear her gasp softly under her breath.

"I was lucky. I blacked out somewhere in there so I don't have any recall of the actual impact. When I woke up, I was in the back of an ambulance, surrounded by paramedics."

"The pain must've been unbearable."

The temperature of the water from the showerhead is starting to drop. I don't want to be here for a cold shot in the crotch.

"Do you mind if we get out?" I ask and feel her stiffen.

"Oh, I'm sorry. I shouldn't have—"

"No, no, it's not that. The water's starting to get cold. Why don't we continue this discussion in bed."

When she extricates herself from me, I'm immediately cold. It's still hot as hell outside but the air conditioning in this house is ridiculously low and now that I don't have hot water beating down on my chest, I'm feeling the chill. I get out first, and hand her a towel from a shelf over the toilet. I grab another, first drying myself with it and then slinging it over my hips like a loincloth.

"Nice," she says with an appreciative smile when I'm facing her again.

"You're not so bad yourself. That towel is barely big enough to cover your T&A."

She scrunches her nose. "T&A?"

"Tits and—"

"Oh, okay, okay. Got it," she says, holding out her hand to stop me.

"Sorry, was that too crude?"

"No...just a little 'horny fourteen-year-old boy,' that's at all."

"Ah, well there you have it, then," I agree sheepishly.

She goes to the bed, which she proceeds to straighten and fluff after our rather athletic encounter has left it disheveled. Then she pulls back the corner of the comforter, slides in under the sheets and pats the empty spot next to her. I comply, ditching the loincloth along the way. When I'm with her under the covers, I pull her to me so that she's resting in the crook of my arm, her head on my shoulder. She snuggles in, draping both her left arm and leg over me.

"So, your parents..." I begin quietly.

"Ugh, please."

"They love you, don't they?"

She shrugs. "Who the hell knows? Nate, I'm almost twenty-five-years-old and they pay all my bills. They tell me what to play and where. They've had my career mapped out for me since I was four. Jesus, I never even wanted to be a pianist!" Alex grows very still in my arms as soon as the words are out of her mouth. "I—I don't know why I said that."

"Because it's true? That might explain why you freak out on stage. If you're saying it's *never* felt right, I mean."

"It felt right today. With you."

It did, and that's just as big a mystery to me as it is to her.

"I was in the hospital for over a year after the plane crash," I say, taking a sharp detour in the conversation. "All that time spent staring at the same walls, the same faces. My aunt was there—and she was amazing—but it was just all that *time*. There's a reason why solitary confinement is considered torture. If you spend enough time inside your own head, you start to get a little...crazy."

She flips herself over onto her stomach so she can look me in the eye.

"Stop it. Don't say that. You're not crazy, and you weren't in solitary confinement. You were a scared little boy."

"Alex, when you have nothing but time on your hands, the mind can take you to some dark, dark places. At first, all I could think about was my family and the horrific, hellish way they died. Terrified and in agony. God, my sister, Annike...was just a kid and her life was over, all because her big brother had to be a superstar. If it weren't for me, they wouldn't have been on that plane."

It's taken me more than a decade to say that out loud. And, in the end, it wasn't to a psychiatrist or a reporter or even my aunt. It's to a woman I barely know. A woman I suddenly can't stand the idea of being separated from. Whom I can't fathom hiding anything from. Is that possible? Oh, Jesus. This cannot be that "love at first sight" bullshit in all those romance books... Can it?

"You listen to me," Alex hisses. She gets up from her reclining position to straddle me, her body sitting across my stomach. Her naked body. On my naked stomach. "Your family loved you. They were on that plane because they wanted to support you—to be there when you competed. And again, you were a child. They died loving you. Being proud of you. Don't you see, Nate?" She bends at the waist and leans forward so that her face is right over mine, her breasts brushing against my chest. Her naked breasts. On my naked chest. "I'm so, so sorry that you lost them, especially that way. And, you may hate to hear this, but the press was right. You were—you still *are* a miracle. You've endured, despite all of this tragedy. And now, you're finally going to finish that journey that you started when you won the gold medal."

I look at her skeptically.

"Believe me when I tell you that's not something my parents would ever do," she informs me. "I'd give anything to have someone love me enough to follow me halfway around the world just to watch me play."

"What? How can you say that?" I ask incredulously. "I read that your parents are with you everywhere you travel, every place you compete or perform."

She's shaking her head before I'm even finished. "No. They don't travel with me because they're proud of me or excited for me. They travel with me to ensure that I don't embarrass them. To keep me from doing anything stupid, like getting friendly with a competitor or drinking the night before a recital. They want to be there to do damage control if necessary."

"Isn't that love? I mean—in a weird, kinda twisted way?"

"My mom, she loves me...I think. But not enough to protect me from him. His word is the last word. For her. For me. He's a goddamned bully and we're both terrified of him. Of what he's capable of."

"And what is he capable of?" I ask, feeling myself tense up. "He's never...hurt you or your mom, has he?"

When she shakes her head, her beautiful, long dark hair swings from side to side. Her dark eyes are sad, suddenly.

"No. He doesn't need to lay a hand on us to hurt us. He knows how to cut to the bone with his words, Nate. He's a real son of a bitch. I can't even believe that we're related."

"Will he come looking for you?" I can't believe how this single question has my guts twisted up in knots.

"If he figures out I'm here, he'll come for me. But it'll take him a while to figure that out."

"And what will you do when the summer's over?"

"I don't know. Are you asking me if I plan to go back to New York?"

"I'm asking you what this is, Alex. Because, maybe I'm crazy, but this feels like something. I mean, unless I'm way off base here..."

"No, you're right," she agrees quickly. "I don't think it's nothing either. But *is* it something? I don't want to presume...you know...that it's anything serious. It can be a casual thing if we want it to be."

"I don't think that's what I want, Alex."

She looks confused.

"What's what you don't want? I've lost track. Do you want something...or nothing?"

Rather than talking about it anymore, I reach up, grab her by the waist and push her back. Just a little bit. She gazes down at me, clearly puzzled, thinking I'm pushing her away. But I'm not. I'm pushing her closer. And when her butt feels my hard cock behind her, she gets it, too.

A broad smile fills her beautiful face.

"My, my, my, Mr. Calloway. Aren't we the overachiever!" she says coyly.

I shrug. "Maybe."

"Hmm. Well, you know, we have two choices here. I could get up and go fetch us another condom. Or..."

"Oh, I like that option very much. But, just out of curiosity, what's the 'or'?"

"Or this."

In the blink of an eye, she's managed to scoot herself up and over my erection so that she's now sitting on my calves facing it. She lowers her head, takes me in her warm, moist mouth and I forget everything. Including my own name. And that's something.

CHAPTER 19

*Alex*

"Alex?"

His voice is a husky whisper in the darkness.

"Hmmm?" I murmur from the adjacent pillow, eyes still closed.

I wonder how he knows I'm awake? That I've been awake for some time now, in spite of the fact that we haven't slept a full hour between us since we hit the sheets last night.

"What do you think will happen when your parents find out you're here?"

When my lids flutter open, we are face-to-face. What a nice face to see next to me. This guy is growing on me, that's for sure.

"I'm hoping they don't find out. But...if I'm honest, I know my father is looking for me. And he's furious. Like spontaneous-human-combustion-level furious."

"He'd be that mad that you went away to study for the summer? It's not like you're hanging at the beach for three months, working on your tan and sipping fluffy pink drinks."

This makes me chuckle.

"I like the sound of that. Can we go now?"

He lifts an eyebrow that tells me he's not budging on the topic that easily. I sigh and continue.

"Yes. And no. I mean, yeah, he'll be pretty pissed that I blew-off his plan to supervise my recital prep all summer. But there was this thing that happened before I left..."

When I pause a little too long, he scooches closer until our noses touch and he looks like a very attractive cyclops.

*God, I hope I don't have dragon breath!*

"Go on," he coaxes.

"So, I sort of hit him."

"You... You hit your father?" He pulls back a little to get a better look at my expression.

"Well, I didn't punch him. But I did slap him."

"Wow."

"Yeah. Wow is right."

"What did he do?"

"Oh, he just stared at me, incredulous, this bright red outline of my hand on his cheek—"

"No, I mean, what did he do that *made* you slap him? Must've been pretty bad. Unless you have some super-scary temper that I don't know about..."

I offer a weak chuckle, not really wanting to get into the details of that awful morning but doing it anyway. Because I haven't told anyone about this. And I need to. I mean, Nate Calloway's already been inside my body. Might as well let him hang in my head for a bit, too.

"He pretty much told me I wasn't good enough at anything to support myself, including flipping burgers."

"Ouch."

"It was reflex. I was exhausted and wrung out from the night before—because that's when he pulled this stunt, early on the morning after my clusterfuck of a performance at Carnegie. I was doing an excellent job of making myself feel like shit, I didn't need any help from him or anyone else, for that matter. If I'd been a little more rested and a lot less beaten-down, I'd have done what I usually do—just ignored him. Let my mom smooth things out later."

"But you didn't do that."

"No."

"You hauled off and slugged him."

"What? No…"

"I'm just teasing," he says, poking me in the stomach with his index finger until I'm laughing and squirming. "But I wouldn't want to be alone with you and a baseball bat in a dark alley."

"Yeah, well, believe me, when Wyatt first tracked me down, it was in a dark alley and I'd have given anything for a baseball bat at that moment. I thought for sure he was going to rape me, kill me, and cut me into little pieces. Not necessarily in that order."

Nate opens his mouth to say something, stops, shakes his head and changes his mind. "Yeah I'm not going there. But seriously, you're going to have to see them at some point. I mean, unless you're planning on going to ground. And, if that's the case, I know a guy who knows a guy who can get you a whole new identity."

I tilt my head to one side, considering him.

"I can't tell whether or not you're kidding."

Nate raises his right hand, as if he's being sworn into office.

"I assure you I'm telling the truth and nothing but the truth, so help me God."

I grin at him, my eyes taking in the slopes and valleys of his face cast against the moonlight streaming through the window.

"And why would you need someone with that particular skillset?"

He shrugs.

"There have been times when it was better that no one knew my name. So, I occasionally avail myself of an alternate ID."

I make the move from my pillow to his, nudging his arm up so I can slip under it and rest my head on his shoulder, draping my leg over him.

"Ooooo! A man of mystery! What's your name?"

He looks confused for a second.

"Umm...Nate Calloway..."

"No, silly!" I swat at him and watch as his brilliant white teeth practically illuminate the room when he smiles. "What's your fake name? Your pseudonym. Your *nom de plume*."

"Oh! Oh, that! Michael. Michael Holloway."

"Okay, I get the Holloway part, it's kind of like Calloway. But what made you choose Michael?"

"They been calling my 'Nate, the musical miracle' for years now. I never thought it had the right ring to it. But Michael..."

"Miracle Michael," I muse. "Michael the Musical Miracle. Yeah, I get that. Good choice." Without warning, I swing myself up and over his torso so that I'm straddling him, looking down.

"You know," he begins thoughtfully, "I think I might just feel a miracle coming on..."

When I feel him stir beneath me, I know just what he means.

* * *

"Nope, nope, nope. Hold up, hold up," Wyatt calls out over us as we butcher Claude Debussy's *Petite Suite* for the third time.

We may have been off to a great start the other day—when we were playing an easier piece—but there's no room for hesitation, or flubs, or "off" timing in this one. I look at Nate who quirks an eyebrow and shrugs. It's making me crazy being this close to him. I can smell his scent—that clean, fresh, masculine smell of a recently-showered man. And I can attest to just how recent his last shower was, as I was present for it this morning. Not to mention the one that we squeezed in during the middle of the night after a particularly sweaty bout of...practicing. Oh, yeah. We were taking our practicing very seriously last night. So much so, that Nate had to drag me out of bed this morning for my solo lesson with Wyatt.

Right now, I take a long, deep breath through my nose, trying to inhale him into my lungs. That's when I feel him giving me a gentle nudge with his foot. When I look up, he shoots me a warning glance and gives an almost imperceptible shake of his head. I guess he's trying to tell me that this isn't a normal, everyday, non-sleeping-together gesture that people utilize.

But I'm not worried about Wyatt noticing anything out of the ordinary. It would appear he's got other things on his mind. Things that have him rubbing his temples in a gesture I've come to recognize not as frustration or impatience, but as thoughtfulness. The wheels are turning in his blond head right now...and I see the moment the idea comes to him as clearly as if a light bulb appeared over his head.

Then he's over to his desk, clicking and scrolling and printing. Less than a minute later he's back with a single sheet of paper in his hand and a shit-eating grin on his face. He leans across the top of the piano with his elbows so he can address us.

"So, the *Petite Suite* is based on poems by a nineteenth century guy named Paul Verlain. I thought that maybe, just maybe, if we get back to the source material, you'll get the gist of what Debussy was going for." Behind Wyatt's back, Nate rolls his eyes. "This first one is *En Bateau*. And for those of you who don't speak French, that means sailing. But this isn't just any random boat on the water. This particular little craft is carrying a pair of lovers..."

*Seriously? He couldn't possibly...could he?*

"It's dusk and they're having a romantic sail on a glassy lake. Very romantic."

*Shit, shit, shit. Maybe he does know.*

"So that's what I need from the two of you. I need for you to be lovers. On a boat. On a lake. At dusk," he says, watching us expectantly from across the Steinway grand. "Do you think you can try that for me?"

I can actually hear Nate gulp from next to me. When I glance his way, he looks a couple of shades paler...but he's nodding his agreement.

"How about you, Alex?" Wyatt asks.

Is he mocking me? I examine his expression carefully. Uh-uh. He's being sincere.

"Um...yes, Wyatt. I can give that a try," I reply evenly.

"Excellent!" he says, standing up straight again and rubbing his hands together excitedly. "Okay, so you guys start and I'm going to read some lines of the poem as you play. Let's see if maybe that makes a difference in your musical inter-pretation."

Wyatt still hasn't gotten us a second bench, so we're still squashed together on the one—not that I mind. God knows every part of Nate has been squashed up against every part of me at some point in the last week. Our upper arms are touch-ing...our thighs, too.

"Okay, here we go," he says, giving us a slow countdown to match the languid tempo of the music. "Three...two...one..."

He is the lower half of the keyboard, I am the upper. And from my fingers flow the gentle waves upon which my boat is sailing.

"Meanwhile comes the moon and beams," Wyatt says

slowly, just loud enough for us to hear him over the piano, "as the sailboat gaily skims briefly over waves of dreams."

The water ripples upward from the bass at my left to the treble in my right. It comes as one continuous wave. My simple melody floats above him—sometimes inserting itself right in the middle of his trajectory, so that his hands flank my left and my hands flank his right. We are deliciously entangled. Until we're not...

"Meanwhile, up comes the moon; the bark gaily sails round the little park. Over the water, dreaming, dark."

We extricate our tangled limbs for a quick recap before taking off into a game of hide-and-go-seek. Our hands play and chase, taunt and tease their way up and down the keyboard. But we're not done yet. Wyatt has one last stanza— the conclusion to our little tale of love on the water.

"Moon emerging; Small boat on short journey. Glide on water, dreaming."

A dreamy little sequence provides a bridge for us to return to where we began, floating and carefree, gentle waves rippling underneath our sailboat. We trade the melody between the bass and the treble, echoing here and there until, at last, we slow and soften until we're no longer there anymore—the boat just a distant memory as the last chord dies away.

Wyatt is so happy he looks as if he's about to throw his hat up in the air and break into a line dance on top of the piano. I think he'd do it, too, if the damn thing didn't cost fifty-thou-sand-bucks. Nate and I sit back, both of us breathing hard, considering what a gentle, low-key piece we've just played. His fingers brush against mine on the bench, well out of Wyatt's line of sight.

"Excellent!" he exclaims through his huge grin. "Abso-lutely stunning! How'd that feel to you two?"

Nate and I look at one another and shrug in tandem.

"Pretty good," he says. I can tell he's holding back, afraid that showing too much enthusiasm will give us away somehow.

"Yeah, the poem really helped," I add with a nod.

Wyatt is still grinning when he comes around to our side of the piano and, standing behind us, wraps one arm around each of our shoulders, inserting his head between us. When he speaks again, the grin is still there, but his voice is much softer and coaxing. Almost...conspiratorial.

"So, how long y'all been knockin' boots?"

# CHAPTER 20

# Nate

"Oh my God—I thought I was going to die right there—in his studio!" Alex gasps as she rubs my bare chest lazily.

I pull her closer against my naked body under the sheets. "Well, I can't imagine it was any more mortifying than having a meltdown on stage at Carnegie Hall," I muse.

She considers this for a long moment. "Yeah...I'm gonna have to go with less mortifying. But mainly because Wyatt was so...you know...so *easy* about the whole thing."

"Yeah, there's something about that guy. But let me ask you—as a girl—"

"Woman," she corrects me with a point of her finger. "I should hope you can make the distinction, considering what we just spent the last hour doing."

I can't argue with that. "Sorry, *woman*. So, as a woman, do you find him...you know...hot?"

She snorts and looks up at me with a smirk. "Seriously? You're asking me if I find a man my father's age hot?"

"Yes."

The smirk dissolves into a sheepish smile. "Yeah...kinda..."

"I knew it! I've seen him around women. They just like gravitate toward him. I mean, what *is* that?"

"Oh, well, the cowboy thing is a big plus."

"Really?" I scour her face for some sign that she's pulling my leg.

"Really. There's like a whole sub-genre of romance books involving cowboys."

My turn to snort. "You're making that up!"

She shakes her head earnestly. "No, no, really. Also, for men in uniform—cops, military..."

"Funny, I never pegged you for a romance reader. Or a reader at all for that matter..."

"Actually, I'm not. My mom is."

I don't know why, but I find this totally scandalous. "Your mother? Madeleine Mickelson? *The* Madeleine Mickelson? The goddess of piano reads cowboy romance?" Alex giggles and the sweet sound sends a jolt of electricity to my groin. I clear my throat and try to redirect my thoughts—for a little while, at least. "I mean, when does she even have time?"

"Well, it's not like she's playing twenty-four-seven. And God knows she spends enough time in airports. And, really, if it's a choice between talking to my father or reading about smooth, tan, six-pack abs, there's no competition."

I take a peak under the sheet. "Hmmm...no six-pack here," I observe with a pouty face.

She gives me a playful nudge.

"You've got plenty of other...attributes. So, anyway, back to your initial question—yes, I do find Wyatt to be very attractive, though he's more in my mother's wheelhouse than mine."

"Maybe you should introduce them?" I suggest with a sly smile and watch in amusement as her face scrunches up.

"Please—I wish. If my mom hasn't left my father yet, she never will."

"Is he that bad?"

"Worse. I don't know how he managed to get her to marry him in the first place. God, he's such a...a..."

"Micromanager? Controlling jerk?" I offer helpfully.

"Dick. He's a total and complete *dick.*"

I burst out with a deep belly laugh and she moves her soft, warm hand to where my abdomen is rising and falling.

"A little harsh, no?"

"No," she assures me emphatically. "He's mean, manipulative, shallow—I'm not convinced he isn't a sociopath, Nate."

I'm not laughing anymore. "What? Why would you say that, Alex?"

She shrugs. "I've done my research. He ticks a lot of the boxes. No empathy, self-absorbed, manipulates everyone to get what he wants, treats his wife and daughter like trophies rather than people."

"Huh. Wow. You've really given this some thought."

She nods slowly. "I've had twenty-four years. My mom's had thirty. She just rolls with it and tries to keep things as smooth as possible between the three of us. Unfortunately, that usually entails giving in to his ridiculous demands."

Alex has already told me about her father's plan for her to move back home for the summer and study with them. Truth be told, I'm having a little trouble being totally sympathetic— given the dearth of parents in my life—but I'm smart enough to keep my mouth shut and nod my head in understanding. It's what she needs. And I need her.

As soon as I register the thought, I suck in a breath so quickly that it makes her sit up and look down on me.

"Hey, you okay?"

"Yeah..."

"What *was* that?"

"Nothing," I lie. How can I tell her it was my reaction to a momentous revelation that has no business being anywhere in my universe? Ever. Period. *Need* her? I hardly *know* her! And, since when do I need anyone?

"That was *so* not nothing," she says dubiously. "Come on, Nate. Were you thinking about your parents? I'm sorry—I shouldn't be complaining about mine..."

Thank God—she's thrown me a life raft. "Yeah, that's okay. It just...it just hits me sometimes. But let's not talk about all that right now. This summer is about us. About getting better acquainted." I lean down in an attempt to capture her lips and get things moving in a more...active...direction. But she puts two fingers to my mouth, her dark eyes seeking out mine.

"I think...this summer is about getting better. Period. On the piano. In our heads. This—" she removes her touch before I have a chance to suck those fingers into my mouth, waving her hand at the room around us. "This...this thing with us is a really nice unexpected bonus."

I feel my heart sink. Damn. Why do I do this to myself? Why should I think that this is anything other than a summer fling for her. Before I can pretend to be all cool and nonchalant, she rolls on top of me, placing her palms on either side of my head and leaning down close to my face. She smiles.

"Well?" she asks.

"Well what?"

"I'm waiting for you to call bullshit."

Oh...I am so confused now.

"Bullshit on...?"

"I'm not stupid, and neither are you. I know you feel it, too. There's something indescribable between us. I just can't... I can't quite figure out how I got along without you all these years."

I have nothing to say to that, so I don't even try. In one fast and fluid movement, I flip her over onto her back so that she's caged in under me.

"It's fast," I point out.

"It is," she agrees solemnly.

"I do feel it."

She smiles up at me with an adoration that snatches the breath from my lungs. "I know. And, whatever it is, I say we just go with it and see where it takes us."

"I like that suggestion," I murmur as my lips meet hers.

Finally. I sigh with the relief of it. Of her.

* * *

When I wake at three in the morning, the bed beside me is empty. And cold. I know this because I put my hand on the sheets. So, she's *up* up. I get to my feet, pulling on a pair of sweatpants and wander out into the hallway, making a pitstop in the kitchen so I can chug a bottle of water. From here, I can see the jumping, jerking play of light spilling out from the living room, which tells me she's watching TV. Not that I can hear it, she must have it on low so as not to wake me. Probably some late-night horror movie or something. Not much else on at this hour. Five-hundred freaking channels and there's never anything on. At least, nothing worth getting up in the middle of the night for.

I pad along the carpet and pause just shy of the entrance to the room. I can see her from here, her face silhouetted by the light of the screen. Whatever it is she's watching has her totally rapt and it gives me a chance to really see her. To study her fine features. The long, dark hair is wild and unruly, tumbling down her back and shoulders as she sits there in my over-sized t-shirt. I feel some more lascivious activity coming on and consider the practicality of jumping her right there on the couch.

"Hey, what could possibly be more entertaining than a

night in bed with me?" I tease as I step all the way into the darkened room.

She looks horror-struck. Terrified. Guilty as fuck. For a split second, I think I've caught her watching something naughty. Not that I would've minded. Hell, I'd have made a bowl of popcorn, grabbed a box of condoms and joined her. But, when I glance over my shoulder to see what it is that she's seeing, it takes me several seconds to process. At first, it makes no sense. That can't be... can it? Oh, it is. It most definitely is. Laid out in front of me in all of its flat-screen, high def, surround-sound glory, is the day my life ended.

The day I didn't die.

# CHAPTER 21

# *Alex*

I'm so engrossed with what I'm watching that I don't hear Nate leave the bedroom and make his way down the hall. When I realize he's behind me, I jump up guiltily—like a teenager caught in front of a steamy movie.

"I—I'm sorry, Nate... I couldn't sleep so I was just going to watch a little television and this was on... I just... I couldn't stop watching." And I mean it. The sheer coincidence of this particular documentary being on at the same time I'm up with a bout of insomnia...well, the odds are pretty slim, if not astronomical.

He doesn't say anything, just stares, transfixed, at the scene unfolding on the screen. And then he's sinking to his knees and collapsing into a heap on the floor like a wilting flower. On the screen in front of us, NTSB investigators are combing the wreckage of a flight. His flight. Nate picks up the remote and raises the volume when a silver-haired expert on aircraft disasters begins to speak. He's retired now, but spent the better part of a year investigating the crash of flight 7079.

*"It was the worst site I've ever been on—even now. Nothing compares to the devastation in the field that night."*

Then the film cuts to footage of the aftermath. There is debris everywhere—big chunks of the twisted metal, seats ripped from the floorboards and flipped over. A child's shoe. And smack in the center of it all is the burnt-out hull of the fuselage, like a charred skeleton smoldering in the middle of the field.

"Here, let me turn this off—" I say, reaching for the remote, but he shakes his head and shrugs me off.

Now it's a shot of the tail section, overdubbed by the mellifluous voice of the narrator.

*"Miraculously, when crews came upon the wreckage of the tail section, they found a single survivor. Alive, though critically injured, a barely breathing twelve-year-old Nathaniel Calloway had been in the aft lavatory when the plane crashed."*

And there he is. But it's not the broad, strong, confident man I've come to know so intimately. I'm looking at a child. Frail, bloodied, and bruised as he's extricated from the grim scene on a stretcher. One slender arm hangs down, having escaped the blankets that swaddle him. Then, suddenly, we've gone back in time a few days to see Nate as a happy, healthy twelve-year-old performing flawlessly at the Rossi International Piano Competition. His fiery rendition of Tchaikovsky has the huge audience on its feet, applauding wildly before the last note has died away. The camera cuts to the ecstatic faces of his parents as his little sister jumps up and down. Nate reaches out and touches the image of their faces with his finger. But they're gone a moment later.

*"In an instant, Nathanial Calloway lost everything and everyone dear to him. In an instant, Nathanial Calloway became a symbol of hope for an entire nation,"* the narrator informs us. *"Dubbed the 'Musical Miracle,' Nathanial stayed in the public eye for years after the crash, the press providing regular updates on his progress to a country hungry for a miraculous survival story."*

And now video of a young boy on crutches as he makes halting, painful progress down a hallway.

*"Doctors never expected Nathanial to walk again—but he did. And, while he went on to live a quiet life in the Midwest with his aunt, the public's interest in the Musical Miracle has never waned..."*

I drop to the floor and wrap myself around him. Not just my arms, but my entire body drapes around his, as if I can absorb him into me. As if I can take on some of his pain and give him even the slightest bit of relief from the hell that he dreams of every night. I feel him shake beneath me and I realize he's crying.

"Shhh. Shhh, it's okay. It's going to be okay," I soothe him. "You don't have to be alone anymore, Nate." At the sound of my words, he grabs me around the waist and clings to me, his tears soaking through my nightshirt. "It's okay, Nate." I lift his tear-stained face and press my lips to the damp skin. First his eyelids. Then his forehead. His jaw line and Cupid's bow. When my mouth finds his, he latches on hungrily. As we kiss, my hand reaches around behind me, feeling along the floor for the remote. When I find it at last, I turn the thing off so he can't be haunted for a single second longer.

"I haven't ever..." he begins, pulling back just far enough so he can speak. "I mean, I knew it was out there—the producers asked to interview me—but I never saw it. Never wanted to see it. And my aunt did an amazing job of keeping the pictures and video out my sight..."

"Wait, wait, wait...are you saying you've never seen any photos or video of the crash site?" I ask, holding his head in my hands. He shakes his head and closes his eyes. I pull him to my chest and run my hands through his thick, dark hair. When he speaks again, his voice is muffled by my body.

"I've always told people I had no recollection of the crash.

But it must've been in there—somewhere in my head—because now that I see this, it's all come flooding back to me."

Oh, dear God. The last shred of merciful ignorance he's been clinging to for the last fifteen years—ripped away just like that. *Why the hell didn't I just turn the TV off? Or change the channel? Why was I riveted by this tragedy? Suddenly I feel like a voyeur—some kind of sick, rubber-necking looky-loo who can't help but slow down as she passes the scene of a fatal accident.*

I hold his head and I rock him back and forth, back and forth, until I'm not sure who's comforting who anymore.

We don't talk about it again. Any of it. Somehow, we find our way back to bed and spend most of Saturday there, holding one another under the covers. We ignore the concert hall and the practice rooms. In fact, we don't so much as mention music or piano or Wyatt or anything of any real substance. Instead, we curl up on the couch and binge watch *Game of Thrones* (his pick) and *Outlander* (my pick). The two series are just steamy enough—and we're just randy enough—that we end up going through the better part of a box of condoms before the weekend is over. It isn't until Monday morning, when I'm seated at the piano in Wyatt's studio, that I realize the price of our weekend "off the grid."

He's got the heel of his right hand pressed against his forehead now and he's shaking his head.

*Shit. This doesn't look good for me. Maybe if I'd bothered to warm-up before our lesson—to run a scale or two... but I didn't. And my cowboy/piano professor is in one foul mood this morning.*

"Alex," he starts slowly when he finally removes his hand from his head, "I thought we had an understanding—the two of us. I'd take you on as my student. For free. I'd spend my entire summer helping you to work through this thing that's holding you back. In exchange, you'd work your ass off for me. Because, here's the thing, Alex, I can't want this more than you do. And I'm beginning to think that's the case here."

"No. No, no, no, Wyatt—you've got this all wrong. I had a bad weekend—we had a bad weekend. I'm sorry. I do want this, I swear it..."

But he's not having any of it.

"Maybe this was a mistake. Because, not only are you fumbling and stumbling over material that you should have memorized by now, but I suspect this fling between you and Nate will also impact his playing."

"Come on, Wyatt. That's not fair and you know it!" I object, unwilling to take the blame for something that hasn't even happened yet.

"No? Huh. Hold on a second." Wyatt leaves me sitting at the piano watching after him as he steps out into the hallway. The sound of his boots on the linoleum floor fade away as he leaves the studio wing. It only takes him about five minutes to return with a very confused looking Nate in tow.

Wyatt gestures to the bench and I scoot over so Nate can join me.

"What the hell's going on?" he mutters under his breath.

"Don't ask," I caution. "He's in a bad mood and he's really, really pissed."

If our professor overhears this exchange, he doesn't say anything. Instead, he slaps some music down in front of us. I realize with growing alarm that this was the piece we were meant to work on over the weekend. Except that we didn't. We haven't played so much as a round of Chopsticks since Friday afternoon and now he expects us to play the *Danse Macabre* with some measure of success.

We are so screwed.

"Alrighty then, you two," Wyatt says as he walks around to the other side of the piano so he can stand right over us and watch as we play. Or whatever the hell it is we're about to do. "You know the music—everyone knows the music—death dancing, corpses rising from the grave, skeletons rattling, right? So, this arrangement for piano four-hands should be a walk in the park, right?" He doesn't wait for us to answer. "Wrong. It's one of the trickiest arrangements I've ever come across. But, since you two don't seem to think you need to put in any practice time over the weekend, I assume you think you can just waltz in here and sight read it. Am I right?"

He's glaring down at us now. And, while I've had time to adjust to this nasty side of Wyatt McFadden over the last hour, Nate has not. And he's not nearly as diplomatic—or contrite —as I am.

"I don't remember saying that, Wyatt. This weekend was an exception. You know me better than that. You know both of us better than that—"

"Spare me the bullshit, Nate. Just lift the lid of the piano."

"What? Why?" I ask.

When Wyatt sneers, every trace of his boyish good looks and charm evaporates.

"If you'd bothered to even look at the score, Alex, you'd know that it opens with one of you plucking on the wire itself to simulate the clock striking midnight."

I tighten my mouth into a sharp line, afraid that if I open it even a fraction I'll say something that I'll regret. Or, worse, spill the beans about Nate's little breakdown this weekend. That's definitely not my story to tell so if the man sitting to my left doesn't care to bring it up, I'm sure as hell not going to.

Nate gets up, props the lid and glances down at the music. Without another word, he starts plucking the piano wire. Once, twice, six times...twelve. He sits down and plays the creeping chords that pave the way for my entrance in the treble end—the part usually reserved for the violin in the orchestra version of Saint-Saens' Dance Macabre. It's not bad. I'm not bad—considering this is the first time I've seen the music. Wyatt was right—it's a piece that we all know but it's not one that was written for piano so, while I kind of know what it sounds like, I've never actually had to work my way through it. Still, I do a reasonably good job holding the melody line together while Nate accents in the bass. In fact, that whole thing is sounding reasonably good. That is, until the opening fiddle lick returns with a much stronger pulse and faster tempo...and with Nate playing in tandem. It requires complete synchronization—which we'd have had if we'd taken even a few minutes to play through it. But we didn't. And, so, we don't.

Nate's a split second behind me, causing an echo effect. Out of the corner of my eyes, I see Wyatt's jaw harden and his nostrils flare.

He. Is. Pissed.

"Enough!" he yells loud enough to make the both of us jump on the piano bench. "Just stop. Stop, stop, stop."

"Wyatt, man—"

Wyatt holds up a hand, stopping Nate mid-sentence. He takes a deep breath, closes his eyes for a moment and, when he addresses us again, he's clearly working to keep calm.

"Okay, so here's the thing," he begins softly. "When I was a few years younger than you, I was in piano duo. And a damn good one, too. Oh, it started off innocently enough—we were paired up by the piano faculty for a department recital my junior year. And I'll be damned if we didn't have amazing chemistry, the two of us. So amazing that it spilled out of the practice room and into the bedroom."

I shift uncomfortably on the bench. This is not a side of Wyatt that I care to explore.

"We fell in love. And we played our asses off. It was great...until it wasn't. A few nasty bumps in the road and our personal lives were impacting our professional lives. It got ugly and we lost a lot of credibility over that. I'm not saying it's impossible to have a relationship and play together. I just want you to be aware of what a slippery slope you're on. Because, in the end, you might turn out like me—thinking about her and what might have been. Thinking about how you had it all and then fucked it up every single day of your life."

Holy. Shit.

# CHAPTER 22

# Nate

We're both so stunned by this rare glimpse into Wyatt's mind and his personal life that we just stare at him, waiting silently for him to reveal something else. But he just eyeballs us with a mixture of irritation and pity and regret that has me even more rattled than before.

"Um, Wyatt," I venture after a long pause, "could we—can I please speak to you...privately? *Please?*"

He looks as if he's going to tell me to fuck off, but, in the end, he simply nods and waves a dismissive hand in Alex's direction.

"Alex, take the music and head to the practice room. Hit that spot with the metronome—you're getting too fast too early. It'll build but not quite that soon."

"Okay, Wyatt," she murmurs softly, standing and pulling the sheet music from the bridge of the piano. "I—I'll go do that now. Maybe I can come back and see you after lunch?"

He shakes his head. "No, it's okay. Spend the afternoon working it separately and together and we'll start again in the morning. Okay?"

It's his way of apologizing. I think.

Alex nods and leaves, shooting me one last questioning look over her shoulder. My God she's a beautiful woman. How the hell did I get so lucky? The thought makes me wince. Hasn't that always been my problem? Too lucky? Lucky enough to win the Rossi competition. Lucky enough to survive a plane crash. Lucky enough to be right here, right now.

Once we're alone, I get up off the bench and pull a chair up to Wyatt's desk. He's planted himself there and is scanning his email absently.

"Wyatt, something really crazy happened this weekend. It threw everything off...I couldn't even leave the house. We stayed in bed all—"

His head whips around and he's glaring at me now. "Nate, I really do not need to hear the details of your extracurricular activities."

"Hey, man, will you just shut the fuck up for a second and listen?" I snap and wait to see if he's going to kick my ass to the curb. He doesn't. He just sighs with some irritation and nods for me to go on. I do.

"I came across that shitty docudrama bullshit on TV. The one about—about the plane crash that came out right around the tenth anniversary, you know? I saw a lot of stuff I'd managed to avoid seeing all these years. The accident scene, footage of them pulling me out. Some media clips from the competition. My parents..."

He's on his feet before I can even finish telling him, looking down on me looking up at him.

"Jesus Christ on a pogo stick, Nate! Why on God's green earth didn't you just say so? I'd have understood!"

I stand, too, so that we're eye-to-eye.

"I know you would have. But, dude, you were being kind of a dick, you know?"

He blinks hard. And then he bursts out laughing, throwing his head back so far that the cowboy hat slides right off of it and onto the floor. I start to laugh, too, and, before I know it, we're both laughing so hard there are tears running down our faces. Only my tears turn into something different somewhere along their journey from my eyes, down my cheeks and to my chin. At some point they morph from tears of laughter to tears of anguish. He knows it. He sees it, and he hears it. And soon I find myself in his tight embrace. It's different from when Alex holds me. Very different. Wyatt's hug brings with it the reassurances of a man who has lived and experienced and learned.

"You're okay, Nate," he says quietly as he pats my back. "It was just a matter of time, son. You can't hide from that horse-shit forever, you know. Eventually it comes looking for you."

Feeling a little more in control, I pull back from him, looking down at the floor as I use my sleeve to paw at my soaked face. It's so fucking embarrassing—and frustrating—this riptide of emotions that keeps pulling me under. Every time I think I'm clear of it, I'm overpowered again.

"Yeah, yeah, I know," I mutter, willing myself to meet his bright blue eyes. The anger and irritation are gone from them now, replaced with concern. Not pity, thankfully. Never pity from Wyatt—and for that I'm grateful. "But listen, it's not Alex's fault. She was helping me keep my shit together, man. Just don't take it out on her, okay? I did this."

A small, sad smile crosses his face. "Boy, you are good and smitten aren't you?"

"I...uh...yeah. I guess there's no point denying it. I've known the woman all of five minutes and now she's under my skin. I have no idea what I'm going to do when she goes back to New York." I'm stunned by my own admission. The thought was always there, in the back of my mind, but this is the first time I've managed to give voice to it.

"That's exactly the way it happens, Nate. So fast and so sneaky that you never see it coming. You don't have any time to protect your heart," he says knowingly.

That's when I realize—he's talking about that woman. His duet partner. He never did get over her. It's why he's still alone. It's why he doesn't perform himself.

"What happened?" I ask him. "What happened to her, Wyatt?"

For a second I think I see something flicker in his eyes—but then it's gone so fast that I can't even say for certain that it was ever there.

"Better things than me, Nate. Better things than me."

* * *

Wyatt's words plague me over the next two weeks. They *should* make me want to hold on tight to this beautiful, brilliant woman who's wandered into my world and thrown my life into a holding pattern. Instead, they make me think about that long-ago relationship with Lindsay—how I trusted her with my heart and paid for it dearly. I'm not a stupid guy—I know how this ends. She goes back home. I go back home. We keep in touch for a little while and eventually one of us will move on—most likely her. I'll go back to being alone. And lonely. But for now...

"What are you thinking about?" she asks me through a mouth of General Tsao's chicken.

"Nothing."

"That is so not nothing. You're like a million miles away."

I shrug. "Maybe I'm wishing you'd eat that naked. Since we're in bed and all."

Alex rolls her eyes and pokes my ribs with her chopsticks. "Yeah, it's all fun and games until someone gets sweet and sour sauce in their navel," she warns and then pops the food into her mouth. Her beautiful, full, soft mouth.

"I promise you, Alex," I say, raising my hand as if I'm taking an oath. "If *anything* lands in your navel, I will personally remove it. With my tongue."

"Ugh!" She makes a disgusted face as she chews.

I tackle her then, prying the wooden weaponry/cutlery from her hands and flattening her on the bed, her body pressed tight against mine.

"Your mouth says 'ugh' but your eyes say, 'ooooooooohhhh,'" I tease as I start to kiss along the extended column of her neck. She grunts and swallows. "Well that's quite sexy..."

"Nate..." she gasps when the food has finally cleared her esophagus. "God, Nate..."

"Uh-huh?" I murmur distractedly, locating the delicate dip of her collarbone. Jesus, she's like this frail little bird. Her bones are so tiny...and dainty. How can they possibly be strong enough to support her? This makes me think of her elegant wrist. I pull it up and encircle it with my thumb and forefinger.

"What?" she asks, curiously lifting her head just enough to peer down at what I'm doing.

"Nothing. It's just you're so fragile. And strong. At the same time. How's that even possible?"

Her lips tip up into a half-smile. "You always know just what to say."

"I do?" Huh. Wonder how I managed that?

"Yeah, you do," she assures me, pulling her arm from my grip so she can use it to pull me back down to her face. To her mouth.

Her tongue on mine is so gentle that it shouldn't be sexy. But it is...although there's only so much 'gentle' I can handle before I'm exploring and stroking and teasing without benefit of hands. Those are too busy holding her face still, as if she might pull it away, denying me this divine access at any second. And I couldn't stand to have that happen. But she doesn't. Instead, she sighs against me; into me. She literally infuses me with a tiny piece of her soul and it leaves me wanting more. So much more.

In a heartbeat, I've managed to wrestle the shorts from her long, tan legs, panties going along for the ride.

"Unhhhh..." she groans beneath me. A signal that I'm on the right path.

Reluctantly, I allow our faces to separate long enough to pull off, first my own T-Shirt, and then hers. But my eyes never leave hers for a second. Christ, the way she looks at me—looks through me—as if she knows my heart. As if she could possibly conceive of the hell I've been through and still love—

I break off the thought before I can finish it. It's way too dangerous to allow it to see the light of day. Or the dark of night, as the case may be.

"What?" she asks again, though this 'what' is decidedly different from the last one.

I shake my head. "Nothing. You're just so..." More head shaking. There are no words for what this feeling is. Because I can't readily define it. It's a cross somewhere between ecstasy and pain and desperation and contentment.

Holy shit. I'm in fucking love.

"I love you," I blurt before I can stop myself. And then I hold my breath. Will she laugh? Will she pretend I didn't just say that incredibly ridiculous thing? Will she—

My runaway thoughts are stopped short by the way she yanks me to her with a force I didn't know she possessed. And then all bets are off. The only thing standing between us are the cargo pants I'm wearing. I can't get them off fast enough— for either of us. She's pushing. I'm pulling. Fuck, I'm never going to wear underwear again. Way more trouble than it's worth at a moment like this. When I'm finally free of my cotton restraints, I don't waste a single second burying myself in her warm, silky, wetness. She throws her head back with such force the headboard slams back against the wall.

"Oh...Oh, God, Nate... Nate..."

"I love it when you say my name," I tell her on an upstroke.

"Nate. Nate, Nate, Nate," she murmurs over and over again and it's making me absofuckinglutely crazy as I slam into her again and again. I've never been this rough, but she's not objecting. Quite to the contrary, actually, as she pushes up off the bed, forcing me back onto my knees, and straddles me. Like she's sitting in my lap. Dirty style.

Some garbled semblance of a groan escapes my throat but it's about all I can manage as she begins to rock herself back and forth, up and down, taking control of every ounce of her pleasure. Our pleasure. And she's not taking her sweet time, either. With her face right next to my ear, it's impossible to miss a single audio cue. Her sighs and whimpers morph into a gravelly moan. In a matter of seconds, she's panting harder and harder as she rides me in a corresponding fashion.

I'm a goner—all control ceded to the stunning woman atop me as she reaches her peak with a keening I've never heard in my life. It pushes me right over the edge, my own orgasm exploding against a veil of starbursts that leave me dizzy and disoriented for a full minute while we both return, reluctantly, to the earthly bounds of this bed.

I'm still trying to catch my breath when she begins to pepper my face with tiny little kisses.

"Don't, I'm a sweaty mess," I object, laughing as I turn my face away. But she's not having it. She secures it with both of her lean but strong hands, her lips pressing to my skin with even more fervor.

"Don't care," she manages to murmur between brushes. "I can't...I don't ever want to let you go..."

We stay like that, with me inside of her, until she's decided that I'm not going to jump off the bed and run away. When we finally separate, I realize with dawning horror that things are quite a bit messier than they should be.

"Oh, shit... Alex, we didn't—"

"Use a condom? I know," she informs me calmly.

"I'm sorry—you know? You *knew* and you didn't say anything?"

She smiles at me as she allows herself to drop back against the pillow.

"I'm on the pill, Nate. Have been for years."

"Oh." I'm not quite sure what to do with this information.

"We didn't know each other at first so...I couldn't risk, you know, getting anything from you... just in case you had a whole gaggle of piano groupies or something..."

I snort at the visual and she continues.

"But now..."

"Now?"

"Now I know you. And now I love you."

I never realized that when they say your heart "skips a beat" it really does skip a beat. But now I know it. And now I know her.

And now I know she loves me, too.

I am so screwed and I just. Don't. Care.

# CHAPTER 23

# *Alex*

He's in this hole-in-the-wall shop off of Los Brazos when I spot him behind the cover of an old Shostakovich LP. Abner Beckett blends in with all of the other hipster-villagers in Manhattan but here, deep in the heart of Texas—where weird reigns supreme—he sticks out like store thumb. I set down the vintage Van Cliburn I'm holding and turn slowly, so as not to draw too much attention to myself. I've managed to inch my way to within a few feet of the shop door when someone comes in, causing the little bell to tinkle—and making Abner Beckett glance up. And down. And up again, almost immediately. His pale gray eyes narrow suspiciously—he knows me, but he doesn't know how he knows me. Until he does.

I'm out the door before the perfect "O" of his stunned, open mouth can formulate an audible thought. But he's fast for a short guy in jeans in a-hundred-and-five-degree weather and I know by the sound of the tinkling bell that he's in hot pursuit. So to speak.

"Alexandria?" he calls after me but I've shoved earbuds in and bop my head a little, feigning an inability to hear his nasally little voice. "Alexandria Mickelson-Fitch?" he tries again.

I'm almost clear—almost—until the very polite young man with the guitar out in front of the coffee shop stops in the middle of his Leonard Cohen cover to get my attention. No way I can ignore him as he points behind me.

"There's a guy trying to get your attention, miss," he says.

I try not to look too pissed off with him as I reluctantly turn in the direction of the approaching man and pluck the silent buds from my head.

"Yes?" I say, pretending not to have a clue who he is.

"You're Alexandria Mickelson-Fitch," he informs me, panting a little as the heat and the exertion catch up with him. In the half-second I have to reply, I weigh the wisdom of denying my identity, coming to the conclusion that it's not a good idea to make an enemy of an arts critic.

With a sigh of resignation, I nod. "Yes. I am. And you are...?"

He's not offended that I don't know him—even though I do. I suspect he likes the air of mystery that surrounds him...the idea that he's an invisible defender of classical music, moving unseen among the masses as he passes judgment.

What he *is,* is a goddamned coward.

"Abner Beckett—,"

"Oh! Of the *Times*? *That* Abner Beckett?" I smile with faux excitement.

It works. He's grinning so hard his scrawny little goatee practically touches his earlobes. "One and the same. I didn't know you were in town. Are you giving a performance somewhere?"

"Ah...no. My mother is from here originally and I like to come back every few years for a visit."

He studies me carefully and I wonder if he's going to grill me for inconsistencies in my story. But he doesn't. What he does do, however, is more terrifying than I could have ever imagined.

"Alexandria, may I buy you a cup of coffee?" he asks with a nod toward the shop we're standing outside of.

"Uh...sure...?"

"I don't bite, you know," he kids and, for a just a moment, I see him as a regular guy, instead of the pretentious, pompous windbag that I assume him to be. Maybe I'm wrong. "Unless I'm writing a review that is!" He smirks and snorts at the same time.

Nope. My assumptions aren't going to make an ass out of me today.

I give a lame chuckle and follow him into the coffee shop. Five minutes later, we're seated in a quiet corner—me with a latte, him with a huge mocha-strosity that requires a straw as wide as PVC pipe to get it down.

"So," he begins amiably, poking a hole for his straw in the three-inch whipped cream cloud, "how've you been feeling since your recital?"

"Fine, thank you," I say, using a sip of coffee for a period.

"I understand you already have a new date lined up," he ventures.

Do I?

"I do."

"And it's quite an ambitious program!"

It is?

"It is."

If he's waiting for me to elaborate, he's going to be waiting a long time—because I have no clue what the hell he's talking about. But he's not stupid. He takes a different tack—one that leaves me with little room to circumvent his fishing.

"What's the date again? I want to be sure I've got it on my calendar..."

Little. Shit.

I force myself to remain completely placid, even though my heart is about to pound out of my chest. One wrong move and I'm this guy's next exposé.

"Oh, hmmm…" I quirk an eyebrow and pretend to think hard. "You know, my father's moved the date around a few times already. To be honest with you, I'm not sure what we settled on. But I'd be happy to confirm that with him and get back to you, Mr. Beckett…"

"Please, please, call me Abner," he coos in way that makes my stomach turn.

"O-Okay…Abner…"

"You know, I can do a lot for you, Alexandria," he continues in the smarmy tone. "I'm a man with consider-able…reach. A few well-chosen words from someone like me and your career is set. On the other hand…" Oh, he is *not* trying to shake me down! The little weasel! "I sometimes find myself with an extreme dislike for someone. And that can be a hard thing to disguise in my writing."

"Oh? I thought journalists were supposed to remain objec-tive. Although, I suppose you're not really a journalist…"

He bristles even as he affixes a tiny smile to his face. "I consider myself to be a journalist."

"I'm sure you do." Why am I antagonizing him? There's nothing—and I mean nothing—good that can come out of this. I stand up and glance at my watch as if I've suddenly real-ized what time it is. "I'm terribly sorry, Abner, but I have to go—"

When his hand wraps around my wrist, it's slick from the condensation on his glass. It doesn't feel anything like when Nate held my wrist. He made me feel like a fragile beauty. This guy makes me feel like there's a manacle tethering me to this table.

"Do you, Alexandria?" he asks. "Do you really need to leave so soon? I think we were just getting to know one another. Of course, my hotel is just around the corner. Perhaps we could continue this discussion there? It's a bit more private..." His voice tapers off—not because the innuendo is clear, but because he sees something behind me. Something that makes him scowl.

"Everything okay over here?"

I don't need to see the person to whom the deep voice belongs to know that he's big. I can tell by the way Abner has to crane his neck to look up at him. And I can feel the heat rolling off of him as he stands directly behind me.

"The lady's just fine, thank you, Mr. Cowboy," Abner informs him coolly. "You can just shuffle along to your square dance, or sheep shearing, or whatever it is you guys do down here."

Oh, bad idea. Very, very bad idea. The guitar player stops playing. The other patrons stop chatting. Even the incessant hiss of the milk steamer goes silent and it feels as if all eyes are upon Abner Beckett, chief music critic for the *Times* and jackass-at-large.

The stranger reaches around me and grabs Abner's arm at the wrist. I notice the full sleeve of tattoos that runs from the top of the man's hand to the bottom of his elbow. "You'll wanna let go of her now, son," he says.

Abner only tightens his grip, making me wince in pain. "First of all, I'm not your son, asshole. Second, we weren't done with our conversation. Trust me, she *wants* to hear what I have to say."

As nice as it is to have a white knight ride in to save the day, I'm thinking it's high time this cowgirl started roping her own cattle...or baling her own hay...or whatever other western metaphor is appropriate for this situation. So, I twist my head in the direction of the register where the barista looks poised to jump right over the counter and throw a few punches if necessary.

"Sir, does that video camera work?" I ask him with a nod toward the lens with the blinking red light up in the corner.

"Yes'm, it sure does."

"I'd be real grateful if y'all could send a copy of that to the police," I say in my best Texas drawl. "And to the *Manhattan Times* newspaper. In case you didn't know, he's Abner Beckett —a real important writer up there. Those folks don't take kindly to their writers making them look bad."

"That Beckett with on T or two?" the still-unseen man behind me asks.

"Two. B-E-C—" Before I can finish spelling his name, Abner has released my wrist and stood up so quickly that his metal chair clangs to the floor loudly.

"All right," he spits at me quietly. "All right, I'm leaving. But you'd better get ready for the shit storm that's about to rain down on you, Alexandria Mickelson-Fitch. You and your mother and your dick of a father. Soon the whole world is going to know what a fucked-up bunch of losers you are."

I laugh because I just can't help myself. "Oh, Abner, that horse is already out of the barn, buddy. If you think my father being a dick is 'breaking news' then maybe you'd better find yourself a new profession. Everyone knows it, dude—and no one gives a shit."

"This isn't over—"

The threat is cut short when my cowboy security detail finally steps into my line of sight long enough to put a hand around the journalist's scrawny neck.

"Oh, I'd say it's good and over. I'm given this little lady my phone number. And if I hear you so much as breathed in her direction, I'm gonna come a-lookin' for you Abner B-E-C-K-E-T-T of the *Manhattan Times*. So why don't you just make yourself scare afore I decide to see you back to your hotel room myself. You know, the private one. 'Cause you and me, we could find plenty to talk about, Abner."

I watch with perverse satisfaction as the blood drains from Beckett's face. He gives a single nod and walks out of the shop as quickly as he can and still call it walking.

"Oh, my God, I cannot thank you enough!" I say with clear relief when he's gone and I'm finally facing my guardian angel.

He's probably near sixty, with tanned skin and a face that's been weathered by too many summers in the hot Texas sun. When he smiles, it reaches all the way to his soft hazel eyes.

"Happy to help, Miss…Alexandria, was it?"

"Yes, sir. But you can call me Alex," I reply with a grateful smile of my own.

"Here…" he reaches into his wallet and pulls out a business card for me. "Don't you hesitate to call on me if I can be of any assistance, Alex."

"Thank you," I say again, giving him an impulsive kiss on the cheek. He blushes and walks out of the shop as time and sound resume again all around us. I glance down at the card in my hand and pocket it for future reference.

* * *

"Are you *insane?*" Nate demands incredulously. "Why would you ever agree to have a cup of coffee with him? And then, why would you antagonize him like that?"

I can't believe what I'm hearing. I practically ran all the way to the concert hall so I could tell him what happened. Explain how scared and angry and relieved I was feeling. Here I thought he'd be furious on my behalf—worried even. But he's actually going to pin this debacle on me.

"Nate, I didn't do anything wrong…"

"No? Well, now he knows you're here. It won't be long before he figures out why. That leads him to Wyatt. Which leads him to me, Alex. Jesus Christ! How could you have been so careless?"

"I—I don't..."

"Abner Fucking Beckett! He's been after me for an exclusive for years! Oh, god, if he puts the two of us together..."

"What? What if he puts the two of us together?" I demand. "What then, Nate?"

He glares at me across the piano. "You know what."

"Do I? Tell me, Nate."

I'm pushing too hard, but I'm pissed and I just don't care.

"He's going to tell the world where I am, what I'm doing. He's going to write about how I'm a washed-up has-been. He's going to ruin any chance I have of making a comeback, Alex. Thanks. You've pretty much just ensured that my life as a pianist is over."

I feel the sting the same as if he'd slapped me with his hand rather than his words. Not a week ago he was telling me he loved me. Now he's telling me I've destroyed his life. But something's changed since I got here—since I started working with Wyatt. I'm done being the victim. I won't do it for my father. And I won't do it for Nate, either. So, I square my shoulders, take a deep breath and stand tall. When I speak, my voice is clear and calm, my tone even.

"Nate, I love you. But I will not let you lay this bullshit at my feet. Your life as a pianist was over the second that plane went down. Not because you couldn't play after that—but because you wouldn't. And you still won't. I'm sorry if you think I did something wrong this afternoon—and maybe I did —but it doesn't have anything to do with you. Because not *everything* is about you, Nate."

"I can't believe you would say that to me," he hisses. "I thought—you said you loved me, too... And now you think you can just—you can just say that shit to me? Like what happened to me was just another setback?"

"No!" I object. "No, no, Nate!" I rush to be close to him. "I need for you to hear me. You spend all this time talking about your comeback...but you never make any plans for it. It's always somewhere, out there in the future. When you're ready. When the press isn't watching. When people have forgotten. When, when, when, when. There's always another 'when,' Nate. You've got to stop this! You're not living your life, you're hiding from it..."

"Stop it!" He yells so loud that my ears ring. "Jesus Christ, will you just stop it?"

I stare at him, feeling my gut churn and face flame, unsure of what to do next. I work to keep back the bile that's rising in the back of my throat.

Nate stomps around the stage now, pacing and running a hand through his already tussled hair. When he spins around to face me again, it looks wild, like his eyes. It only takes him a few seconds to close the distance between us, approaching so quickly that I take an involuntary step backward, expecting him to crash into me. He's scaring the hell out of me and he doesn't even realize it. Or maybe he doesn't even care.

"You have no idea," he begins, biting off each word as if he's fighting to stay in control. "Your life has been a fucking cakewalk compared to mine. Yeah, yeah, your daddy's an asshole. You're mom's weak. Poor little Alexandria. Poor little rich girl. Doesn't have to do anything but play the piano. No job. No school. No obligations. Well, aren't you just the lucky one?"

And just like that, my fear evaporates. The churning stomach, the flaming face—they're the perfect match for the wave of rage that crashes over me.

"You arrogant, self-centered son of a bitch!" I screech at him. "How dare you speak to me like that? I'm the one who was accosted and threatened today and you make it all about you! I tell you my deepest, darkest feelings and you throw them back in my face! Why? Why did you tell me you loved me, Nate? Why when it's so obvious that you're incapable of loving anyone?"

"Ahem!"

I'm not sure if we were so loud that we didn't hear Wyatt come in or if Wyatt was so quiet that he snuck up on us. Either way, he's standing there at the foot of the stage, looking up at us.

"I'm done, Wyatt," I say quietly. "I can't do this anymore. I'll stay on and study with you solo, but I can't—I won't spend another second sharing a piano with him."

"That makes two of us," Nate mutters.

Wyatt considers us for a long moment. I wait for the cowboy wisdom. I look for his affable nature and comforting smile. I don't get any of them. What I do get is even more frightening than my encounters with Abner and Nate put together.

"Unacceptable!" he yells and slams his hand down on the stage hard. "You do *not* get to bail on one another—or on me! That is one thing I will not tolerate. I've invested too much time and energy on the two of you and you will see this through. I don't give a damn if you hate each other, if you can't stand the sight of each other. You will get your asses on that piano bench and you will be at every lesson. You will practice. I did not just waste an entire summer on two ingrates. Understood?"

I nod. Nate nods. I'm shaking and I'm pretty sure he is, too.

"Good!" Wyatt yells up at us. "Now get home, both of you! I want you in my studio on time tomorrow, prepared to work until your goddamn fingers bleed on the keys. And then you'll work some more. Got it?"

I nod. Nate nods. I'm sweating and I'm pretty sure he is, too.

"No phone calls or texts or smoke signals—I don't want the two of you talking tonight. I'll be supervising your rehearsals until you can get your heads out of your asses. Jesus Christ on a fucking pogo stick! I have never in all my years doing this come across two musicians who deserve each other more than you two do. For the first time—ever—I regret offering to help. I'm wishing I'd never heard of you. Either of you."

Wyatt's still shaking his head and muttering under his breath as he turns around and stomps up the aisle and toward the exit of the concert hall, leaving us staring after him.

"Go home!" he calls out as he lets the door slam closed.

I nod. Nate nods. I'm crying and I'm pretty sure Nate is, too.

# Alex

"I like having you around again," Ellie says as she serves me a plate of pasta and joins me at the table in her kitchen. "I've missed seeing your face."

I give her a weak smile. "Thanks."

After an extended stay at Nate's apartment, I've spent the last six nights in a row back here at her house—where I plan to stay for the foreseeable future.

We eat in companionable silence for a couple of minutes and I wonder if she knows. I wonder if Wyatt told her about the blow-up with Nate. How we're on a rigid schedule of supervised rehearsals and lessons. How he doesn't joke with me anymore. How Nate and I both seem to do nothing but irritate him. If she knows any of that, she doesn't say.

"You know, your mom and I were best friends," she says quietly. I look up, but she's busy examining the spaghetti she's wrapping around her fork. "Good lord, she was beautiful. And laughing—always laughing. That girl just had a way of making everyone around her smile." I stare at her, fork poised halfway to my mouth. "Something wrong with the food?" she asks when she notices.

"Uh...no... I just... I didn't realize you knew her that well," I confess.

"Oh, I knew her real well. I was at her wedding. And I came to see you in New York the week you were born."

The fork clatters as it falls from my hand and hits the bowl.

"You—you did?"

She nods solemnly.

"We were going to be stars together, her and I. We'd go to Juilliard for grad school and take the world by storm. I wanted to be a concert pianist—play with orchestras all over the world. She wanted to be a recitalist and give concerts in all the grand salons of Europe. We'd get a flat in London as our home base and travel from there. Date handsome men in every country but always come home to each other. We were like sisters, Ellie and I."

With my mouth hanging open and my eyes wide with shock, I'm sure I must look rude at best, ridiculous at worst. Still, Ellie keeps regaling me with tales of the mother I had no idea I had.

"But then everything changed. She fell in love and I knew our little fairytale was just that. Oh, sure, I was disappointed, but she was so happy—how could I not be happy for her? That she'd found something so special..."

I'm having a hard time imagining my parents in that kind of a relationship. Could he have been so very different back then? Or maybe it was her... What had changed?

"Was it me?" I blurt.

Ellie's dark brows knit together in confusion. "Was what you, honey?"

"Am I the reason things got so bad between them? Why he got so mean and she just...just did whatever he told her?"

She opens her mouth to say something then seems to think better of it. Her long slim arm slips across the table and her touch brushes gently at the fingertip-shaped bruises on my right wrist.

"You should put a little ice on this," she says.

"Did he ever love her?" I ask, still thinking about what she's just divulged.

"Your father? I think so. In his own way... But men like Hugh are wired differently, Alex. Their entire identity is wrapped-up in what they do, who they are, who other people think they are. And when you live your life like that, you start to forget the things that really matter."

"She never fights him. She just lets him do whatever. He treats me so badly. And she lets him." My voice is small now—tiny, like a child's.

"He's a hard man to go up against. But you already know that, don't you?"

I nod because I can't speak. If I try to say another word, I'll just start to cry again. And I don't want to cry anymore. It's all I seem to be able to do lately. But she doesn't require me to speak.

"It's been a long time since I've spoken to your mom but my guess is, the same way that Hugh has forgotten what really matters, Madeleine has forgotten that *she* really matters. And you... Well, you do matter—to both of them. I know that beyond a doubt, Alex. They're just so lost in trying to sort out what's real and what's for show that you've somehow gotten lost in the shuffle, honey. But now you're a woman. You're old enough to put the hurt behind you and move on. It's time, Alex. It's time for you to take your life back and be the woman that you want to be. Sweetheart...do you even want to be a pianist?"

She's looking at me with so much intensity that I'm certain she must be able to see right through me. She'll know if I'm lying, so I tell her the honest-to-god's truth.

"I wasn't so sure when I first got here. But now...I think I want that more than anything," I whisper.

She smiles. "Good, because I think you're about the best pianist I've ever known."

"What?" I can't disguise the shock I feel. Surely, she's kidding...

"I'm serious, Alex," she assures me, as if she can read my thoughts. "There's a grace and an ease to your playing that your mother never had. Or me. Or even Wyatt. You're the pianist we all *wanted* to be, Alex."

"No...please, don't say that..."

"Why not?" she asks.

"Because I'm a failure. I'm a fraud. What good is a professional pianist who can't play in front of an audience?"

"Who says you can't?"

"You know! You know what happened to me at Carnegie Hall..."

"Yeah? What about it? You had a bad night. We all do. Even the almighty Hugh Fitch himself has made some very big, very public flubs on that million-dollar Strad violin of his. It's one of the reasons he demands perfection now."

"What? When?" My questions come out as gasps.

Ellie just smiles at me across the table, her warm hand still covering mine. "Uh-uh. You'll have to get your mom to tell you that one."

"But...but I—"

She shakes her head.

"Sorry, Alex. Now, what about Nate?"

"What about him?" I ask cautiously. She quirks an eyebrow, waiting for an answer. Somehow, I think we'll be here until the wee hours if I don't give her one. "He hates me. He thinks that idiot Abner Beckett is going to find out he's here and tell the whole world that the Musical Miracle is nothing more than a has-been."

"Oh, my. Well, that's a bit dramatic, isn't it? And maybe a tad narcissistic? I mean, considering you're the one Beckett wrote about in the *Times* and you're the one he man-handled down at the coffee shop..."

Ah, so Wyatt *had* filled her in after all...

"Right? I know! But that didn't even seem to bother him! He was so busy accusing me of ruining his big comeback... The comeback he's never going to have..."

"Oh, he'll have it alright."

"You think?" I ask, her clear confidence making wonder if she knows something I don't.

"Absolutely. Wyatt will never let him slip back into obscurity again. Once Wyatt McFadden has his claws in you, he never lets you go. Ever."

I consider asking her if that includes the mystery woman, but then it occurs to me that maybe *she's* the mystery woman. Maybe Ellie broke Wyatt's heart and he's still not over it, even though they've been friends all these years. I make a mental note to run this theory past Nate. And then I remember that I can't. Because Nate's a jerk. And because *he* broke *my* heart.

"I love him," I say in a voice barely above a whisper. "Nate —not Wyatt," I clarify.

Ellie smiles. "I know, honey. I know."

"I didn't think it would be like this—the pain. Even when it's good, there's pain. And when it's bad...my God, it's agony."

She nods knowingly. "Yup. Sounds like love to me."

"What do I do?"

"You wait, Alex. He'll come around. Or he won't. And if he doesn't, your heart will mend and you'll move on. It's all you can do."

"Wyatt never moved on," I say, watching her reaction. And I get one.

"What do you mean?" she asks, suddenly on guard.

"The one that got away. He told us about her."

She looks taken aback. "He…he did?" I nod. "Huh," she says thoughtfully.

Oh, God, it really is Ellie! I keep my features neutral so she doesn't suspect that I know her secret. "I mean, he never said who she was. Someone from a long time ago, I think…"

"Yeah, a long time ago. Well, I suppose you've got me there, Alex. Wyatt is the exception to that rule about moving on. But that won't be you, sweetheart. You're too smart and too strong to be held back by anyone. Your heart is your own, Alex. That means you never give it away, you just lend it out from time to time and you take it back when you need it."

I nod as if I understand, but I don't. Not really. How could she hurt Wyatt so badly and not see what it's *still* doing to him? Maybe that's why she has an out-of-town boyfriend— so as not to rub it in his face. Still… When she pats my hand, I come back from my thoughts to the cold pasta in front of me.

"I'm going to heat these up," Ellie says, grabbing first her bowl, then mine. "Then we're going to take them into the living room and eat on the couch so we can watch the Lifetime Movie channel."

"So, we can what? Why would we do *that?*" I ask, horrified by the idea.

She smiles. "Because, Alex, there's nothing like a little woman-scorned, baby-sitter-in-danger, and switched-at-birth to remind you that things can *always* get worse."

I laugh for the first time in a week and it feels so good that I want to cry again. But I don't.

# CHAPTER 25

# Nate

After a week of watching and waiting—of scouring every inch of copy written by Abner Beckett and every social media post he publishes—I finally allow myself to relax a little. If he knew I was here in Austin, he'd have outted me by now. But he hasn't. Nor has he made any mention of his run-in with Alex. Though, if I were him, I probably wouldn't either. Being taken down a peg by some random cowboy and a barista doesn't look great for a guy who has a following like Beckett does. Still, it doesn't make things any easier between Alex and me.

I overreacted, I know it; she knows it; Wyatt knows it. Still, I can't bring myself to apologize. Nor can I make myself stop thinking about her. It's a clusterfuck of epic proportions— one that only gets worse as the days go by. Wyatt makes good on his threat to supervise our rehearsals so we spend hours on the Saint-Saens with him sitting in the corner, scowling at us over his laptop. He doesn't intervene as we snip and snap at one another, working slowly through the intricacies of each measure of music. Between Alex and me, our words are sparse —limited to brief exchanges about how to approach a phrase or tempo. The chill makes its way into our playing and I find myself stumbling again and again.

We're working a particularly tricky section when Alex stops playing suddenly, throwing up her hands in irritation. "Seriously?" she huffs.

"What? What did I do now?" I demand defensively.

"You know what you did! You've been purposely dragging the tempo since we started playing."

"Wyatt...can you please tell her that I'm not dragging, *she's* rushing?" I ask, hoping for a little back up.

"Come on you two, enough with the fussing," Wyatt chides from his desk where he's looking at his email but listening to everything happening behind him at the piano. "Let's try that again at your entrance, Alex."

She shoots me a nasty glance before nodding and taking a deep breath. "One...two...three..." she whispers and begins. I echo the melody a second behind her. We run up and down the keyboard in tandem in one fluid motion. Until we're not so fluid. Alex's fingers trip up and, rather than righting herself and getting back on track, she stops and slams her hands down in frustration. "Dammit, Nate! You're too close to me! I can't—I can't move, I can't breathe..."

"Hey! I didn't do shit!" I object angrily. "Stop being such a fucking Diva, *Alexandria,* " I spit back at her.

When Wyatt's hand slams down on top of the piano we both start. Neither of us noticed him getting up. And now, his normally placid face looks as if there's a thunderstorm brewing in it. "You know what? I've just about had it with the pair of you! And I'm starting to think you were better off when you didn't know one another! You love each other—your playing gets sloppy. You hate each other—your playing gets sloppy. Playing four-hands is all about communication and you can't even stand to be on the same bench!"

We're staring at him—agog, agape, and aghast—neither of

us daring to utter a single syllable. He's red from the neck up, making his white-blond eyebrows practically glow. His blue eyes have turned icy and hard. Holy shit. This guy is furious. He opens his mouth to lay into us again when there's a knock at the studio door.

"Go away!" Wyatt hollers. "Now, let's try this one more time. And don't you even think about stopping—" The knocker tries again, only louder. "Not. Now!" he bellows so loudly that Alex actually shrinks toward me.

And then it's a pounding that makes Wyatt curse under his breath as he storms toward the door. He grabs the knob and pulls so hard that the door flies inward, slamming against the wall. Standing in the doorway is a woman in her forties. She's tall and lean, with shoulder length chestnut hair that's threaded with bits of silver, and big, deep brown eyes. Wyatt is standing there, frozen and silent. He's looking down at her. She's looking up at him.

"Who the hell is *that?*" I murmur under my breath.

Next to me, Alex cranes her head to get a look at the mystery woman, unable to see from the angle at which she's sitting. But that only lasts for a second because he steps aside, a wordless invitation for the woman to enter. There's something about her...about him. I realize in a flash that this must be *her.* The one that got away. The one he never got over. In the instant it takes her to come through the doorway, Alex gasps and jumps to her feet so quickly that the music we've been reading catches the breeze she's created and scatters everywhere, pages floating down onto the rug like huge, flat snowflakes. Something is very, very wrong here.

"Mom!" Alex gasps.

And that would be it.

I should have seen the resemblance immediately. "Mom? This is...your *mom?*"

She shoots me a horrified look and nods, all of the color

drained from her face. I join her in standing and am about to say something—though I'm not quite sure what. And I never find out because Wyatt gets there first.

"Hello, Maddy," he says softly.

Holy fucking shit. I may have missed the connection between this woman and Alex, but I most certainly didn't miss the one between her and Wyatt. This is the "her" who haunts his dreams. Clearly Alex has not made that connection.

"Maddy?" she echoes. "*Maddy?*"

Now Alex and I are both staring at Wyatt. Who's staring at Madeleine Mickelson. Alex's mother.

"Hello, Wyatt."

* * *

Of the three of us, Wyatt seems to be the least surprised by the sudden appearance of Madeleine Mickelson Fitch.

"You're looking lovely, as always," he says, lopsided grin up and running at full speed. "To what do I owe the honor of your presence in my humble studio?"

The twang in his voice doesn't jibe with the formality of his words. This is getting more surreal by the second. But she's not having any of it. Madeleine shakes her head and shoots him a look that I can't interpret. Clearly Wyatt can, though, as he quirks a knowing eyebrow in her direction before she spins around to face the piano. Us. Alex.

"Well, young lady, I hope you've had fun playing hide-and-go-seek, leaving your father and I frantic, wondering if you were dead or alive."

Oh, please. Dramatic much?

I wait for Alex to express the same sentiment, but she only looks down at her hands like a toddler who's been caught with her hand in the cookie jar.

"Six weeks!" her mother rants indignantly. "Not so much as a text or an email! We were worried sick!"

And I believe that, to look at this woman, her expression alternating between anger and relief. She loves her daughter; that much is clear. Not exactly the monster I was anticipating, I have to admit.

"Alright, alright," Wyatt interrupts with a hand on her shoulder. A very gentle hand.

*Did he just give her upper arm a squeeze?*

"You!" the woman spits, all traces of relief evaporating. "You knew I'd be worried! Why didn't you get in touch? How could you, Wyatt? Is this...is this some kind of revenge thing?" she accuses, eyes narrowing and lips pursing.

This. Chick. Is. Pissed.

From next to me, Alex's head snaps up and her brows knit in confusion. She's so busy feeling guilty that she hasn't taken the time to wonder what the hell it is that's going on between these two. Because, whatever it is, it obviously predates her.

"Now, Maddy, I saw Alex's performance at Carnegie Hall and I knew I could help her get her playing back on track. It was her decision to come here and she didn't think you and Hugh would approve—"

"Approve? Approve! Of course, we wouldn't approve! Alexandria had a very comprehensive plan in place for the summer. And then you come along and just talk her out of it? Really, Wyatt!" She shakes her head in disgust, but he doesn't appear to be the least bit phased by it.

"I didn't talk her out of anything, Maddy. You know me well enough to know I'd never do that—"

"Yeah...and just how well *do* you know one another?"

All eyes swing to Alex, including mine. She's not looking like a chastised child now, with her hands poised on the bridge of the piano. When I look up at her, I flash upon an image of us—in bed. And her—on top

So *not the time, Nate!*

"We went to school together," Madeline Mickelson tells her daughter, not offering any additional information. Which is foolish, because if there's one thing that Alexandria Mickelson-Fitch is not, it's stupid.

Nope. She definitely knows how to put two and two together to come up with—

"Were you by any chance Wyatt's duet partner?"

Four.

Madeleine and Wyatt exchange a quick glance. "Uh...yes, for a time..." her mother says.

"Look, Alex, I'm sorry I didn't disclose that to you early on, but I didn't want you to think this was about anything other than me helping you. If I'd told you, you might not've come all the way down here," Wyatt explains contritely, then turns back to Alex's mother. "And, like I said, that's all that was on my mind, Maddy, I swear to God. I knew I could help her—I knew it in my heart. She's a damn fine pianist and you should hear the progress she's made here!"

Maddy looks toward us dubiously. "Funny, I don't recall there being any four-handed pieces on Alexandria's program."

"Funny, I don't recall choosing a program. Or a date. Or agreeing to do another performance at all!" Alex shoots back.

"Since when do you speak to me like that, young lady?" Maddy demands.

"Since I finally realized I'm a grown. Ass. Woman."

Before I can think too much about it, I give a little fist-pump behind the cover of the Steinway so no one can see me but her. She does and I'm rewarded with an almost imperceptible nod. I'm starting to realize what it was that Alex has been trying to tell me all summer long. This is not your standard parent/child drama. What's going on right here, right now, with her and her mom is something much darker and deep-seated. I can only imagine how her father fits into this equation. Speaking of which...

"You should know that your father is on his way back to New York," Madeleine hisses at her daughter in response and I notice Alex's hands clench into tight, white-knuckled fists.

"Isn't he in France? I thought he was going to be teaching at that music festival all month..."

"He was. But now that we know where you are, he insisted on coming here right after he performs tonight. He'll be home sometime tomorrow."

Wyatt removes his cowboy hat and scratches his platinum-blond hair, head tilted to one side in an unspoken thought. "And, just out of curiosity, how did you come to find Alex, here?" he asks.

"Why do you keep calling her 'Alex'? Her name is Alexandria!" Madeleine says, her voice rising again. She takes a deep breath, getting herself under control before speaking again. "If you must know, it was that horrible Abner Beckett."

*Little shit!*

"He made a point of finding me when I was teaching at Juilliard yesterday. He demanded—*demanded*—to know what you were doing here."

"And, what did you tell him?"

When I ask the question, everything stops. It's like they all forgot that I was here in the room, a silent observer just taking in the layers of dysfunction and peeling them apart.

"Who *are* you?" Madeleine Mickelson Fitch is the one demanding now.

I look up at Alex. She looks down at me and nods—I can trust her mother.

"My name is Nate Calloway, ma'am."

She raises a finger and starts to point in my direction and then stops. "Wait, wait, wait—you're *Nathaniel* Calloway?"

"Yes, ma'am."

Now she looks to Wyatt for confirmation. He gives it with a single nod of his head. She turns back to me.

"You're—you're here studying? With Wyatt?"

"I...uh...yeah, I guess you could say that. I want to play publicly again and it's been...you know...hard. And Wyatt thought he could help me get my head in a good place to do that. So...here I am..."

She seems to consider me for a moment. And then Alex. And then me and Alex.

"You're playing four-hands?" she asks, though the evidence in front of her is indisputable. We're not playing pinochle here.

"I tried a little experiment and put the two of them together," Wyatt pipes up now. "Maddy, you really need to hear them—"

She rounds on him so quickly that he takes a step back, lest she should decide to clean his clock with her dainty little pink-manicured hand.

"I don't need to hear them play. I know how good my daughter is and she does not need anything from you, Wyatt McFadden." Now she pivots back to Alex. "Let's go, Alexandria. We're going to get your things. From...where is it that you're staying?"

Alex's entire body seems to tighten up next to me. "I'm staying at Ellie Dominguez's house..."

Madeleine throws up her hands. "Oh, that's rich. Perfect. First Wyatt, now Ellie. Was anyone else from my past implicit in you running away, Alexandria? Please, tell me now so I can feel betrayed by everyone at once."

"She didn't run away," I say, standing up and trying not to be terrified by the evil eye I'm getting from Alex's mom right now. "She made a decision. She's twenty-four years old. She gets to do that. You can't run away from home when you're an adult."

"Mr. Calloway, I don't know what any of this has to do with you, but I'll thank you stay out of my family's business if you don't mind."

"I do."

"Excuse me?" she barks incredulously.

"I do mind," I repeat. "You can't just show up and drag her off like she's some wayward child. If she wants to stay, she'll stay. If she wants to go, she'll go. Either way, it's her choice and I won't allow you—or anyone else—to bully her."

There's a faint gasp from next to me and I know, without checking, that Alex is staring at me. Wyatt is doing a shit job of hiding his smirk and Madeleine looks as if she'd like to eviscerate me with her eyes.

"And what *do* you want to do?" she demands from her daughter.

Alex takes a deep breath. When she speaks, her voice is a little shaky, but it gets stronger with each word she utters.

"I—I'd like for us to go to Ellie's house. You and I. And I'd like us to spend the night there together. Then, tomorrow, I'd like for you to come and hear Nate and I play, Mom."

I can see the wheels turning in Madeleine's head. She looks at Alex, then me, then back to Alex again. "Fine," she says at last. "Fine. But we're on a plane out of here tomorrow afternoon."

Alex doesn't comment on the last part, but she smiles. "Thank you, Mom. I know you're going to love what you hear..." She makes her way around the piano and wraps her arms around Madeleine who resists for just a second before patting Alex's back.

"Alright, alright. Come on. I've got a bone to pick with Ellie," she mutters.

Alex kisses her mother on the cheek and then looks to Wyatt and me. "Ten at the concert hall?"

"Sure, I'm in," I say with a shrug, trying not to look too interested either way.

But Wyatt's grinning like a blond-haired, blue-eyed fool. "I reckon I might could make that happen…"

I reckon he just might.

# CHAPTER 26

# *Alex*

"I can't believe you," my mother grumbles as Ellie hands her another glass of wine. "You could've called me. Didn't you think I'd care, Ellie? Did it not occur to you that I might want to know where my daughter was?"

Ellie sighs and sinks down onto the loveseat across from the couch where we're sitting. "Mads, I haven't seen you or heard from you since Alex was a baby—"

"Alexandria!" my mother snaps. "Her name is *Alexandria!*" Then she turns in my direction. "Is this how it goes? You run away, change your name? Pretend you never had a family? Are we such an embarrassment to you?"

I snort before I can help myself. "Oh, please! If anyone feels like the embarrassment here, it's me. You and daddy have made it quite clear that I'm nothing but a disappointment to you—as a pianist, as a daughter and as a human being. And, you know what, Mom? You're right. I've failed miserably on all three counts."

I don't even realize that I'm shaking. And that there are tears streaming down my cheeks. I see her face soften and she opens her arms. I slide into them like I did when I was a scared little girl. She holds me and runs her hands through my hair.

"I was so afraid something had happened to you," she whispers against my face. "I thought you'd never come back to me. Why would you do that, honey? Why?"

I cling to her, my face buried in her shoulder, unable to look her in the eye. "You know why, Mom. You know."

She sighs heavily and holds me for several long moments before pushing me back gently at the shoulders so she can peer down into my face. "What have you been doing here? With Wyatt, I mean. Did you know that he and I played together many years ago? Is that why you came here?"

"What? No! I had no idea you even knew one another. He never said a word." I explain how he followed me that night in the rain and how my father's ultimatum forced me to take Wyatt up on his offer. By the time I'm done, she looks stunned. And exhausted.

"You know, I'd thought about sending you here. I almost mentioned it to your father... Well, you know how that would've gone over. And he was never a fan of Wyatt's."

I sit up, wiping at my damp face. "Wait, Daddy...knows Wyatt, too?"

"Of course, he knows Wyatt. I was...you know... I was with Wyatt when Daddy and I met."

"You were...playing piano with Wyatt?" I ask carefully, not sure where this line of questioning might lead me.

"Among other things," Ellie snorts. My mother shoots her an unmistakable warning glare.

"What? What is it that you're not telling me? Were you and Wyatt..." And then it hits me like a freaking Steinway falling from the sky. "Oh! Oh, my God! It's *you!*"

"It's me what?" Mom demands.

"You're the one he told us about! The one who broke his heart! It was you, Mom, wasn't it?" It comes out as more of an accusation than a question. Her split-second hesitation gives me my answer. "Oh...my...*God!* How could he not have told me?"

It's Ellie who jumps in here. "Because he didn't want you to have that baggage, Alex—sorry, *Alexandria*. Wyatt only asked you here because he believes he can help you, not because of who you're related to."

My head is spinning as a few of the pieces lock into place. But only a few.

"So, what was he doing at my concert then? I mean, he told me he was seeing an old friend but he never said who...was that you, Mom? Are you and Wyatt...you know...?"

My mother looks aghast and offended at the same time. "Of course not! Alexandria, is that what you think? That I've been sneaking around on your father?"

"Well it's not like he doesn't cheat on you..." I mumble.

The timing of my comment is unfortunate in that Ellie is mid-sip with her wine and hasn't had time to swallow it. "Goddammit!" she yips, using a napkin to blot at the chardonnay shower that's just sprayed across her throw pillows. "You two are something else," she mutters, shaking her head. "Well, at least it wasn't red..."

"Ellie!" Mom hisses at her old friend.

"Well, she's hit the nail on the head, hasn't she? We both know Hugh's been cheating on you since before this child was even born..."

"Holy shit!" I exclaim. "Is that true, Mom? I mean, I knew about that Angelica woman from the symphony...and his student, the one with the bible name..."

"Esther," my mother supplies.

"Yeah, Esther. But why would you stay with a man who cheated on you from the very beginning?"

"Honey, when you've loved a man—*really* loved a man, you'll understand."

Something in the air changes. It's a palpable shift—as if the thing that's not being said has taken on a life of its own. I think they call that the "elephant" in the room. My mother takes note of its presence.

"Alexandria?"

Ellie is watching me carefully, unable to quash the tiny smile that's tugging at the corners of her deep red lips. "Oh, I think she understands quite well, Mads."

"Please," Mom says, waving a dismissive hand. "Alexandria's never had a serious relationship, Ellie." When I don't reply she seems to reconsider this proclamation. "Have you, Alexandria?"

I could lie. I could downplay the last several weeks. Or I could just come clean. None of these options is especially appealing but since we've got everything else out on the table...

"Yes, Mom."

"Who?" she asks, sounding completely taken aback by this admission.

"Nate."

"Nate?"

"Nate."

"You mean...Nathaniel Calloway?"

I nod solemnly.

"Alexandria, surely you know that young man's history. I'm not so sure that getting involved with someone like that is such a good idea..."

I shrug. "Well, it doesn't much matter because we've broken up."

"Oh?"

"Yes."

She doesn't ask me to elaborate and I don't offer to. "Well, then I suppose that's that."

"Not quite," Ellie, pipes up. "They may not be *together*

together but they're working as a piano duo at the moment, so they have to spend a lot of time together."

My mother shrugs. "I don't see what difference that makes now. We're going home tomorrow and she'll get back into her solo routine again. Do you—do you feel as if Wyatt's helped you, honey?"

"Absolutely," I agree emphatically. "He's an amazing teacher. He really knows how to get the root of a problem and, I don't know, just kind of diffuse it. You know what I mean?"

She's smiling now, a little wistfully. "Yes, actually, I do. Wyatt was always a problem solver. You remember what he was like our junior year, Ellie?"

"You mean when we lost power on campus the night of your recital? He bought every candle in town and handed them out to people who showed up..."

"Right, right!" My mom nods and smiles at the memory. "He stuck each taper into a little paper plate to catch the wax. And he found that candelabra..."

"He *borrowed* that candelabra from the Catholic church down the street," Ellie reminds her.

"Oh! Yes! Boy was that priest angry with him!"

"But it was so beautiful," Ellie recalls wistfully. "You were so beautiful, playing there in the candlelight."

I watch, transfixed by them being transfixed by the memory. At last, it's my mother who breaks the spell—albeit reluctantly.

"Ah, well, that was a long time ago," she murmurs wistfully and then takes a deep breath, wrenching herself back into the here and now. "So, Ellie, got another bottle of wine somewhere?"

* * *

Her voice is nearby—but not in the room. Not in the bed we shared last night after Ellie and I hauled her off the couch after one too many glasses of wine.

Where is she?

I open my eyes and focus. It's morning—early morning by the looks of the sun. I sit up in bed and force my fuzzy head to triangulate the sound. It's coming from outside. Just outside. I get up and pad across the carpet silently, approaching the window from the side so no one will see me.

"No, Hugh! I will *not* do that. I promised Alexandria—"

Whatever it was she promised me has just gotten swallowed up by one of my father's tirades. Jesus, I can hear him yelling from in here. There's a long pause as she listens and, I hope, pulls the phone away from her ear before he does damage to her hearing.

"I told you. I'm going to see her play with this young man and then we'll go to the airport... Hugh Fitch! Don't you dare call that boy a circus freak!"

He didn't! Who am I kidding? Of course, he did.

"No. I don't care. Fine, Hugh, fine. Do what you have to do, but for once I'm putting our daughter's needs ahead of you and your precious code of conduct."

She must've hung up on him because the next thing I hear is her crunching on the gravel outside of the house. I dive back into bed and pull the covers up over my shoulders, pretending to be fast asleep when she slips back into the bedroom, quietly closing the door behind her. She slips under the blankets next to me and turns inward on her right side so that we're facing in the middle of the bed. I can feel her eyes on me.

"Mom?" I mutter, as if I've just now woken. "What's going on?"

"I was just thinking about when you were a little girl. Your feet didn't even touch the ground when you sat at the piano. You'd play for hours and hours..."

"I loved it," I agree. "I was never happier than when I was playing."

"What happened, Alexandria?"

I feel my face furrow in confusion. God, I really need some coffee. "What happened with what?"

"When did you stop loving it? When did it become this...this *thing* that you're so afraid of?"

"Uhhh...wow, yeah... I don't know, Mom. Somewhere along the way, I guess. I mean, I've always been a little nervous when I perform but it got worse after Grandma died. She used to keep me balanced. You know what I mean?"

She nods slowly. "I do. She did have a way about her. Especially the way she could handle your father."

I snort. "Yeah, you could say that. She knew how to put him in his place, that's for sure."

She offers a wan smile. "Grandma was never a fan of Hugh's, I'm afraid."

"That can't have been easy for you."

She shrugs. "No one said marriage would be easy, Alexandria."

"Okay, well, turnabout is fair play, right? What happened to *you*? When did *you* stop loving *him*?"

She looks taken aback by the question, as if it never occurred to her that I'd notice the steady crumbling of their marriage. "What makes you think I don't love him?"

"He's an ass, Mom. And he treats you like garbage."

"Alexandria Elizabeth Mickelson-Fitch! Don't you dare speak about him that way! No matter what's happened between him and me, he's always loved you as best he could."

I give her my most skeptical look. "Really, mom?"

She purses her lips together and I can see this conversation is over. "You should get a move on if I'm going to hear you and Nathaniel Calloway play before we go to the airport."

"I'm not going home."

I don't know where the words come from. Or the decision, for that matter. I hadn't really considered the option of just saying no. But here I am doing just that.

"Alexandria—"

"Alex, Mom. I go by Alex now. New attitude. New name. New me."

"I'm going to strangle Wyatt when I get my hands on him," she mutters, shaking her head in disgust.

"Why? Because he's been helping me to play better than I ever have? Because he's helped me to see that I'm an adult who can make her own decisions and be responsible for her own choices? Mom, you should be patting the guy on the back, not strangling him."

She considers me for a long moment before she speaks again, her tone cool, calm and determined. "Young lady, once we get your debut behind us, you can do whatever you please. But for now—just until Carnegie Hall—I need you to get with your father's program. He's worked hard to get you this second chance. Please."

I sit up and swing my legs over the side of the bed, my bare feet hitting the carpet. I wiggle my toes, examining the pink polish.

"Can we get pedicures together, Mom?" I ask, apropos of nothing.

"W-what? What on earth are you talking about?"

I grab her hand, which is resting on the bed next to me, and I hold it in both of mine. "Remember we used to get them? And then you'd take me for high tea. Sometimes we'd see a show. Oh, we had so much fun! Why don't we do that anymore, Mom?"

Her face softens with the memory and a slight smile pulls at her lips.

"Yes, those were good days, weren't they? I don't really know why we stopped. It just seemed like you were always working up to some big performance and we couldn't spare the time…" She sighs. "Speaking of which, that young man will be waiting for us if you don't get dressed. Now."

I drop her hand, grab a few things from the dresser and head toward the bathroom, stopping before I'm fully through the doorway. "I'm not going, Mom," I repeat and then disappear with her staring back after me. We don't discuss it again. In fact, we get ready and drive over to the concert hall in silence—each of us deep in our own thoughts.

"What's he like?" my mother asks as we make our way through the lobby of the music building. "Nathaniel Calloway, I mean. He's been off the radar for so long…"

I nod my understanding. "I know. He's…he's a really spectacular pianist. Better than me. Maybe as good as you."

"Well, that wouldn't be too hard these days, I'm hardly in my prime. "Twenty-five years ago, maybe…" she muses.

"You know, at first, I was attracted to him."

"To Wyatt?" her voice jumps about an octave. "Wyatt McFadden? Alexandria, he's old enough to be your…" she stops before she can finish the sentence. "Anyway, I assume you've moved past that little crush. And then…Nathaniel. Do you want to tell me what happened?"

"You were right last night. Nate's got some serious issues. But I…I just… I can't. I'm sorry."

I'm relieved when she doesn't press the issue. We resume our walk down the hallway in silence, save for the clacking of her sensible heels on the shiny tile floor. I can't help but notice that she knows exactly where we're going. As if she's walked this route a thousand times before. And, for all I know, she has.

"Ah, there they are!" Wyatt calls out to us from the stage when we walk through the door and down the aisle.

The concert grand piano is centered in the middle of the

stage and Nate is already seated on his side of the bench. He doesn't look up as we approach.

"I'm going to listen from down here," my mother says, using her chin to nod toward a row of red velvet seats. "You go on up and get started whenever you're ready."

I walk to the far end of the stage, taking the three steps up and crossing to where Wyatt is standing, waiting for me to join him and Nate.

"Good morning, Alex," he greets me with that cheeky, crooked grin. Yes, indeed, older men can be hot. "Why don't you get yourself settled in and I'm just going to skidaddle back into the wings so as not to be a distraction to either of you or your mother."

"Okay…" I agree, wondering what kind of a distraction he thinks he'll cause as I take my spot to Nate's right. We don't acknowledge one another's presence.

"Alrighty then, how's about we do the En Bateau?" he suggests, pulling the music from the top of the piano and setting it up on the bridge for us.

"Really?" Nate asks, surprised. "I thought you'd want something a little more…you know…flashy."

"I agree," I pipe up. "If we want to really impressive my mother…"

But Wyatt is shaking his head. "Nope. This one'll do just fine. Now let's have it."

And then he's turning his back and walking away. For all intents and purposes abandoning us. I look at Nate. He looks at me.

"Well, you heard the man," he says at last, straightening out the music and sitting up, poised to play.

Oh, hell. It's not like I can object if he's not going to. I glance out into the house nervously, and see my mother just sitting there, calmly awaiting the beginning of our performance. Suddenly I feel as if I'm back on stage at Carnegie and my breath starts to pick up.

"Hey," Nate says quietly. "Hey, hey—what's wrong?"

"I—I don't think I can do this..."

"Uh-uh. No way. Come on. You are not going to freak out on me now, Alex," he says sternly.

"What the hell do you care anyway?" I hiss back at him as quietly as I can.

He stares for a little too long and his jaw hardens. "You're right. I don't. Come on, get your shit together."

"God, could you be *more* of an ass?"

"Just play!" Wyatt yells from backstage. I take a deep breath and put my hands on the keyboard. And then we begin.

# CHAPTER 27

# Nate

When the last bit of the last note fades away into the concert hall, there is silence. Alex and I are both staring down at our hands, still arched over the keys. She's the first one to pull away and I follow suit. Neither of us has been brave enough to so much as sneak a glance at Madeleine. But she didn't stop us while we were playing, so I guess that's something. Finally, it's Wyatt who breaks the spell, his cowboy boots clacking against the boards of the stage as he makes his way towards us with a grin. A grin that's not for me. Or for Alex. Now we both turn on the bench to follow Wyatt's gaze.

At last, Madeleine stands up and makes her way down the aisle toward us, stopping at the base of the stage. As I look down into her face, I see it clear as day. This woman is seriously spooked. She's pale and slightly shaken, looking as if she's just seen a ghost. Alex doesn't miss the change in her mother's appearance. She stands up and walks around to the front of the stage, dropping down to sit with her legs dangling so she can be at eye level with Madeleine.

"Hey, mom? What's wrong? Are you feeling alright?"

Madeleine shakes her head slightly, and wipes her face with her hand. Christ! Is she crying?

"Ummm, no, honey, I'm fine. Really," she assures us.

"But...why are you crying?" Alex asks, her voice full of alarm.

"I can't...I'm just...I'm so proud of you," she manages to say at last. But there's something that's not quite right here. She may very well be proud of her little Alexandria, but that's not what this is about. I'd put money on that one.

"Well, Maddy, what're y'all thinking?" Wyatt asks softly—the only one who seems to be unconcerned by the woman's emotional response to our playing.

"I thought they were...just breathtaking," she says softly.

"Really, mom?" Alex asks, scooting up onto her knees and throwing her arms around her mother's neck. "Really?"

Madeleine nods and tears continue to stream down her face as she pats Alex on the back. "Oh, Alexandria, I had no idea... You play so beautifully, honey, but this—this is a whole other level..."

"They're somethin' special, aren't they, Maddy?" I'm a little startled when Wyatt's voice comes from directly behind me. "Well played," he leans down and murmurs, giving my shoulder a firm squeeze. "Now, I want Maddy to come to my office and take a look at the program I'm proposing. Why don't you two take a little break and meet us in the lobby in...oh...say twenty minutes? Pulled pork tacos and prickly pear margaritas are on me this afternoon!"

"Oh, dear god, I'd forgotten about those tacos!" Madeleine says, smiling now as she extricates herself from her daughter. "There were just a couple of small things...but really, baby, I'm so, so proud of you."

Alex is all smiles as she returns to the piano bench and we watch Wyatt and Madeleine disappear together backstage.

"That's really great, Alex," I say. And I mean it. Suddenly

everything with Abner Beckett seems just like what it is—bull-shit. I put a hand on her forearm. "Your mom was right. You play beautifully."

She considers me for a moment, her eyes softer than they've been for a while—at least while she's looking in my direction. "I couldn't have done that without you, Nate."

Now that I wasn't expecting. "Of course, you could."

She shakes her head and grabs both of my hands. "I'm sorry. I'm so sorry that I haven't tried harder to understand what it is you're going through. But you've got to know, Nate —I'd never do anything to hurt you. And playing with you, like that, just now, it's so special..."

All at once the last shards of ice melt within my veins. I can't stay mad at her. And, the fact is, I never really was mad at her. I was mad at myself. And I was scared. Scared about what Beckett might write and scared about my growing feelings for this woman I've known for less than a season. I open my mouth to try and explain all this to her, but there simply are no words. There's only emotion as I grab her face in my hands and pull her into me. She doesn't resist.

Quite the opposite, actually. And by the time we separate, we're both breathing heavy, staring at one another in bewil-derment.

"So...what does this mean?" she asks, breathlessly.

I shrug. "I think it means I'm sorry I screwed it all up and I swear to God I'll do my damnedest never to push you away again."

"Never again? Like...ever? As in...the future?" she presses uncertainly.

"Yeah. I guess so. Considering I can't wrap my head around the idea of not kissing you tomorrow and next week and next month and next year..."

She hops into my lap, straddling me on the piano bench so that we're face-to-face, only a couple of inches apart. I can see every striation in her rich, brown eyes and it's positively hypnotic.

"Then let's not," she declares with a nod of affirmation. "Let's not *not* kiss tomorrow and next week and next month and next year."

"You know long distance romances can be tough," I caution, even though every cell in my body is rejoicing with the knowledge that she wants me in her life as much as I want her in mine.

"No."

"Well, yeah, they kinda are..."

She shakes her head. "No. We're not going to do that."

"Do what?"

"Long distance."

"Alex, we can't stay here forever..."

"No, you're right. We can't. But you can come back to New York. With me. And we can play...together."

On reflex, I take a sharp breath in. "Are you suggesting that we keep playing as a piano duo?"

"I am. I mean, we can still do solo and chamber stuff, but, yeah. I think maybe we should be a team. Permanently. In fact...oh, hell, Nate, I'm just going to spit it out— I think we should make our Carnegie Hall debut *together*."

"Together? Like in the fall? *This* fall? Oh...Jesus, Alex," I murmur. "I don't know..."

Her beautiful brow furrows in concern. "What? You don't want to?"

"No, I didn't say that... It's just, I have a bit to prove, you know? After all this time, I think I need to stand on my own first. Then, maybe..."

Before I can even finish the thought, she's wriggling her way off of me—and I don't like that one bit. So, I grab her by the waist, gently but firmly.

"Hey... Hey, hey, hey...wait, Alex, don't be angry..."

"Why? Is it that you don't think I'm good enough? Is that it?" she demands, all sweetness gone, replaced by hurt masquerading as offense.

"No! Ugh, God...how can I explain this to you? Look, Alex, what you're proposing—I just don't think it's the way back for me. Not yet, anyway. Carnegie Hall is huge and I thought I'd ease into my comeback. You know—a little tour with some nice, low-key venues at liberal arts colleges..."

"What? Are you insane?" She uses my shoulders to push up and off of my lap. "Nate! You're back already! Why waste another day? Why not do this *with* me? Then you won't be alone. Ever. I'll always have your back. You'll always have mine. Oh, come on, Nate. Please?"

Crap. How can I say no to her?

The answer is: I can't.

"O-okay," I agree reluctantly. "If you really—"

"Oh, Nate! That's wonderful! I'm so happy!" She grabs my hand and pulls me to my feet with a strength I didn't know she had. "Come on, let's go!"

"Go where?" I ask, allowing her to drag me away from the piano.

She smiles this witchy little mischievous smile that pings my radar even as it pings my groin. I'm so screwed. So very, very screwed.

"Mom, Wyatt! You'll never guess what Nate and I have decided—"

I'm right there, behind Alex as she throws open the door to Wyatt's office without the obligatory knock. She really shoulda knocked. Because what we see when the heavy door swings open is something we can never un-see.

It's Wyatt. He's got Madeleine pulled into a tight embrace.

She's clinging to him like he's the last life vest on the Titanic. They're so intent, so...intertwined...that they don't immediately realize they have witnesses. Until they do.

"Mom!" Alex gasps, her hand flying to her mouth. "And...Wyatt? Wyatt!"

I should be surprised. And I am...sort of. But not really. Madeleine is, clearly, "the one that got away." And, clearly, Wyatt has no intention of letting her slip through his fingers a second time.

"Oh!" Madeleine exclaims, lips red and swollen from some serious action.

"Uh...hey..." Wyatt joins her, a little flustered but still with that goofy, off-kilter smile.

"Mom?" Alex repeats as she walks inside the office. I follow, closing the door behind us.

"I...uh...Alexandria... It's not...You know, it isn't—"

"What it looks like?" I ask, unable to keep the smirk out of my tone. Or off my face. I'm rewarded with a simultaneous glare from Madeleine and snort from Wyatt.

But it's really Alex who everyone needs to be focusing on because, near as I can tell, she's about to blow. Her face has gone from flat white to glowing red and her breath is coming in jagged bursts. Oh, shit. This is not good.

"I can't believe you'd do this..." she whispers.

At first, I think she's talking to her mother. And then I realize she's not. It's Wyatt. And his smile is falling—fast.

"Wait...no, Alex, you don't understand...I've known your mother for a long time. And we were...well, you know... If Hugh hadn't—"

She starts to shake her head violently from side to side.

"No. No, no, no," Alex spits, shutting him down immediately. "You don't get to say his name."

Before he can formulate a response, she spins around, running right into me. Hard. And fast. It takes every ounce of strength and balance I have not to let us tumble to the carpet.

"Come on," I whisper softly into her ear. "You come home with me. We can sort this all out later."

She's nodding because she can't speak anymore—she's too busy crying. I catch Wyatt's anguished expression over Alex's shoulder and mouth the words: "It's okay." He nods in return, letting me know that he knows that I've got her. That I won't let anything happen to Alexandria Mickelson-Fitch. That, as of this moment, I consider it to be my solemn task on this earth.

# CHAPTER 28

# Alex

When my phone buzzes for about the hundredth time, I smack it off the nightstand and it flies onto the carpet with a dull thud.

"It's not the phone's fault," Nate mumbles from next to me.

"Sorry, I didn't mean to wake you."

He throws the covers off and sits up, bracing his back against the headboard.

"Come here," he says, his arms open as his hands gesture for me to slip into them. I do, resting my head on the smooth, hard plane of his chest. I can hear his heart beat through the layers of flesh and bone. It's a strong, steady sound that immediately calms my frazzled nerves. If his heart could survive everything it's been through—all that it's lost—mine can certainly overcome this... This what? It's not an obstacle, exactly. More like a complication, I suppose. A confusion. Is that a thing? A "confusion"? I'm slightly startled when Nate speaks, the booming bass of his voice filling the cavity of his chest where my ear is still pressed.

"I'm sorry I was such an ass about Abner Beckett," he says

softly. "That was just stupid. And then I let my pride keep me from apologizing. I've had a really fucked up life, Alex. I'm not sure that us playing together would be the best thing for you."

I full away from him abruptly and sit up so that we're face to face, rather than face to pecs. "What are you saying?" I demand, already feeling defensive. "You don't want to play with me?"

"No! That's not what I—" Nate rests his hands on my shoulders. "I'm saying that maybe you're better off getting your debut out of the way first. I don't think you appreciate the amount of baggage that comes with me making a public appearance, Alex. This should be all about you. Not me. Or my comeback. We have all the time in the world to be a duet…" The tears that I can't hold back anymore slip down my cheeks and stop him short. "Oh, fuck it," he murmurs, pulling me back to him and pressing his lips to the salty trails.

He kisses all the way up to my eyelids and then makes his way back down toward my mouth with a brief pit stop along the shell of my right ear. By the time I welcome his soft, sweet tongue into my mouth there are no more tears. I press my hand to his heart so I can feel the beat I'd been listening to only a few minutes ago. It's become a lifeline to him. To myself.

I'm not sure at what point his t-shirt leaves my body or where, exactly, my panties have gone, but when his large, warm palms press my flesh there's nothing between my skin and his. And I like it that way. A lot.

I'm straddling him now, the same way I did in the concert hall, on the piano bench, my hands on his shoulders and his…everywhere. We're kissing so intently that I don't even notice his fingers have managed to walk their way down to the soft spot between my legs. His very *clever* fingers. I read that once in a book—someone describing a lover's fingers as clever. Now I understand. It's as if he knows exactly how to touch me. He's slow and gentle, using his thumb and fore-finger to nudge and tease until a keening sound fills the room. It takes a second to realize it's coming from me. I begin to move against him more assuredly, more firmly, showing him without words how I need to be touched. He obliges, his mouth now affixed to my neck as I throw my head back in wanton abandon.

"Please..." I whisper to the ceiling. "Please, Nate... I want you. I want all of you."

I whine with the loss of his fingers on my wet flesh, but I'm only bereft of his touch for a moment while he aligns his erection against my entrance. And then he thrusts upward with a force that rips the air from my lungs and sends my fore-head in search of his so we can be connected there, as well. He hasn't uttered so much as a single syllable all this time but I hear his exhalation as he holds me like that, lodged deep inside me, unmoving.

I allow myself to feel him—to envelop his unyielding hard-ness with the deepest parts of my body—until I cannot stand the exquisite torture for a single second longer. I use my knees to pull myself upward, gradually extracting him from me, inch by inch. But not totally. Not all the way. I couldn't... I can't. So, I get as close as I can before using my weight to sink down upon him once more. He fills me again and again in this agonizing ritual, the sound of his breath growing more ragged in my ears. It's clear that he's holding back—for me. I'm quite certain he wants nothing more than to flip me over and fuck me hard and fast but Nate Calloway is letting me conduct this particular symphony.

*Did I really just think that?*

"What?" he rasps. "You look like you're going to laugh."

"Yeah...just the punch line from a joke. Something about a conductor and his baton..."

That's all it takes. He thrusts upward so hard, so fast, that

I cling to him—lest I go flying. "Get ready for the big finale," he murmurs seconds before he captures my mouth in his.

I groan into him, my torso rising and falling—meeting him stroke for stroke until I can feel the first distant rumblings of an orgasm building. I'm not sure if he feels it, too, or if he's taking his cues from me, but what began as a deliciously slow coupling has rapidly ramped up into a frenzied race toward some elusive finish line. My urge to cry out supersedes my need to kiss him, making me tear my mouth from his. Not that Nate seems to mind, he just relocates his warm, moist tongue in the region of my left nipple, which is very conveniently right in front of him.

"Jesus, Nate..." It's all I can manage before it hits me. Every inch of my body tightens from head to toe; inside and out. I'm trembling and convulsing, head thrown back, nails raking his shoulders as he redoubles his efforts—sending me to a place I've never been. A place I never want to leave.

* * *

"Are you sure you're up to this?" he asks me. Again. I nod. Again. "Because, we can just turn right around and go back to my apartment..."

I place a hand on his sweet face, so full of concern. He doesn't know it, but he's more afraid of what might happen in there than I am. And who could blame him? It's not even noon and there are a slew of cars in front of Ellie's house. Hers, my mom's rental, Wyatt's truck. There's even a spare sedan that likely belongs to Ellie's boyfriend. If that guy's smart, he'll haul ass back to San Antonio and wait for the crazy to clear out before he comes back again.

"Come on," I coax, stepping out of Nate's car and slamming the door closed behind me so there can be no more discussion until he gets out, too.

"Alex…" he's scratching his bedhead nervously. "You know your mother is going to try to get you to go home with her."

"I know, Nate. We've been through this already. I'm going to stay here, with you, so we can prep for the concert together. Then we'll go back to Manhattan and stay at my place until we figure out where we want to go next."

This is the plan we worked on all night. After the multiple mind-blowing orgasms. I had no idea sex could be like that—and I have absolutely no intention of going back to basic and boring. Ever. That means this will be the last man I ever share a bed with. Ever. And I'm okay with that.

We'd sent the text around four in the morning when we were a little punch-drunk and a lot tequila drunk. "Liquid courage" I think they call it. Maybe liquid stupid would be a better descriptor. Either way, issuing a command performance this morning for all parties concerned had to be done. Now, as we quietly climb the three steps onto Ellie's tidy front porch, I can hear the voices coming from inside and one of them stops me dead in my tracks.

"What is it? Alex?"

I hold up my finger to indicate that Nate should hold on for a second. Let me hear. Let me process. Let me flip out.

"She has a right to know!" Ellie hisses.

*Who? Me? What the hell are they talking about?*

"Stay out of it, Ellie!" comes a growl in response. Oh, yeah. That's the voice I thought I heard.

"Hugh—" my mother begins to protest.

"Hugh?" Nate whispers from next to me. "*Hugh* Hugh? Like your father, Hugh?"

I can only nod.

"No, Madeleine," my father spits. "This is none of her goddam business. Alexandria is our daughter and we'll make those decisions. And you know what? I think it's time we left. All three of us. As a family. Let's go, Madeleine. We're going to get Alexandria from that...that washed-up freak's house. Right. Now."

"Hugh, I think maybe you'd best settle down before you get in your car and go anywhere." That's Wyatt's calm, sensible voice. "And as for young Nathaniel, well, I think if you'd give him a few minutes of your time, you'd realize he's neither a freak nor is he washed-up. In fact, when the two of them play together it's...it's magical..."

"Why the hell are you even here?" my father bellows in response. "What's the matter, Wyatt? Run out of broken-down little has-beens so you had to kidnap my daughter? Or is this just your way of trying to get into Madeleine's pants again? Is that it, *cowboy?*"

Oh. My. God. This is getting worse by the second.

"Hugh!" My mother begins but is cut off, once again, by her husband.

"Shut. Up. Madeleine," he warns her.

I don't even realize that I've opened the door and walked into the house until I'm standing there, watching them. But they're so wrapped up in what's unfolding that no one notices me—or Nate standing next to me—except for Ellie. She shakes her head slightly, indicating that we should stay where we are and not get involved. Yeah, right. Let's see how long that lasts for.

"Hugh, I'm going to suggest you take a step back."

"Oh? And why is that Wyatt? She's *my* wife. She chose *me*, remember?"

An awkward pause.

"Hard to forget, Hugh," Wyatt says quietly.

"I'm sure it is," my father snarls, a cruel smile tugging at his lips.

"Stop it right now, Hugh!" Mom demands, but we both know that he doesn't respond well to demands. He swats her away like a pesky fly.

"I'll bet you think about it every day, don't you? How you had her and then you lost her. You couldn't give her what she needed. If she'd stayed with you she'd still be here in this freak show of a town, teaching nobodies. So, she hitched her wagon to *my* star and left you behind. Poor, poor Wyatt. Alone all these years—pining for the woman who slipped through his fingers. What you don't know, Wyatt, is that taking her with me is my biggest regret. She's been nothing but a disappointment to me. Nothing but a second-rate pianist trading on my name and reputation. You should be *thanking* me because you dodged a bullet. She's as frigid in the bedroom as she is at the piano..."

*"Daddy!"*

Suddenly all eyes are upon me as I stalk toward my father. "Daddy, please, Wyatt really helped me, Daddy. I think...I think you're going to be very pleased with how well I'm playing. I wanted to get better so I wouldn't embarrass you again." I'm pleading with him, tugging his arm with my hand. I'm a little girl again, begging her daddy to love her. Knowing, all the while in my heart-of-hearts that he never will. Not really.

"Ah. So, there you are. A little harlot like your mother, aren't you? Did you really think I'd let you just run-off with some fucktoy and leave me looking like a fool back in New York? No, no, no, my dear. That's not how this works."

"Yeah, I think you should reconsider that train of thought." I'm not sure at what point Nate followed me across the room, but his voice is directly behind me now.

My father looks positively maniacal, his eyes wide, nose flaring and that smile. That bloody fucking smile that he just won't lose.

"Well, well, Nathanial "The Musical Miracle" Calloway, I presume. How very industrious of you to find your way into my daughter's bed. I mean, really, I should be commending you—what better way to ensure your return to the classical music scene than to ride my daughter's...coattails all the way?" The pause is positively obscene and it makes my face redden even more. "You're smarter than I'd have given you credit for. Or, maybe not—perhaps it was Wyatt who hatched up this little plan? Did he throw you two together and tell you how to win her over? She's a sucker for a wounded bird, just like her slut mother..."

Things go very quiet and still—as if someone has hit the pause button. As if the air itself is waiting to see whatever it is that's going to come next. Finally, it's the sickening sound of Nate's fist connecting with my father's face that restarts the clock, slamming everything back into motion with a deafening, dizzying ferocity. My father looks stunned, wiping at the sticky wetness streaming from his face and holding his fingers up to examine it. And then something extraordinary happens. He smiles.

"That wasn't very smart of you, young man. In fact, it was quite foolish. Let's see how you like having your mug shot plastered all over the international news after I file assault charges against you. Oh, how the world would just love to hear the next tragic installment of the pathetic little life of Nathaniel Calloway! And good luck getting anyone to come hear you play after that. That is, if you ever had the balls to play in public—which I seriously doubt. Of course, there are those people who just can't resist a good carnival side show..." My father looks gruesome, blood coloring his teeth red and dripping down onto his crisp, white shirt. His nose and mouth are already swelling. He's right. If the police come now, they'll arrest Nate on the spot.

"Daddy, please, no," I whisper, grabbing at his hand and trying to divert his attention back to me. "Daddy, you can't do that. You wouldn't do that..." But we both know he would. And we both know he will. Unless I act fast. So, I play the only card I have. "Daddy, just stop. Stop now and I'll come home with you," I blurt out before he can get another word in. Before anyone can stop me. "I'll move back home. Now. Today. I'll work on the concert and I'll get it right this time—I swear it. But only if you leave Nate alone."

"Alex..." Nate's got a hand on my shoulder, trying to get me to look at him. But I can't so I won't. "Don't you do this," he hisses at me. "Don't you *dare* sacrifice yourself for me. I don't need it. And I sure as hell don't want it."

"Don't you?" my father spits—literally—blood spraying from his mouth as he bites out the two words. Then he looks at me looking at him.

"Please, Daddy," I whisper, drawing upon every ounce of willpower I have to ignore Nate—to stay turned away from those eyes that have the power to turn my head and heart to pure mush. If I look at him now, I'll never be able to do what has to be done. "I just want to go home. Please just take me home..."

Hugh Fitch is a lot of things—including a terrible father. But, perhaps his favorite role is that of "master." Luckily for me, I've had a lifetime of supporting him in my role of the submissive, dutiful daughter. He grumbles something resembling his assent under his breath.

I'm in motion before anyone in the room can stop me. Including myself.

# CHAPTER 29

# Nate

She's gone.

Just like that—not so much as a kiss goodbye. I was so sure after last night... What? That she really does love me? That she'd give up her destiny to be with someone like me? Clearly, I had that all wrong. The Mickelson-Fitch family was packed up and pulling out of Ellie Dominguez's driveway within seven minutes flat, Hugh still holding a washcloth to his seeping face.

I tried. I tried to follow her. To plead with her until, finally, it was Wyatt, who dragged me outside where we waited. And then we watched. Alex offered a tiny, apologetic smile through her tears but it was too late by then. My heart was closed—slammed shut, double-bolted, tripled-barred and arc-welded shut. For good this time.

"So, I'm thinking about November sixteenth," Wyatt is saying from his desk as he glances between his computer screen and the calendar/blotter on his desk.

"What about it?" I mutter disinterestedly picking my way down the keyboard in half steps.

He turns to look at me over his shoulder. "What have we

been talking about for the last twenty minutes, Nate? For your recital date! I can get you a spot at the Austin Performing Arts Center for that night. It's not Carnegie, but the acoustics are spectacular and you'll likely fill the hall—" Whatever it is that he sees in my reaction makes him stop short. "What?" he asks slowly, those freakishly-blue eyes narrowing in suspicion. "What is it, Nate?"

I shrug noncommittally and allow my fingers to start the walk up the keys again. C, C#, D, D#...

"Nathaniel!" He barks so abruptly that I halt my ascent and stare at him.

"What? I heard you, Wyatt. November fifteenth."

"Sixteenth!"

"Whatever," I mutter in annoyance.

Wyatt spins around in the chair so that his entire body is facing me and then he stands up, closing the distance between us in only a few long-legged strides, the telltale clack of his boots muffled by the Oriental carpet under our feet. He stands, facing me, just on the other side of the piano. He could grab me by the collar, drag me onto the strings and drop the lid on me in a matter of seconds. If he really wanted to. And right now, I'd give those odds about sixty-forty in favor of it.

And still, I couldn't give a shit. I just quirk a challenging "what's *your* problem?" eyebrow at him. Maybe not my smartest course of action, given the look I'm getting in response.

Make that eighty-twenty in favor of the piano/coffin lid scenario.

"Get your head out of your ass, Nate." His voice is a menacing whisper.

Mine is a snide muttering. "Fuck you, Wyatt."

We eyeball one another for a long moment and I see it all there. He's furious with me, but also with himself. We both screwed this up and neither of us was able to do a damn thing to make it right. And still, we sit here pretending everything is still hunky-fucking-dory. Finally, he takes a long, slow, deep breath. The kind that you have to force yourself to take so you won't do something else. Like kill your student.

"Look, Nate, I get it. I really, really do. More than you can even imagine—"

"Oh, I can imagine," I inform him coolly.

"Can you, now?"

I nod. "Absolutely, Wyatt. You think you know what's going through my head right now. You think I'm sad and lonely and depressed, like some lovesick teenager whose girl ran off with the captain of the football team. Only, I'm not. Because that's not my story, Wyatt, it's yours. You're the one who got thrown over by the big dick on campus. You're the one who's been hiding out here for decades replaying the whole thing in his head over and over and over again. And wouldn't you know it? The mother of all second chances falls in your lap—pun *totally* fucking intended, by the way," I sneer, getting to my feet and leaning across the piano on my forearms. I'm just getting warmed up.

"You got to play the part of the hero to Alex and to Madeleine—by association, didn't you? You —how do you say it, Wyatt?—oh, yeah, you did a little 'spit swapping' in hopes of a little 'boot knocking.' But it didn't quite go as expected, did it? You lost her a second time. And to the same douchebag, no less. Only this time it's worse because she *knows* he's a douchebag and she goes back to him anyway!"

My voice has grown progressively louder. And even though I'm fully aware of the fact that I'm taunting the one person who has stood by my side in more years than I can remember, I just don't give a shit. I mean, I've got the Molotov cocktail in my hand, why not just light the sucker and lob it right over the fence?

"And now you think we can just pretend that it's okay—

that the whole damned summer never happened. That we can just pick up where we left off and you can keep licking your wounds and consoling yourself with this idea that you're some fucked-up savior for fucked-up pianists like me. Yeah, well, guess what, Wyatt? It takes one to know one."

He's gone very still through this little diatribe of mine, his face barely changing, save for the occasional reflexive blink. He's staring at me flatly. No emotion to be found anywhere in his appearance or his demeanor. No indication that he's even the least bit affected by what I've just spewed. Until he opens his mouth to speak, that is.

"You can leave now, Nathaniel," he says in a cool, flat, monotone.

"Whatever, Wyatt," I mumble, shaking my head and pulling together the music on the bridge of the piano.

"No, you can leave the music. That's one of my copies," he says, holding out his hand for the score.

"Dude, what? You think I'm going to skip the country with your crappy Mozart sonata? I'll bring it back with me tomorrow," I say, holding the pages out to him.

He snatches them out of my hand. "No, you won't. Because you won't be here tomorrow, Nate. I'm done with you. I'm done with your bullshit. I'm done with your self-absorbed, self-destructive bullshit."

Nasty as things have gotten between my teacher and me, they've never gotten this far before. Suddenly I'm feeling a lot less smug and a lot more insecure.

"Wyatt, man—"

He turns his back and walks to the door, pulling it open and holding it, nodding out toward the hallway. "Goodbye, Nathaniel."

I could grovel. I probably should grovel because even I know I've crossed a line. But I won't. Not now, not ever.

Because groveling is for people who have something left to lose. Something to grovel *for*.

I am not one of those people. Not anymore.

* * *

I've always looked at stupid, rash people who make stupid, rash decisions and wondered, "Dude, why can't you just man-up and apologize?" But now I'm the stupid, rash one and I get it. I'm wrong. I know it. And I just don't give a shit. Not about her, not about the piano, or Wyatt or anything. Not even myself. And you know what? That's okay. Because I'm sitting on a very nice bank account which allows me the freedom to sit at home, on the couch and watch Dr. Freakin' Phil all day long. I tell myself that I do it just for the mockage factor, but I secretly suspect it has more to do with the fact that his Texas accent reminds me of Wyatt.

I'm surprised I've not heard a word from him. It's been three weeks and I'd have thought he'd have reached out by now. It's just the kind of guy he is. But, clearly, I've managed to burn the last bridge connecting me to the world of classical music. Oh, sure, I could try to make a comeback on my own— and I'm certain the press would be all over it. But without Wyatt's steadying presence, I just don't think I can manage it. Maybe I should've thought of that before he threw my ass out.

When I dragged myself back to my Minneapolis apartment, I found that nothing had changed. Everything was exactly the way I'd left it—save for the pile of mail that had been collecting on the floor just inside the front door, under the slot. Other than that, every spoon was exactly where I'd left it. Even my alarm clock—which I'd neglected to unset before I went to Austin—went off at seven-thirty every morning, without fail and had for the duration of the summer.

These are the kinds of things that happen when you don't have anyone to share your life with.

The very idea galls me. I was just fine before I left for Texas. I was perfectly content to be alone and on my own. I like my own company. But goddam her. And goddam him, too. They reminded me what it's like to have people care about what happens to you...and then they stopped caring.

Well, fucking lesson learned.

I toss another empty pizza box on top of the piano. It joins myriad beer bottles and crumpled up, dirty napkins and half-eaten bags of pretzels that I've parked there over the last days and weeks. Alex and Wyatt aren't here to be confronted, but the piano is. And I want to make it suffer. I want to denigrate it for everything it's done to me. For everything it gave to me and then so callously took away. I want this hunk of wood and metal and strings to feel an inkling of the pain I experience every day of my goddammed life.

But, of course, it can't feel.

I wish I were so lucky.

# CHAPTER 30

# *Alexandria*

"That son of a bitch!" I wince when my father slams the paper down on the kitchen table. "I don't know what the hell you did to this man, Alexandria, but he is bound and determined to drag our name through the mud."

It's Abner Beckett. Again. He's been goading me in his column. Again. This time, the asshole has gone so far as to speculate as to how far I'll get in my recital before I choke. According to him, I won't see the intermission, let alone still be standing for an encore. But Beckett's an amateur misery-maker in comparison to Hugh Fitch and I have a feeling he's going to be sorry if he doesn't knock it off—and fast.

"I'm sorry, Daddy," I murmur contritely for the third time this morning.

I could elaborate about how Beckett's a vindictive little man, and how he accosted me in Austin, and how this isn't my fault but I've already tried that. To no avail. My father hasn't stopped being furious with me for a single second since we left Texas over a month ago, no matter how hard I try to placate him. And I do try. I do everything that's expected without complaint. I spend every waking moment at the piano and every sleeping one in my childhood bed. I don't go out. I don't watch television. I don't read or surf the web or text. Not anymore, anyway. Not since I don't carry a single dollar bill in my wallet or a cellphone in my purse. Not since my laptop was confiscated and the wifi password changed. Not since I went under house arrest.

Oh, I managed to get some email and texts out to Nate the first month, but when he didn't respond I finally gave up trying. Now, it's just easier to pretend that it's impossible to contact him than to face the fact that he doesn't want to hear from me. And why would he? I told him I loved him—that I'd be by his side no matter what—and then I abandoned him. True, I couldn't see any way around it at the time. But now... if I could just find a way to leave here. To go to him. But I don't. Because I'm sure he must hate me and I couldn't bear to see that in his face. It's just...easier this way. The grueling, monotonous routine, the daily humiliation from my father and the mounting terror over my upcoming recital are all preferable to Nate Calloway's disdain. His hatred.

I take a sip of my coffee and sneak a glance at my father who's still muttering and shaking his head as he peruses the newspaper.

"Daddy..."

"No."

I tilt my head to the side in confusion. "I haven't said anything..."

He levels his hardest, coolest stare on me. "Whatever it is, the answer is no."

I press on, unwilling to give up quite so easily. "I just thought maybe I could ask Nate to join me for one number on the recital. Maybe just an encore—"

"I. Said. No."

I close my eyes, take a deep breath and try again. "It's my

recital. My debut. Don't you think I should have a say in the program?"

"Alexandria, I will not tell you again. I don't want that flying freak show anywhere near you or Carnegie Hall—or anywhere else for that matter. I forbid it."

"They really are quite exceptional, Hugh," my mother says as she comes into the kitchen and starts to fix her second cup.

"Stay out of it, Madeleine. We agreed you're going to leave this matter to me."

"We did no such thing," she objects, spinning around so quickly that the coffee sloshes over the rim of the half-filled mug in hand. "You made that proclamation all on your own."

"I'm sitting right here," I interject flatly. "You guys can see me, right?"

"Oh, we can see you just fine," my father replies. "But what I want right now is to *hear* you, Alexandria. You'd better glue that backside of yours to the piano bench today until you can play that Bach forwards, backwards, upside-down and inside-out. Understood?"

I'm about to nod and slink out of the room when my mother intervenes unexpectedly.

"Actually, I need her to go uptown for her last dress fitting," she informs him.

This comes as a surprise to me, I thought the last fitting was five days ago. My recital is in two days—it's a little late now to be worrying about hemlines and bodices, but I don't contradict her. Anything to get sprung from this apartment for a couple of hours. My father harrumphs as he gets to his feet.

"Fine. But I expect you to make up the time tonight. You've got a dress rehearsal tomorrow afternoon."

My mother smiles sweetly. "Alexandria will be ready, Hugh."

Another harrumph, this one tempered with a little snort.

Has he always been so hateful? Why hadn't I seen it before? It's as if the time away—the time in Texas—gave me a perspective I've never had. And now it nags at me. Something niggling at the back of my brain. Something not quite right between him and me.

"You'd best get a move on," my mother says, shaking me from my thoughts.

"Okay..."

"And maybe you can stop by the bakery on your way back? I thought I'd make a nice pot of minestrone for dinner and you know how much your father likes a crusty loaf of semolina with that..."

I see his shoulders relax slightly.

"Oh! And I'll bet you'd like an apple strudel, too, Hugh, wouldn't you?"

Is that a non-scowl on his face? Not exactly a smile but a long way from his usual sneer. Damn she knows just how to work this man.

"Of course, Mom," I agree, getting up and following her out of the kitchen. "Anything else, Daddy?" I ask over my shoulder, taking a page out of her book.

"Cupcake," he grumbles.

"Red velvet?"

He grunts. I'll take that as a yes.

I'm slipping on my sandals in the vestibule when my mother hurries over to meet me.

"Let me give you some cash for that, Alexandria," she says over her shoulder—clearly for my father's benefit. But the twenty-dollar-bill isn't the only thing that she presses into the palm of my hand. It's wrapped in a small slip of paper.

I open it up and glance down.

Grind Café.

. . .

I open my mouth to say something, but my mother shakes her head and presses her index finger to my lips before I can get the words out.

"I need you back here in two hours, honey. Don't be late!" she says a little too loudly. Then, in a whisper: "And for, God's sake, don't forget the bakery!"

My head is still spinning as I step out into the bright morning sun and start the ten-block walk to the Grind. It can only be Wyatt. But why would he be here? And why would my mother be willing to risk my father's ire by facilitating a meeting between us? This doesn't make sense. That niggling thing again—it's going on in the back of my head. What would be so important that he'd come all this way to see me? Clearly, he and my mom are still in communication. He could have passed along a message or a letter. She could have managed to arrange a phone call between us when she knew my father would be out. So why the four-hour plane trip for lunch at the Grind?

As I walk past the windows of storefronts—drugstores, the wholesale jewelers, the wigmaker, the tobacconist—I go through that last day at Ellie's house. Those seconds when I first walked in. Before they realized I was standing there. That I could hear see them. And hear them.

*"She has a right to know..."* Ellie had said.

She *me?* I have a right to know...what? What does one have the *right* to know? Who they are. Where they come from. Who their parents are...

I stop, one block short of Broadway, and gasp out loud. All around me, irritated people are pushing past me, shouldering me roughly as I block the path to wherever it is they're hurrying to at ten-thirty on a Tuesday morning.

It's that niggling in the back of my mind. My mom. Wyatt. My mom and Wyatt.

Oh. Oh, God. Is it possible?

All this time I've spent wondering how it is that I could be the child of such a bastard. Someone so different from me. Maybe, just maybe, the answer is that I'm not. And suddenly, I'm seeing everything as it might have been. My mom and Wyatt. Then Hugh Fitch sweeps her off her feet—promises her the moon and the stars if she'll just entrust him with her future. She's not sure. And then, she finds out she's pregnant. She knows Wyatt will give up everything. *Everything.* In an instant, he's saddled with a family and no way to support them—all dreams of becoming a concert pianist leveled under the weight of the domestic burden.

Oh, god, it's all so fucking tragic! But it makes perfect sense. And it explains everything.

I start to pick up speed—my mind whirring with each step that brings me closer to him. To the man who was supposed to raise me. The man who would have truly loved me— the man sitting in the booth at the back of the bustling restaurant. I rush to where he's sitting, examining the menu, waiting to see the look on his face when he sees me. I'll know it. I'm sure of it.

"Wyatt..." I begin breathlessly.

"Alex!" He jumps up and embraces me. "Well aren't you just a sight for sore eyes!"

"Wyatt, it's you, isn't it?" I blurt. "That's what you came to tell me, right?"

He looks at me, white-blond brows crinkling. This is not the deep, soul-searching, all-consuming gaze I was hoping for. It's confusion.

"It's me...what?"

"You're...you're my father," I hiss. "Aren't you?"

The words are no sooner out of my mouth than the waiter is there, pot of coffee at the ready.

"You want something to drink, miss?" he asks.

"Uhh...no..."

"We got three breakfast specials, a tofu hash with vegan scramble—which I do not recommend—a flight of pancakes including peach, apple, and red velvet—which I do recommend, and a—"

"I'm sorry—would you...could you just give us a minute?" I ask, hearing the desperation in my own voice. If I have to wait for this guy to finish, *I'm* going to turn into a quivering bowl of tofu hash. Right here. Right now. And it won't be pretty.

The guy shrugs, takes his pot and moseys on over to the counter so he can complain about me to the woman serving up slices from a glass-encased pie stand.

"Alex, sit down," Wyatt says gently.

"No, just...just tell me," I say.

"Sit. Down," he says more firmly this time.

Conditioned from the weeks I spent obeying this man's every instruction, I drop into the red vinyl booth across from him and watch as he eases back in. He leans across the table, hands clasped together. When he finally speaks again, his voice is slow and soft.

"Darlin' I'd give my right arm to be able to say yes to that question. But, I can't. Because it's just not the case. And, believe you me, that will always be one of my greatest regrets. I'd have been the luckiest man on the planet to have you as a daughter. I can't tell you how many times I looked at you— watched you and listened to you play—and thought 'Hugh doesn't deserve this child.' And he doesn't. Not that you're a child anymore, Alexandria..."

The sound of my given name from his lips is almost more than I can bear. Because it means it's over—this last faint hope

—the final straw that I just had to clutch at—is no more. I'm not Alex anymore. I'm Alexandria. Alexandria Mickelson-Fitch. Daughter of Hugh and Madeleine. The supreme disappointment and anguish must be written across my face in neon judging from the way Wyatt is peering at me.

"I just...I'd hoped..."

His smile—though still lopsided—is filled with the regret he's spoken of. It's there, as real and true as the heaviness in my heart.

"No, honey," he replies softly. "Afraid there's no way. Your mom and I were well past our relationship when you were born. I'm sorry, but Hugh Fitch is definitely your daddy. But you already know that, I think. Deep down."

Of course, I do. I always have. But I was willing to overlook the obvious so I could, if only for a few moments, pretend I was someone else. Something else.

I sigh deeply and manage a sad smile of my own.

"I'm sorry, Wyatt. I didn't mean to just..."

"Nope. Nope, nope, nope," he says, shaking his head firmly. "No apologizing here. You're safe here with me. You can say anything. Now, tell me, how are you doing?"

I shrug.

"You mean besides the fact that I'm so desperate to escape the hell I'm living in that I'm willing to cling to the fairytale of my 'real' father? Yeah, pretty good, otherwise."

Now he's got that impish grin going on.

"Funny, word on the street is that you're sounding better than ever."

"Hah! Clearly, you're not getting your 'words' from the *Manhattan Times*!"

Wyatt waves a dismissive hand.

"Don't you worry about Abby Beckett."

"Abby? You call Abner Beckett *Abby?*" I ask in disbelief.

"We all called him that back on the competition circuit."

"What are you talking about?"

"Oh, yeah. Abby Beckett thought he was gonna be the next great pianist. Fancied himself somethin' special. Oh, he was special, all right! The first time I came across him was at the regional auditions for the Rossi in New York City. That boy was sweatin' harder than a whore in church. In July. Wearing a fur coat."

I can't help but break my stunned expression long enough to chuckle at my professor's colorful imagery. Just the idea of Abner Beckett on stage, nervous...oh, but apparently there's more...

"At any rate, poor Abby was wearing a white shirt with nothing underneath but the skin God gave him. By the time he played and stood up to face the committee, the whole auditorium was privy to every mole and hair and nipple. All three of them."

My jaw drops and I can actually feel my eyes growing bigger in their sockets.

"What? You're making that up!" I accuse.

Wyatt just shakes his head, the grin remaining at full wattage.

"Oh, my god! How...how embarrassing for him!" I say. "But...how did he play?"

"Meh. Let's just say I coulda spent a decade of summers working with Abby Beckett and he'd a still been mediocre. And smug. And a sombitch."

"Wow... I had no idea..." I murmur.

"Ah, well, ancient history. I just wanted to give you a little insight into why he's such a jackass. Sour grapes, you see. So, to watch someone with so much talent fall apart before his very eyes...well, that makes a guy like Abner downright gleeful."

I nod, the additional intel giving me a broader understanding of the nasty little man.

"Well, as much as I appreciate the laugh, Wyatt, I'm wondering what you're doing here."

He sighs and sits back against the booth's bench, folding his arms across his chest.

"I'm worried about you, Alex."

"I'm fine," I say.

He looks dubious.

"I've been in touch with your mother. With Maddy," he informs me.

"Uh-huh." I didn't know but I'm not surprised.

"And...she seems to think that there's something wrong."

"Huh." News to me.

"In fact, she's the one who asked me to come here and speak with you."

My brows shoot up. That was a risk, to say the least. If my father had any clue...

"Jesus, Wyatt, my father will kill us if he thinks— Oh, god! Are you...are you and my mom having *an affair?*" My volume drops dramatically on the last part of that question and I actually look over my shoulder, half-expecting Abner "Triple Nipple" Beckett to be hanging over the back of the booth, recording us with his iPhone.

Wyatt blinks hard but shakes his head

"No, Alex. We're not. But let's just say we've renewed our acquaintance. And she's real worried about you."

I turn my head away and look across the room at nothing in particular the room.

"If she's so worried, she should do something to get my father to back off a little."

"Now, Alex, that's not fair and you know it. She's in just as deep as you are. Only Hugh has *you* to use as a pawn against her."

My gaze snaps back to him and I wave a dismissive hand.

"Please," I say sardonically. "I've lost a lot of respect for my mother through all of this, Wyatt."

He sighs, as if this is something he, too, has grappled with.

"We all make bad choices," he tells me softly. "And, in all fairness, your daddy sold her a bill of goods when they were first together. Promised her the moon and the stars. Swept her right off her feet."

This gets my attention.

"So..." I begin tentatively, leaning forward slightly, "he did love her, back then, I mean?"

The look that crosses my teacher's face is a little sad. And regretful.

"I can't say for sure. Oh, he cared for her—no doubt about that. And he was attracted to her. He'd a been nuts not to be! But I think what he saw in Maddy Mickelson was the perfect partner. She was brilliant and ambitious. And willing to follow him to the ends of the earth. By the time she realized who he was—what he was—it was too late. She was in too deep. Married, bound to him professionally and pregnant with you."

"Wyatt, if things were really that bad, she should've just taken me and left him."

"Not that easy. Hugh was a powerful man in the arts community, even back then. He could have destroyed her reputation and her career. He'd have found a way to leave her penniless, too, I'm sure of it. And she had you..."

I can't say, honestly, that any of this comes as a surprise. Over the years, I've gleaned bits and pieces of my parents' history together. And I've certainly experienced his particular brand of manipulation firsthand. At the end of the day, though, none of this really matters.

"I'm fine," I repeat, knowing full well that there's nothing he'd be able to do if I said I wasn't. "I'll be fine. I'll get through this recital and move back into my apartment and then do my damnedest to get away from him."

"All right, fair enough. But are you sure you'll be able to get through the recital?"

"I am."

Another lie.

"I see. Because, I might be able to wrangle us a practice room at Juilliard..."

"No. No way. Dad will go ballistic if he finds out. And he will, Wyatt. He'll find out and then he'll go on the warpath."

"I'm not afraid of him, Alex," Wyatt assures me firmly.

"It's not you I'm worried about," I blurt.

And there it is. The elephant in the café.

He nods his understanding.

"How...how is he?" I ask tentatively. "How's Nate?"

Wyatt shrugs.

"Damned if I know. We had a little falling-out of our own and I sent him packing back to Minnesota."

Suddenly, I'm sitting bold upright.

"You did what? Oh, no! Wyatt, he needs you!"

The man looks down at his hands, folded on the Formica table.

"I know that. But I can only do so much, Alex. And Nate wasn't anywhere near ready to commit to performing. I'm thinking more and more that he might never be. That's he's just too damaged to—"

"No!" I cut him off a little too loudly. "No, don't say that! He can do it, Wyatt. I know he can!"

His smile turns wry.

"Well now, only problem there is that you're not the one who needs to know it."

He's absolutely right. As long as Nate believes he's washed-up, it doesn't matter what anyone else thinks he's capable of. I start when I feel the warm touch of his hand on mine. "But it's not Nate I'm here about, it's you. Come back with me. I'll help you get on your feet. Your mama and I have talked about it. She won't fight you."

I'm shaking my head before he's even finished the thought.

"I can't, Wyatt. I appreciate it, but I just can't. I need to do this. I'll—I'll pull it off...and then it'll all be done. He'll be happy."

Wyatt takes a very long beat to consider me, sitting across from him.

"Will he, Alex? Will he ever be happy? I mean, what happens after Carnegie Hall? Your first tour, maybe? The Rossi? When do you get to decide what's best for you? 'Cause, near as I can tell, Hugh's got it all planned out for you. And, god help you if you don't abide by his plan."

In that instant, I see it all so clearly. Wyatt is absolutely, horrifyingly accurate in his depiction of what comes next. I've been tiptoeing on eggshells for weeks now, waiting to just get over this one hurdle. Only...this is just the first of many hurdles. A lifetime of them.

I shake my head slowly with the dawning comprehension of my situation.

"Holy shit. Either way, I am well and truly fucked. Unless..."

It's the second epiphany that really rocks my world. For a moment, everything and everyone fades away as I see a different scenario unfolding in my mind. One where my father loses. One where—

"Alex?" Wyatt is peering at me, his face crinkled in concern. "Unless what?"

"Uh...nothing. Just that I'll have this Carnegie Hall thing behind me. And then he'll probably back off. It's good, Wyatt. Really."

Even I can hear the lie in my tone. Those icy blue eyes

make micro-sweeps across my face, scrutinizing my every twitch. Shit. He knows exactly what I'm thinking. I see it on his face an instant before I hear it from his lips.

"Alexandria Mickelson-Fitch," Wyatt begins softly, slowly. "Are you planning to do something rash? Like throw the recital?"

"What? No!" I laugh a little too quickly. "Why on earth would I do something like that?"

"Because you want to embarrass the hell out of your daddy. Because you'd rather just tank your career once and for all than live like this. Because...because it's exactly what I'd do in your situation if I were your age. But I'm not, Alex, I'm older. And wiser. And I know...there's no coming back from something like that. Not a second time..."

I just smile ruefully because, for the first time, I've come to the realization that maybe playing under these circumstances is worse than not playing at all.

Maybe, next time, I won't want to come back.

# CHAPTER 31

# *Nate*

I have no clue when the storm began, but the sound of torrential rain, crashing thunder, and howling wind has been plaguing my dreams for what feels like hours and hours. At some point, though, that ruckus gives way to another one. Pounding and ringing. Ringing and pounding. They are punctuated by someone calling my name loudly. At some point, I realize that I'm not dreaming all this. It is, indeed storming outside. And there is, in fact, someone banging on my front door.

With great effort, I finally manage to haul myself out of bed with the specific intention of beating the crap out of whoever it is that's standing there. Bang-bang-bang. Ring-ring-ring. They're as good as dead, this cookie-selling girl scout, pamphlet-peddling missionary, or daytime-deadbeat counting census-taker, so I hope he or she is enjoying their last few moments of oxygen. I'm literally seeing red by the time I get my hand on the knob, flip the deadbolt and yank the solid oak slab open on the mini-monsoon that's happening out in front of my house.

"Jesus Christ on a pogo stick!" Wyatt McFadden hollers

over a particularly loud clap of thunder. "You gonna let me in Nate or you waitin' for Noah's fucking ark to come by and scoop me up?" he demands, water rolling off the brim of his cowboy hat.

He's so unexpected—so out of place—that I can only stare at him as I step aside and allow him passage into the foyer. He shucks his jacket, removes and shakes out the hat and yanks the boots from his feet, leaving him looking more like a damp Ken doll that's been left out in the rain than a concert pianist.

"What are you doing here?" I ask when I finally find my voice again.

He quirks an irritated eyebrow at me. "Funny, that's the same question I've been asking myself since I landed in this godforsaken place this morning. You got a coffee pot somewhere?"

I nod and he follows me into the kitchen where I pull down a pair of mugs from the cabinet and pop a K-cup into the Keurig. I add the sugar I know he likes and scrounge around in the fridge for a few creamers that I stole from MacDonald's last time I was there. When the machine has spit out the last of his dark roast, I hand him the mug and make a cup for myself, black. Wyatt's eyeballing me—taking stock of my appearance from head to toe.

"You don't answer your emails."

I take a sip of coffee without responding.

"Or your texts. Or your goddamn cell phone. I can't believe I had to get on a plane and, even then, it took you damn near a half hour to let me in. I was about to call the police and tell them there was a cadaver in here." He stops, looks around the kitchen and twitches his nose in disgust. "Very well might've been, considering the stench."

I slam the cup down on the counter and find the where-withal to start pushing back. I certainly didn't ask him to come here.

"What do you want, Wyatt?" I bite out through gritted teeth.

"I want you to get your head out of your ass and get your shit together. Then, I need you to go somewhere with me."

I scoff. "I'm not going anywhere."

His face darkens. "I'm not fucking around here, Nate. I need you. Alex needs you."

I feel my heart lurch right into my throat at the sound of her name, but I force myself to maintain an apathetic appearance.

"Sorry to hear it," I mutter. "I'm sure it's nothing her parents can't buy her out of."

"You can drop the 'I don't give a shit' act with me, Nate," he replies. "We both know you care more about that young woman than anyone else on the planet."

Do I? Maybe. Probably. But that doesn't matter anymore. Nothing does.

"I couldn't care less," I mumble petulantly. He just stands there, just staring at me. "What?" I demand. "What do you want from me, Wyatt? What is it that you think I can do for her? Because, from where I'm sitting, she's bound and determined to play her father's little game—be his devoted daughter."

"Is that what you think?"

I shrug. "What am I supposed to think, man?"

He rolls his eyes at me and mumbles something unintelligible under his breath.

"What was that, Wyatt?" I'm so fucking tired of all this. Of him. Of my entire, wasted life.

"I said you're an ass," my teacher/former-friend informs me. "And a goddammed fool. You're a foolish ass."

"Seriously? *I'm* an ass? Seems to me she's the ass. Her father—Hugh fucking Fitch—is the ass. And *you*, Wyatt McFuckingFadden. You're an ass. So, why don't you just put your little cowboy boots back on and two-step yourself right back to Texas?"

"Nate, I'm here to help her. And to help you. Can you see yourself, man? Do you realize just how low you've sunk over the last month?"

I throw up my hands in exasperation.

"Are you fucking kidding me? Dude, you're the one who kicked me to the curb! And now...now you're here, looking to assuage your guilt. And I couldn't care less about that, either."

He looks at me for a long moment then takes a sip of his coffee. The only sound I can focus on is the pounding in my head. I turn my back long enough to find the bottle of Tylenol and knock back a few, along with a gulp of warm, flat beer from last night. Or the night before that. Or maybe it was the night before that. I don't recall. And that's just fine with me.

"You're right," I hear him say behind me in a considerably quieter tone. "And I regret that mightily. You needed me and I sent you packing. It's just that you hit a real sore spot for me, Nate. You've guessed by now that Madeleine Mickelson and I had a relationship years ago—before she met Hugh. But I was a stupid, stubborn fool and I let her get away. I've regretted it every day since. It haunts me. Some "piano whisperer" huh? I can't even help myself. But...I can help you. I don't want you to have to live with the same regrets that I do."

"I don't regret a thing," I reply coolly. He laughs at me and it's infuriating. "You know what? Fuck you. Fuck her!"

All at once, his face grows stormy.

"You said you love her. Was that a lie? Do you really, truly not give a flying fig what happens to her now? 'Cause she's about to make the biggest mistake of her life, Nate. And, near as I can tell, you're 'bout the only one who can talk her out of it."

I spin around now with a sneer so dark and a glare so hard that I see him wince.

"How fucking dare you!" I bellow, totally losing my shit. "I did love her! I begged her to stay in Texas with me! I'd have done anything—*anything*—to convince her to leave home once and for all so we could be together. But she left, Wyatt! She chose her father over me. She turned her pretty little ass right around and walked away like I was nothing to her. Like I was some trailer trash summer fling. Like none of it ever happened. But it did happen! I know it happened!"

Wyatt gets to his feet and moves in my direction slowly, cautiously.

Smart.

He doesn't look afraid. At least, not afraid of me. More like he's afraid *for* me. Which makes me wonder just how psychotic I look and sound. Must be pretty bad considering the way he's approaching. Like I'm some woodland creature that needs coaxing out of the woods. When he finally gets to me, he puts his hands on my shoulders with a weight that's strangely comforting.

"Nate, you've missed something really big here—really crucial," he begins in a soft, low voice. "She didn't choose her father over you...she chose *you* over herself."

I open my mouth to say something—to dispute this claim. But I can't. It's like I'm going back to the beginning of a movie after having already finished it. I know how it ends and that changes every little detail. Everything is a clue. Everything is significant. Everything is colored by the ending that I now know.

Holy. Shit.

"Alex still loves you, Nate," Wyatt is saying. "And I believe you still love her. Believe me when I tell you Hugh Fitch woulda ruined your life if she'd stayed. Alex knew that his threats about calling the cops on you were dead serious. And he's got pull. He would have ended any shot you had at a comeback."

"What comeback?" I blurt and twist out from under his grip. "You don't comeback from where I've been, Wyatt. That's how all this hell began. I should never have survived that plane crash. Now, it's like I live between these two worlds. Don't you see it?" My tone has morphed from rigid fury to crumbling desperation. "Can't you, Wyatt? My life was meant to end that day in the field. A few more minutes in the smoking rubble and I would have been dead, too. That's the way it was meant to be. What fate had intended all along. Only someone fucked it all up. And now... well, now I'm doomed like some goddammed zombie. I'm like that opera— The Flying Dutchman? I'm fated to spend all of eternity sailing into the wind—battling the apocalyptic storm until I'm too exhausted to go on. But it'll only be the beginning, Wyatt. Don't you see?"

By the time I realize I'm sobbing, he's there again, pulling me into his chest. Big, strong hands patting me on the back. He's murmuring words I can't understand—words meant to soothe, I think. But none of it makes sense in the garbled haze of my mind. Because I'm not like him. I'm not like anyone else on this planet. I exist in the space between dead and alive. And I'd give anything right now to be able to take that last step. To allow the abyss to swallow me whole and give me the dark and empty peace that I long for with every cell of my soul.

We don't speak as he sits on the lowered toilet seat just on the other side of the shower curtain. I can't see him, but I can feel his presence there. I should be mortified. I should be enraged. I should be... what? I don't know. I'm just numb for the moment and it's a relief from the constant ache that fills me. I turn the thoughts off and allow the scalding water to rain down over my long-unwashed hair. Once I've finished scrubbing the detritus from my body, I reach out, find the big, fluffy towel hanging from a hook on the wall and dry myself, wrapping it around my waist once I've finished. When I step out, Wyatt is still sitting there, next to a fresh cup of coffee that he's made and placed on the countertop next to the sink. I take a sip before running a comb through my sodden hair. Then, I pull out a new razor and some shaving cream, managing to hack my way through several days' worth of stubble with only a few tiny nicks.

"I took the liberty of packing a few things for you," he says as he follows me into the bedroom, where a small, wheeled suitcase and garment bag are laid out for me on the bed, alongside a pair of jeans, sweatshirt, socks, t-shirt and underwear.

"I can't go anywhere with you, Wyatt," I tell him quietly. "There's nothing I can do to help Alex."

"No, Nate, you're the *only* one who can help Alex."

I spin toward him, my face half-lathered, half-shaved. "And why is that?"

"Because what we need right now is a miracle. And you, my friend, are the only one I happen to know personally."

"Wyatt, I am not a miracle. What *happened* to me was no miracle. It was a curse."

"Son, I'm not talking about that plane crash."

My head is spinning now. If not that, than what?

"I-I don't understand..."

He smiles at me then. It's a knowing smile. One that tells me he sees something I don't. Something important.

"Don't you see? You and Alex both came to me this summer so that I could help you. But, in the end, you helped one another. You helped her to see she *could* do it on her own. She helped you to see that you didn't *have* to do it on your own."

I can only stare at him as this sinks in.

"I...I love her, Wyatt."

He rolls his eyes.

"No shit, Sherlock! Now hurry up and get that face mowed so we can get a move on."

"When do we have to leave?" I ask.

"Whenever we get to the airport. We'll buy seats on the first flight out to New York."

"Where will we stay?"

"That doesn't matter at the moment," he says flatly.

"No?"

He shakes his head firmly, mouth pressed tight.

"You know, you haven't asked me what it is that's going on with her."

"It doesn't matter," I inform him. "If she needs me, I have to go to her."

Because he's right. I love her. More than anything.

CHAPTER 32

## *Alexandria*

I'm wearing the dress. It's not the perfect dress, but it's the one I really wanted—the one with the sweetheart neckline in a rich garnet. From where I'm standing in the wings, I register an excited buzz out in the hall. Word around town is that, thanks to Abner "Abby" Beckett, they're actually taking bets on whether or not I'll make it through the recital this time around. The sound fades as I emerge on stage, replaced by polite if not exactly enthusiastic applause. There's no concertmaster for me to greet since there's no orchestra. Turns out not even Hugh Fitch has the juice to secure an entire symphony after his daughter ruins one of their Carnegie Hall performances.

So, it's a recital, as opposed to a full-on concert for my second "debut." Which is probably for the best, anyway, seeing as how I won't have to worry about ending anyone's career but my own. So, I'm all alone as my heels with each of my strides toward the Steinway. When I finally arrive, I place one hand on its enameled surface and bow.

One Mississippi. Two Mississippi. Three Mississippi...

My smile is a little sweet, a little hopeful, and a lot

resigned. It's hardly the perfect smile, but at least this one's honest. A true reflection of the emotions roiling in my gut. I look out into the audience, this time taking note of the specific faces peering back at me, as if I'm a dancing bear at the circus. They have no idea what I'm about to do...and they just can't look away. Forget about the bear analogy, this is definitely more like the two trains speeding towards one another on the same track. I'm both of them. And I'm headed for myself at a breakneck pace that can only mean certain disaster.

The smile falters a little as I spot my parents, seated down front to the far right—my father on the aisle so he can be back-stage in an instant to whisk me away should I dare shame him a second time. Next to him, my mother looks pale and wan, even as she tries to smile at me encouragingly. A quick scan of the rest of the floor seats and I can just make out several high-profile musicians and classical music administrators who didn't bother to come the first time around. Clearly the train wreck is a hot ticket tonight. And then, sitting in the middle seat in the middle section is my good pal, Abner Beckett.

Abner's been taunting me in the paper as of late, making sure to plug the performance until every last ticket was sold. He'd drop in little comments about my "greatly anticipated 'make-up' debut" and how my true skills "remain to be seen." He's smirking at me now and—oh, no, he did *not* just wink at me! What a bastard! I have to work extra hard to keep the smile that's plastered to my face from souring. Instead I just close my eyes and turn away, taking my place on the piano bench.

Until this very moment, I hadn't realized how roomy it is without Nate next to me. I can't feel the press of his thigh against mine as his fingers move in tandem with mine...or the brush of his hands as he lifts his wrists in between mine. And that brings to mind the feel of his hot breath against my ear, soft and panting as he brings me to ecstasy...

Oh, hell. I realize I've got my head turned away from the audience as I glance down at the empty spot beside me wistfully. How long have I been caught up in this little reverie? Long enough for people to be shifting in their seats, but not long enough for them to take up the murmuring again. Not that it matters—they're going to be murmuring in a minute, anyway. That is, if I go through with it. And, quite frankly, I can't think of a single reason not to. It is truly the very last thing that I have control over.

There's my answer. I take a deep breath, raise my hands to the keyboard and...nothing. They rest there, waiting to begin the roll and ebb of the Moonlight Sonata. But they're unmoving. And with each second that ticks by, they become more firmly rooted to the keys upon which they're resting. My heart is screaming at me to move—to just pick up my hands and play. By my head reminds me that the point here is to fight that urge. To fight...the fight. At last, I pull them back to rest in my lap. Now the murmur is starting.

I can almost feel the schadenfreude radiating from the section where Abner Beckett is seated. He's likely got his little notebook and pen out, capturing every moment of my momentous fall. This is it, I realize. The last time I'll ever be in this position again. Because as soon as I get up from this bench, it's over. Everything that I've worked my entire life for. And you know what? I don't give a damn anymore. Because none of it matters without...

The murmur has turned into a full-on gossipfest right here in front of me. Oh, come on! I know it's bad, but it's not *that* bad. At least, not yet, I mean I haven't even stood up and run off stage yet. I brave a little glimpse out of the corner of my eye and realize no one's looking at me. What? No, they're looking at something behind me. I crane my neck around in time to see the flutter of the stage right curtains; to hear the clack of shoes on the boards.

Oh, hell. My father has come to take me off the stage. Well, this should make for a lovely photo op for Abner's column tomorrow morning. Except that my father is one of the people looking away from me in the audience. And his face is a brewing storm of rage.

What the hell...?

The instant he steps out on stage, clear of the wings, clear of the black velvet drapes, there is a collective gasp from the audience. I jump to my feet so quickly that the bench tips backward and crashes to the floor. But no one seems to notice. They're all too busy talking and twisting. More and more are taking out their phones and taking pictures, shooting video. I hear his name everywhere, all at once.

*"Nathaniel Calloway?"*
*"Is that...?"*
*"Oh, my god...I think it's..."*

"Here, let me help you with that," he says, bending down to right the bench and position it.

I can only stare at him, eyes huge and mouth hanging open. I must look like a fish, but I don't care. He's absolutely breathtaking in his tux—all broad shoulders and long, lean limbs. His hair is tousled, but not messy. Never messy. And his dark eyes are fixed on mine.

"You're...here..."

"Boy, can't get anything past you," he replies with a quirk on his lips.

"But...how? Why...? Nate..."

Nathaniel Calloway—Rossi Competition gold medalist, plane crash survivor, and unexpected love of my life—takes my hand in his and brings it to his lips, barely brushing the knuckles with his soft lips. I gasp. Again. The flash of cameras all around us is almost blinding, but I hardly register them. I can't tear my eyes away from his.

"Why...why did you come?" I whisper.

"I need you."

This makes me throw my head back in an irrational giggle. "*You* need *me*?" I wave a hand at the audience, every member of which has lost all sense of decorum. They're standing and gaping and chattering excitedly. People are rushing forward with their phones. They're taking pictures and shooting video. Twitter must be exploding right now. And more than one reporter has appeared at the foot of the stage to shout questions at him. At us.

*"Nate! Are you back? Is this your comeback performance?"*
*"Nate! Are you and Alexandria a couple?"*
*"Nate! Why are you here?"*

Still holding my hand in his, he turns to face them.

"No, this is not my comeback performance. This is Alexandria Mickelson-Fitch's moment to show you how brilliant she is. Yes, we are most definitely a couple. And...what was the last one?"

"Why are you here?" the woman from the Post repeats.

"Oh, yeah. Well, because I love this woman. And I'm wondering if she'll spend the rest of her life with me."

He doesn't have a microphone and people all around us are chattering and yet every single person in this packed hall hears him. And everything stops.

"What about it, Alexandria?" the reporter asks with a huge grin. Oh, I like this reporter.

I throw myself into Nate's arms and kiss him with every

ounce of passion that I have packed within my body. I give him everything I have. Everything I am.

There is catcalling and shouts of applause all around us.

"Is that a yes?" he asks me when we finally separate.

"I'd say so," I reply with an expression of such pure elation that no one needs to hear the words to know my answer.

"She said 'yes'!" Nate calls out, pulling me to him with one hand while raising the other in an impromptu fist pump of triumph.

And then the hall is on its feet. I haven't even played a note and the applause almost deafening. My father looks fit to be tied. My mother is wiping tears from her face. And then there's Wyatt McFadden. He's just out of sight, standing in the stage left wings. When he notices me noticing him, he pulls his cowboy hat from his head and holds it to his heart, giving a little bow in the process.

"Okay, that's my cue to leave," Nate says.

"What? No! You can't go...we have to play!"

"We will," he assures me. "We will. But for now, it's all you, baby."

Nate kisses my cheek and steps away, holding his hands out in my direction. "Ladies and gentlemen, I'll be back, but right now please welcome my fiancée, the brilliant Alexandria Mickelson-Fitch."

I watch as he slips back into the wings, just out of sight of the audience, many of whom are still craning their necks to get a look at the Musical Miracle. He nods in the direction of the piano with his chin.

"It's all you, Alex," Wyatt calls out over the din all around us. "Show 'em what you got, young lady!"

I look from him, to Nate and back again before nodding firmly, and turning back to the piano and taking a seat on the bench again. Only, this time, it doesn't feel quite so empty. Because, while Nate may not be right here, sitting next to me,

I can still sense him right here, by my side. And that means I can do anything. I can be anything. And, tonight, I want to be a pianist...more than anything.

My hands touch the keys and there is no turning back.

* * *

By the time I get to the end of my recital program, Beethoven's *Moonlight Sonata* has soared, Bach's *Goldberg Variations* have flitted, and Debussy's *Dolly Suite* has charmed—without so much as a missed note. I'm playing better than I have ever played in my life. Probably because I'm feeling stronger, braver...and happier than I have ever felt in my life.

The applause at the end of the recital goes on and on until I indicate that I'm going to sit back down and give an encore. I use my hand as a visor against the harsh, bright stage lights as I peer out into the audience looking for Nate. My gaze alights on my father—who looks doesn't exactly look happy...but at least he's not as furious has he has been. Still, I don't believe he's pleased when I finally just call out from the stage.

"Hey, Nate, you out there?"

"Right here," he says as he waves at me from the wings.

"Come on out."

He smiles and shakes his head.

"Nope. It's your night."

Someone down front catches the exchange and starts the chant, stretching his name out over two syllables. In a matter of seconds, the entirety of Carnegie Hall is demanding his presence.

"Na-ate! Na-ate! Na-ate! Na-ate!"

I look at him and shrug, a sheepish smile on my face. At last, he rolls his eyes and strolls out to an uproarious greeting from row after row. I scoot over and pat the side of the bench.

"What? I didn't bring any music with me," he protests.

"But I did!" Wyatt says, running out just long enough to hand me some sheet music.

It's the *Danse Macabre* and Nate looks more than a little alarmed.

"Alex, I haven't even been practicing," he confides in me softly. "I just...I can't do this now."

Our teacher puts a firm hand on his shoulder.

"Nate, it's now...or it's never. Which is it gonna be?"

I smile and hold out my hand.

He looks at it for a long moment before nodding and taking his place by my side. Wyatt lifts the lid of the piano and plays the part of the clock as it strikes midnight, plucking the single string inside the belly of the instrument until the witching hour has arrived.

And then, we're off.

# CHAPTER 33

# Nate

I t's the most thrilling experience of my life—and the most satisfying. Because, when Alex and I sit down to play together, all is right in the world. I don't worry about how I sound or what I look like. I don't give a shit what people are writing or reporting or saying about me. It's just her, and me, and the music. And God knows there's plenty of that! We move from the *Danse Macabre* to *En Bateau* to a totally improvised four-handed version of *Boogie Woogie Bugle Boy*.

We are on fire. I know it. She knows it. Based on the sheer volume of the audience when the last notes die away, everyone within a five-mile radius of Carnegie Hall knows it. I stand and gesture to Alex who follows suit and takes her solo bow. When she reaches back for me, I take her hand and we bow together. And then, the instant that we're upright again, I pick her up in my arms and swing her around for God and the rest of the world to see. My lips find hers and the swell of sound out in the house doubles.

When they finally allow us to leave the stage, Wyatt is there, waiting, a grin the size of...well...Texas fills his face.

"Hot damn! You two were amazing! Absolutely amazing! I'd like to see Abby Beckett put that in his pipe and smoke it!"

"Ahem."

I half-expect to see the sleazy little man standing behind us, but when I turn it's not Abner Beckett glaring at us. It's Hugh Fitch—the man whose face I punched in not quite five weeks ago.

"Daddy...?" Alex says softly, taking a step toward him.

He looks from her to me to Wyatt.

"Well, looks like you got what you wanted, young man," he hisses my way.

"If you mean Alex, then yes, I did," I agree.

"Her name is Alexandria!" he spits. "And, no, I was referring to her coattails. The ones that you rode in on this evening. How fortunate for you that you got a Carnegie Hall recital, too! And with none of the effort or expense that we put into making it happen. Now you've got yourself a nice little bit of press at the expense of my daughter's career. Because, trust me on this, no one is going to give a damn about you in the morning, Alexandria. You may very well have given an adequate recital, but your freakshow friend over here is all that anyone can talk about. In fact—"

"Stop it!" Alex roars. And I do mean roars. She's loud enough to stop everyone in their tracks. "You don't get to torment me anymore. I'm done. I'll be taking over management of my career and my life from here on out," she informs her father.

"Oh, no you don't, young lady—"

"Hugh Fitch!" Madeleine screeches in a tone that matches her daughter's. "Don't you even think about it! You're done threatening my daughter. And you're done threatening me."

"Is that so?" he sneers back at his wife.

"That is exactly so," she assures him. "Because Alex is moving back to her apartment. Or Texas...or wherever she wants to be right now. And I'm going to the Waldorf. I'll be filing for a divorce in the morning."

His mouth drops open and his brows draw in.

"What are you talking about? No one's going anywhere!" he bellows.

By now, the press corps—which appears to have doubled since I showed up a couple of hours ago—has flocked backstage hoping to get a quote from Alex and me. Instead, they're treated to Madeleine Mickelson's declaration of Independence...and Hugh Fitch's subsequent meltdown.

"Just. Watch. Me," Madeleine says, poking her husband's barrel chest for emphasis as she utters each word.

"Go ahead, Madeleine," he whispers down at her in a threatening tone. "Just try leaving me and we'll see how far you get."

She throws back her head and laughs. A flash goes off somewhere and there are murmurs from everywhere around us.

"Oh, Hugh, I'll get plenty far. I earned half of everything that's in our bank accounts and I plan to collect it. That should be more than enough for Alexandria and me until we each get on our feet. Meanwhile, unlike you, I've got a job teaching at the conservatory, an open invitation to tour with the Walton Quartet, and a contract for a solo recording next year. So, I think I'll be just fine, thank you very much!"

Alex intervenes, closing the short distance between herself and her father. I trail along behind her...just in case.

"Daddy," she says quietly enough so only those closest will hear, "I don't think you want to do this here in public. Why don't you go home, have a drink and get some sleep? You and mama and I can sort this all out in the morning."

For a moment, I think he's going to heed the wisdom being offered up by his only child. That he'll see she's right and give things a night to cool down. But just for a moment, because that's all the time there is before he totally blows it for the last time.

"There's nothing to sort out, Alexandria. Your mother's not going anywhere because she knows as well as I do that there isn't anything more important than our family's reputation. And loyalty."

Madeleine shakes her head, the anger on her face softening into something akin to pity.

"No, Hugh. That's where you're wrong and I will not have our child believing that nonsense." She spins around and points in her daughter's direction. "Love, Alexandria. Love is more important than loyalty or reputation. Love is more important than fame and money. Without love there is nothing—just an empty, wasted shell of a life." Now she turns back toward her husband. "I'm sorry to say, Hugh, love is something you and I haven't shared in a very long time."

And with that, Madeleine Mickelson-Fitch, wife of Hugh, mother of Alexandria, turns on her black high-heels and strides out of Carnegie with head held high...and Wyatt McFadden by her side. For his part, Hugh Fitch watches her go, still not comprehending the magnitude of the loss he's just experienced. Part of me thinks he never will.

* * *

"Lusty passion!" she squeals with delight, bouncing up and down on the bed with the Arts section of the *Herald*. "This one says we have 'lusty passion'!"

I grin up at her, my elbow tucked under the pillow as I watch her—all of her—in motion above me. I like this view very much.

"Score one for lusty passion!" I agree enthusiastically.

"And...that just leaves us with one more..."

We've been saving the worst for last. I hand her the final

paper from the stack that the concierge brought up to the door of our hotel room this morning. With a deep breath and a determined nod, she opens the pages gingerly. I watch her face carefully, eyes moving left to right and down—growing a little wider with each pass. Finally, she looks up at me and starts to read.

"Okay, so what did our old friend Abner write?" I ask slowly.

"He uh..." she begins slowly, softly. "He says... oh, here, you have to read it yourself."

I push myself up on my elbows and rest my back against the headboard. She hands me the paper and I take it from her, locating the column and reading it aloud.

*"It is not my job to make everyone feel warm and fuzzy and good about themselves. Quite the opposite, actually. My job is to be critical—to pick performances and performers apart, look for their weaknesses and expose them. At least, that's what I thought the extent of my job was. Until last night."* I look up incredulously at Alex before returning to the statement. *"I fully expected to be writing a report on the dismal failure of Alexandria Mickelson-Fitch's Carnegie Hall recital. Instead, last night I found myself in the exceedingly rare position of watching the birth of a legend-in-the-making. Ms. Mickelson-Fitch's program was an exceptional amalgam of technique and artistry that gives a glimpse into her bright future...but it was the encore portion of the evening that made me lean forward on the edge of my seat, holding on for dear life until the last note was played"*

I look up at her again. "Holy shit, Alex..."

"Keep reading!" she insists. And I do.

*"Ms. Mickelson-Fitch was joined on stage by the legendary Nathanial Calloway, the last American to take gold at the Rossi International Piano Competition. You may recall that he was the sole survivor of the plane crash that claimed the lives of all others on board—including his own parents and sister. That was*

*the moment when Nate 'The Musical Miracle' Calloway disap-*
*peared from the classical music world. Until last night. Needless*
*to say, there was quite a frenzy when Mr. Calloway appeared*
*after a fifteen-year hiatus from the concert hall stage.*

*"From the moment the two sat down to share the bench, the*
*air crackled with their chemistry. When they began to play, that*
*energy grew and grew and grew beyond anything I could have*
*imagined. Anything I have ever witnessed. Her fiery technique*
*was perfectly balanced by his sublime finesse. Where, individu-*
*ally, they may be exceptional pianists, together, they are one*
*near-perfect musical entity. Bravo to self-professed 'piano whis-*
*perer' Wyatt McFadden for giving us the best of the next gener-*
*ation of great musicians. And congratulations to Ms.*
*Mickelson-Fitch and Mr. Calloway on the start of what I'm*
*quite sure is destined to be a brilliant four-handed career. May*
*you always spend it hand-in-hand."*

I drop the paper, stunned by what I've just read.

"Huh," I say thoughtfully.

Alex's dark, perfectly-arched brows dip downward.

"What's that supposed to mean?"

I shrug.

"I don't know...nothing. It means...you know...huh. Why?
What do you think it means?"

"I think it means you have something else to say. Something that you're not saying," she responds, hands on hips as
she sits up on her knees on the bed facing me.

I pretend to consider this.

"Hmmm...well...let's see..."

Without warning, I lunge forward, tackling her and flattening her slim body underneath mine on the bed. She's
giggling and squirming but she doesn't try to free herself from
the press of my chest. My face is only an inch or two from hers
and her breath is warm and sweet on my skin.

"You're right, there is something else," I admit.

She stares up at me, unfazed and unblinking.

"Yes?"

I lean down and press my lips to hers for just a moment before pulling back again.

"Will you come with me to meet my...family?"

It is the most difficult question I have ever asked in my entire life.

"Of course," she says, smiling up at me sweetly. "Of course, I will."

# Epilogue: Nate

I'm concerned that we won't be able to find it at first, but once we clear the final bend in the long, twisting road, several other cars come into view. We find a place to park the rental car and follow the small stream of people disappearing along a narrow path into the woods. I grab her hand and look at her uncertainly. She smiles, nods and gives my fingers a squeeze, pulling me in the direction of the others. We walk the quarter mile with a rich green canopy above our heads and thick carpet of pine needles under our feet. It smells of Christmas.

People around us are murmuring quietly, reverently, as if we're walking down the aisle of a great piney cathedral. But, as we all emerge from the woods and into the clearing, the mood switches abruptly. Here there are hundreds of other people. They embrace and chat and laugh. Some are taking selfies. Others are showing off pictures of the children and grandchildren and great-great-grandchildren who couldn't make the trip with them.

I have to stop and breathe. For a brief moment it's too much—I think I'm going to have to turn around and go back to the car. But, when my eyes find Alex's, I see that they are calm and unjudging. I feel better instantly.

"It's okay," she says. "We can go if you want."

Over her shoulder, I catch sight of the Flight 7079 memorial sculpture. It reminds me of why we came all this way.

"No," I say, shaking my head, "No, I'm all right."

She smiles and nods her understanding, waiting patiently until I'm ready to take another step. We've barely walked six feet when I hear my name through the crowd. We stop and watch as the petite redhead approaches, her arms open wide.

"Oh, Nathanial!" she gasps when she reaches us. "We've been waiting for you for so very long."

"I..uh...Alex, this is Peggy Moody. Her husband was the pilot. He...he died trying to save us all..."

The woman's eyes being to tear up with her gratitude. She didn't think I knew that about Glenn Moody—that he was frantically trying to right our doomed plane up until the moment it collided with the earth. What Peggy doesn't realize is that I've been doing a long-overdue homework assignment. I've been learning as much as I could about everyone standing in this field—and several others who aren't. Poring over pictures, reading bios, following social media streams and memorial websites.

"Everyone! Hey, everyone!" Peggy hollers above the din. She has an unusually loud voice for such a slight woman and people automatically stop what they're doing and turn to see us. "Everyone, look! Nate's here," she calls out excitedly. "And he's brought..."

"This is Alex," I supply. "My wife."

A collective gasp from the crowd is quickly followed by cheers and clapping. All the while, I cling to my new bride's hand as tightly as I've ever held to anything. She is rock solid as I look to her—those dark eyes a study in tranquil assuredness. She knows. As do I. It's all going to be okay.

And then they are all there, embracing us and welcoming us. Men pat me on the back. Woman squeeze my arm or grab my hand. Every once-in-a-while someone touches my face, as if I'm the last connection between them and those they lost. Which I'm not. But I sort of am. Because I am the face of all two-hundred-forty-seven souls who perished in this field that afternoon so many years ago. I represent what they might have lived to do and see and say and feel. I'm what they might have lived to become.

I am the living, breathing, walking, talking ghost of flight 7079.

With Alex right at my side, I wade into the crowd and allow myself to be swallowed up in their welcoming embraces. I allow myself to belong.

The day I didn't die was a bright and sunny Tuesday.

The day I am reborn is an overcast Saturday.

Back then, I was a child.

Right now, I am a man.

On that fateful day, I lost my family.

On this fateful day, I have found them.


THE END.

# Acknowledgments

Thank you to the amazing people who made ***Counterpoint*** possible...

My sweet husband Tom, love of my life.

My sister, Vanessa, and her beautiful family, Frankie Sr., Frankie Jr. and Ursula.

My amazing family including Janet and Kwaku, Mike and Crucita, Karen and Michael, Bonnie and David, Kim and David, Laura, Michelle, Jessica, Cheryl, Jeremiah, Nathan, Joshua, Hannah, Angel and Noah. I love you all!

My dearest parents—Gregory and Marie as well as my grandparents, Carol and Mario. You gave me a wonderful start in this world, but you left me way too soon.

I'm so very grateful for the women who help me work through the tough times and celebrate the good times. My heart is so full since I met you... Jeannie, Jen, Nika, and Patty.

**Lauren Rico** has earned a reputation as one of the top Classical music broadcasters in the country—introducing listeners to the stories of the great composers. But there came the point when she wanted to start writing some stories of her own, and in less than a decade, she's turned a hobby into several award-winning romance novels. By expanding into the world of Women's Fiction, Lauren hopes to create relatable characters and compelling storylines that will keep readers up all night turning pages. When she's not talking on the radio or tethered to her laptop, Lauren enjoys a quiet but crazy life in a lovely but messy home on Long Island with her husband and rescue pup, Sandy.

Sign up for Lauren's newsletter and be the first to hear about sales, special events, and monthly giveaways! www.LaurenRico.com

# Dear Reader

*Thank you so much for taking the time to read* Counterpoint*! If you enjoyed it, I hope you'll leave a review on whichever book review platforms you frequent. I'm so grateful for your support —you have no idea how much an endorsement from you impacts the authors whose books you read every day. Be sure to check out some of my other titles below, as well as a free sneak-peek of another music-themed romance,* Solo. *And be sure to sign up for my newsletter so you never miss a giveaway or the latest news.*

*With all my very best wishes,*

*Lauren*

Also by Lauren E. Rico

***The Whiskey Sisters*** series (Written as L.E. Rico)

If you're a fan of Hallmark Channel movies, then you'll love the sweet and sassy O'Halloran girls of Mayhem, Minnesota! These PG romcoms are funny and quirky—but don't let the humor fool you! There's a lot of depth to these characters, and a lot of love for family and friends up there on the Iron Range.

### Reading order:

*Blame it on the Bet*

*Mischief and Mayhem*

*Mistletoe in Mayhem (double novella)*

*Mismatched in Mayhem*

### The Reverie trilogy

If you didn't think Classical music could be riveting, think again! The *Reverie* trilogy is a suspenseful rollercoaster ride that's titillating and terrifying by turns. Set at a prestigious conservatory in Manhattan, the stakes are high, and some people will do anything to get their shot at the top. Highly addictive and deliciously dark.

For mature readers only.

### Reading Order:

*Reverie*

*Rhapsody*

*Requiem*

### The Symphony Hall series

Looking for something that's fun and flirty—but also has some dramatic teeth? Don't want to get invested in an ongoing storyline or cliffhangers? Check out these one-and-done stories featuring characters you won't soon forget, and set in the world of Classical music.

Enjoy this free sneak-peek from *Solo*...

KATE

I don't know what I expect to see when I raise the hood of the car. It's not as if there'll be a neon sign flashing *Broken Hose* or *Blown Tranny*—whatever the hell a tranny is. But there's nothing like that. Just the greasy, metallic guts of my old Toyota. I recognize the plastic container that holds the blue washer fluid and the cap that I twist off to put antifreeze in. I see the dipstick I use to check the level on the oil that this bucket of bolts guzzles down and smokes out the tailpipe. But that's it.

"Hey, do you need some help?"

I'm so startled by the voice behind me that I jump and hit my head on the hood of the car. The pain comes in a single blinding flash.

Just great. This is exactly what I need this morning on top of car trouble. On top of being late. On top of freezing my ass off in this parking lot.

"Oh, hey. I didn't mean to startle you. Are you okay?"

The voice is right next to me now, and when I turn to face

it—turn to face *him*, I'm met by some seriously broad shoulders. *Wow*. His concerned eyes are a blend of blue and green that are sexy as hell. His hair, just a little too long in the back, is a sandy blond and he's got a little matching stubble. Like Ryan Gosling. Make that a double *wow*.

"Here," he says, pulling a crumpled McDonald's napkin from his backpack. "It's clean. It's just a little squashed is all."

"I...uh...thanks," I mumble, accepting his offering and his apologetic smile. I use the napkin to apply pressure to my bleeding head.

He looks amused, the corners of his eyes crinkling into the slightest hint of crow's-feet. It makes him look a little older than I thought at first glance. He must be a grad student. No, actually his clothes are too nice. Grad students don't have money for nice clothes. He must be faculty or staff. Older, for sure. But that's okay. I can work with older. "Something wrong with your car?" he asks, his gaze moving between me and my eighteen-year-old Corolla.

I swivel to look down at the vehicle that is the bane of my existence most days.

"It won't start," I say dejectedly.

"And...you know something about cars, do you?" The amusement in his tone tells me that he's wondering why I even bothered to raise the hood and have a look.

I shake my head and immediately regret the movement, wincing through another surge of pain.

"No, I just thought it might be something obvious. A broken hose or something. But it's not anything I can see."

"You know, you really should have that looked at." "Yeah, I guess I'll have to get a tow truck," I mutter.

His cheeky grin grows into a broad smile and he throws his head back, laughing loudly.

"What?" I demand, suddenly embarrassed over something I can't even identify.

"Not the car, your head!"

"Oh. *Oh*." I laugh with him now. "Are you suggesting I have my head examined?" I ask with faux indignation. God! Am I flirting with Hot Older Guy?

"I am, actually," he says, still smiling but not laughing anymore. "That looks like a pretty deep gash. And you know how those head wounds are. They bleed a lot. You might need stitches or something."

He's not wrong. I can feel the blood soaking through the napkin. But at the same time, I can also *hear* the *ka-ching!* of the cash register as I do the mental math on a car tow, car repair, *and* a trip to the ER. The blood will regenerate; the car won't.

"If it's still bleeding in a little while, I will." I lie through my reassuring smile. "But hey, thanks for checking on me."

"Yeah, well, maybe if I'd left you alone you wouldn't have a gash in your forehead," he says, looking remorseful. "Listen, the least I can do is give you a lift. Where're you headed?"

"Oh, the Music building. But it's not too far. I can walk from here," I say, pointing to a cluster of brick buildings barely discernable across a and through some trees.

"Yeah, not too far if you have forty-five minutes to kill." He snorts, closing the hood of my car. "That's all the way on the other side of campus. What are you doing over here? Do you live in the dorms?"

I shake my head. "No, I work in the North Dining Hall. But you know, I'll bet I can catch a shuttle."

"Nope. I just saw it go past. Won't be another one for twenty minutes. Why don't you let me give you a lift? I was headed to the Art department anyway and that's right next door. I mean unless you have the time to wait."

I pull my phone from the pocket of my jeans for a time check. Seven forty-five. That's the thing. I don't have the time to wait. There's no way I'll make it to my eight a.m. Orchestration class if I try to walk it now. And by the time the university shuttle gets me there, I might as well just skip class all together.

I consider the hot guy. I don't know him. Not even a little. What if he's some handsome sociopath who picks up girls in parking lots? With my luck, I'd become a Lifetime Movie of the Week. Some C-list actress will play me as the stupid, unsuspecting girl who gets into the car of the tall, handsome stranger. Next thing you know, my picture is on a poster, they find me stuffed down some drainpipe in Encino, and *Dateline NBC* is interviewing the jurors in my murder trial.

When he extends a hand, I don't have to wonder if my reluctance is on my face. Everything shows on my face.

"By the way, I'm Kevin," he offers.

"Kate," I reply, giving him a quick shake with my free hand.

"Music department, you said?"

I nod. He squints thoughtfully, turning to walk away from my immobilized vehicle.

"Do you know Dr. Markham?" he asks. "Ohhh, yeah. It's his class I've got at eight."

"Seriously?" he asks, eyebrows up, like I might be messing with him.

"Seriously," I say solemnly.

"Well, that's that, then," he declares as he puts a reassuring hand on my forearm and starts to steer me through the rows of parked cars. "I've heard what a dick he can be and I refuse to be the reason you're late for his class. It's the least I can do."

"How do you know him?" I ask, allowing myself to be pulled along. The question is part test, part curiosity.

"I'm a teaching assistant in the Art department. Everybody over there knows him. Or, *about* him, anyway. His dick-ishness is kind of legendary." He grins at me over his shoulder.

I chuckle at the idea of that, but I still can't quite shake the niggling feeling that something's not right with this guy. "So, what are you teaching?" I press, needing just a little more convincing to reset my *stranger danger* radar.

"Art Appreciation for non-majors," he says, edging sideways through two closely parked sedans. I follow him as we cut through to another row. "I get all the business majors who consider the Mona Lisa to be a financial investment rather than a work of art. They'll be lucky if I don't strangle one of them before the semester is over." He laughs and then stops himself with a look of faux alarm. "I'd better be careful or *I* might get a reputation as the next Markham."

"Not likely." I groan, rolling my eyes.

"Well, come on, there isn't much time to get you to class." I stop and look at him.

"Really, be honest with me. Do you mind? Am I taking you out of your way? Because I can walk," I offer with some reservation in my voice.

I get the dazzling smile and the crinkly eyes again. "Kate, please. I really am on my way over there. Same parking lot. You won't be taking me a single foot farther than I was going to go anyway. I swear to God."

I nod, satisfied at last, and follow him through the sedans and small SUVs until we're standing in front of a shiny white BMW X-something or other. Someone's got a little cash, I see. My reflection in the tinted window gives me my first glimpse of the gash on my forehead. "Ughhh," I mutter as I rearrange my long, dark hair to try and camouflage it. But it's no use. I return the saturated napkin to my head and get into the leather passenger's seat with a frustrated sigh.

"I hope you don't mind me saying so, but your ride's seen better days. Might be time for some new wheels," he suggests as he slides into the driver's side and shuts the door. "Just saying."

"Yeah, well, not everyone can swing a bimmer," I counter.

"Oh, come on now," he coaxes. "What are you? A junior?

Senior? You must have family to help you out."

"I'm finishing up my masters, actually," I respond, ignoring the family comment as he pulls out of the lot and onto the main road through campus.

"What? No way!" he says, giving me a surprised sideways glance. "Good for you! Got plans for after graduation?"

"I'm going to sleep. For about a month," I mutter.

"Oh yeah. I crashed at my parents' place for the entire summer after I finished my grad degree and I don't think I left my bed for the first week. What about you? Will you be headed back home to your folks, too?"

"Nope," I say, poking at the napkin over my wound.

"No?"

Oh, hell. I know this trick. He's hoping I'll feel compelled to elaborate. I won't. But it's got me wondering if maybe Hot Teacher Guy recognizes me as the daughter of "Senator Satan" and is fishing for a little info. It wouldn't be the first time a potential date has started out by way of morbid curiosity.

"I'm sorry," he says before I can comment. "I don't mean to be nosy. It's just a bad habit of mine. I meet an interesting, funny, pretty woman and I jump right into the personal details."

"Nah, it's okay," I say softly, his compliments making me feel suddenly bashful.

"Hey, you wanna have coffee sometime?" he asks, quickly looking over at me. He seems a bit taken aback by his boldness, with the lip biting and all.

"Really?" I laugh. "I'm bleeding all over your posh leather interior and you actually want to see me again?"

"Why not? I like being the white knight."

"What? Rescuing the damsel in distress from the parking lot, riding in on your white BMW?"

"Sure." He shrugs. "I'll rescue you from the big, bad Dr. Drew the Dragon, too, if you want. We could run off to the

Pancake Cottage and live happily ever after. Well, for an hour or two, anyway."

"Oh, so tempting." I groan and grin at the same time. "You've just stumbled upon my Achilles' heel."

"Breakfast?"

I nod enthusiastically.

"Well, come on, then! You can get the notes from someone else, can't you?"

I sigh heavily, allowing my mind a nanosecond-long fantasy involving this Kevin guy and pancake syrup.

*Stop it!*

"No, I can't," I reluctantly decline. "I have an assignment due and Markham won't take it if I don't come to class."

He looks a little disappointed, but still determined. "Okay, well, how about a cup of coffee later, then?" he presses.

Oh, what the hell? What else have I got to do except study scores in my apartment and work on my midterm project?

"Um, yeah, I think I'd like that," I agree at last.

"Great! What time are you free?" he asks just as we're pulling into the Arts Complex lot. I notice that it's already full. Even if I had been able to get my car running, no way I'd have found a parking spot. I glance at the dashboard clock: 7:58. If I fly into the building and right up the stairs, I should *just* make it.

"Uh, noon?" I ask as I reach for the visor so I can flip it down and take a quick peek in the mirror. I want to be sure my face is blood-free before I get out of the car. The car which now jerks to a sudden stop, propelling me forward against the seat belt.

"Oh, wait, don't..." Kevin says, reaching toward the visor and sounding suddenly alarmed.

But he's too late. I see it.

My heart sinks, breaks, and explodes all at the same time. This guy is obviously not who he says he is. And I am obviously a fool. I twist around to face Kevin, who looks considerably paler than he was the last time I checked.

"I—uh... That's just a..." he stammers.

"Microphone," I say coolly, examining the small black disc about the size of a button. There's a black wire running from it. When I follow the line, I see how it's carefully tacked around the headliner.

The epiphany or realization or frying pan to the head or *whatever* the hell this is, takes my breath away as everything snaps into crystal clear focus. I'm adding it all up in my head —something I *should* have done much sooner. Along with the slight crow's-feet, I now spot a few threads of silver hair camouflaged by the blond. Then there's the BMW. And the expensive clothes he's wearing. Why didn't I put it all together before? My eyes narrow on him as the last of the pieces falls into place. How could I have been so goddamned stupid? I *know* better.

*So, so stupid, Kate!*

"Who do you work for?" I ask quietly. "I don't know what you mean."

"Who do you work for?" I demand louder this time, a little surprised by the edge in my tone. "The *Post*? The *Sun-Times*? The *Ledger*? Christ! You don't work for the *National Enquirer*, do you?"

Kevin—if that's even his name—takes a deep breath.

His voice is calm and soft.

"Kate, it's not what you think."

"No? Then what the fuck *is* it?"

"I'm a reporter for the *D.C. Courier*," he explains slowly.

Of course he is. Because, why would a good-looking, smart, funny guy want to help me out? Or *ask* me out for that matter?

I take a deep breath and regroup. This is not the time for

self-pity. *Anger*. That's what this situation calls for. Good, old-fashioned rage.

"What did you do to my car?"

Seeing that his cover is totally blown, Kevin tosses charming out the window, replacing it with smugness.

"Not that I'm admitting to anything," he begins coyly, "but you might want to have your battery cables tightened. And, just out of curiosity, why *is* the daughter of a senator—and a presidential hopeful at that—driving around in that piece of shit?"

"You son of a bitch!" I hiss, unable to restrain myself any longer.

"Oh, come on, Katie," he says, turning to me with a conspiratorial grin. My fingers twitch with the temptation to slap it right off his face. "Your father's the most detested politician on the Eastern Seaboard! And, I'm guessing, he's not exactly 'Father of the Year' material. I mean, aside from the clunker you're driving, you're working a crap job. I know you don't have any health insurance. God, you don't even have a winter coat! Does your father know you live like this?"

"What are you talking about? A winter coat?"

I can't follow his line of thinking, so he fills me in.

"Yeah, well, look at you. It's thirty degrees out and you're wearing a hoodie. And, before you feed me some bullshit about leaving your coat at home, I haven't seen one on you in the last six months."

*Wait, wait, wait...*

"Y-you've been watching me for *six* months?" I ask, sounding a bit shakier now because I *am* a bit shakier now. I see, with growing dismay, that this guy isn't your garden- variety journalist out for a quick pic and a sound bite. He's one of a very specific, very tenacious breed known as a stalkerazzi. And that makes him more than a nuisance. It makes him dangerous.

He shrugs, as if reading my thoughts. "It hasn't been that hard, you know. I mean, all you do is go to class and work. No dates. No friends. Why is that, Katie? I'd have thought a pretty girl like you would have some hot trumpet player in your bed by now. And judging by the way you've been drooling over me for the last twenty minutes, I'm guessing it's been awhile since you've had *anyone* in your bed."

That's it, I'm done.

I reach for the handle of the door so I can get as far away from this guy and this car as fast as I can. But the handle doesn't budge. I poke at the button, but he must have some child safety feature so it can't be unlocked from this side.

"Open the door," I say flatly.

"Oh, now, Katie, don't be like that. You know your dad's bill is gaining momentum, right? He's in the spotlight now, and all signs point to a presidential run. I'm just wondering why you aren't a part of his campaign? Come to think of it, why aren't you a part of his *life*? I mean, his only daughter, and him being a widower and all. You're his only family. And yet, you're never anywhere to be seen. You refuse to give interviews. You're never quoted in the press. He doesn't mention you. Ever. Why is that, Katie?"

If he calls me Katie one more time, I'm going to wrap my hands around his neck until his eyes pop out onto the dashboard.

"Open. The. Door," I spit in the most menacing tone I can muster. But he just prattles on, hoping, I'm sure, that I'll give him something that he can use against my father. Against me.

"Near as I can tell, you haven't been home to Virginia in years. You spend the holidays by yourself up in that dumpy little apartment of yours. I mean, I don't know how you do it. What is it, like two hundred square feet? You've got a nice view of the mountains, but still. Put a little color on the walls or something, it's depressing as hell in there."

"You've been in my apartment?" I shriek, but he just keeps talking.

"What are you going to do when he comes here in a few weeks?"

Wait, wait, wait... What did he just say?

My surprise must be on my face because he starts to chuckle.

"Surprised by that, are you? He's part of the panel at a bipartisan town hall that the Poli-Sci department is sponsoring. Word is, he might even announce his intention to run for president."

I close my eyes and take a deep breath. It's time to put on my big girl panties and take back the power in this situation. I pull the phone out of my pocket and snap a picture of him.

"Hey!" he objects. "I didn't say you could do that."

He stops himself and breaks out the obnoxious grin again.

"Okay, okay, I'll give you that one, considering I've done the same thing to you about a thousand times."

The smile fades as he watches my expression darken. Like I said, I've never had a good poker face, so I'm quite sure he's getting the full effect as my emotions pass across my features. Shock, followed by indignation, finally settling on rage. And I must be telegraphing loud and clear because he pulls back a fraction of an inch.

"Listen up, you James Bond wannabe," I hiss. "You're going to let me out of this car and I will *never* see you anywhere near me again. Because, if I do, *Kevin,* I'll call the *Washington Post* and give them an exclusive, including how I was stalked by a rival paper. You don't think they'd just love to discredit you? To paint you as a lame little gossiping tabloid? And after the *Courier* has worked so hard to shake that image.

Your editor won't be happy. And what would that do for your reputation, *Kevin*?"

Something shifts in his features and it's arresting. A cool hardness settles in his eyes and his mouth turns up into a sardonic smile. And just like that, the nice hot guy is gone. This is who he really is, right here. And it's pretty damn scary. I work hard to keep the edge to my own glare. I know his type, and if he gets even a whiff of weakness, I'm toast.

"Oh, Kate, Kate, Katie, Kate," he taunts me in a singsong voice. "Do you really think you can scare me? You have no power and, it would appear, you can't even make use of your father's. So, why don't you just give me something I can use and I promise not to bother you again? For a little while, anyway." He chuckles.

I don't say another word; I just pick up my phone and press nine-one-one. He's looking at me quizzically, thinking I'm bluffing, I'm sure. I put it on speakerphone so he knows I'm not.

"Hello?" I say when the operator asks the nature of my emergency. "My name is Katherine Brenner and I'm being held in a car against my will. I'm on the campus of Shepherd University in a white BMW, Washington DC license plate LVJ 2214. It's parked in the Arts Complex lot in the far northeast corner. Please hurry."

Before I can hang up the phone, the locks click open and he reaches over to unbuckle my seat belt.

"How the hell did you know my plate number?" he asks incredulously. When I don't answer, he decides he's had enough of me. "You want out? Fine. Get out of my car, you bitch," he says, giving my shoulder a rough shove.

My turn to smile now.

"Never mind," I say into the phone. "I'm out. No need to send a car. I'll come by the station later today. I have a picture of the guy and I think I know where he works." I end the call and start to get out. He reaches for me again, but he stops short when I hold up a single finger and shake my head no. "Not unless you want an assault charge," I threaten.

"Oh, please." He sneers. "You won't do it. You won't even follow up with the police. We both know how much you hate the publicity. I mean you're already detested by your classmates and most of your professors. Isn't that right, *Katie?*"

I don't respond. Instead, I open the door and pull myself up and out, snatching the microphone as I go. It unravels in a trail of black wire that leads to a small recorder in the pocket of the passenger door. He lunges forward to grab it, but the seat belt holds him back as I scoop it up and stick it into my pocket.

"I'll be taking this with me," I say, slamming the door at the same instant that he erupts into a screaming tirade. I cross the parking lot at a jog, purposely dodging in and around other parked vehicles, just in case he gets any smart ideas about running me down. When I look over my shoulder again, he's still glaring at me and I can see his mouth moving. Now his window rolls down, and he's yelling something about freedom of the press. I flip him off and run into the building.

My heart feels like it's going to pound right out of my chest. Not because of the jackass I've just left outside, but because of the one who's waiting for me inside. And, God help me, I'm not wrong.

*Solo sneak-peek*<br>*Chapter Two*

DREW

It's easy to hate her. Much easier than liking her. I know it's wrong. I know *I'm* wrong. Katherine Brenner can't help that she's tall, with long, dark hair that falls around her shoulders in soft waves. It's not her fault that her blue eyes are specked with gold and that she has delicate, pale skin. Or that her lips are the color of fucking rose petals. I mean, what's not to hate?

Katherine Brenner is a dead ringer for the woman who absolutely obliterated my heart.

She doesn't think I know that she's there. After all this time, she's still under the mistaken belief that if she slips into the room quietly and takes a seat at the back, I won't even notice she's late. Oh, but I do notice, even with my back turned. I finish writing the details of the assignment on the whiteboard and turn around, my gaze scanning the back of the room until it lands on her.

"You're late, Miss Brenner," I say flatly. "Again."

A blush spreads across her face. "I'm sorry, Dr. Markham," she begins. "I was—"

"Miss Brenner, please spare us the excuses, you've already taken up enough class time."

She responds to my chilly tone by clamping her lips into a straight line and locking her jaw. She doesn't say a word. I cock an expectant eyebrow.

"Well? Don't you think you owe the rest of the students—the ones who bothered to get here on time—an apology as well?"

"I'm sorry," she mutters.

"How about you try that one more time?"

I can feel the resentment coming off her as she gets to her feet, her eyes never leaving mine. It's a dance we've done before.

"I'm sorry to have disrupted the class," she says to no one in particular.

"Fine. You may sit down," I say as I turn back to the board, confident my point has been made.

"Are you sure there isn't anyone else you'd like me to prostrate myself before?" she says just loud enough for me to hear.

There is a collective gasp across the classroom.

With a sigh, I come around to the front of my desk and lean up against it, arms folded, head tilted. Her classmates fidget around us, torn between leaning closer to get a good look, and pulling back to avoid the impending explosion.

"No, Miss Brenner," I reply at last. "I can't think of anyone right now, but I'll get back to you when I do. In the meantime, why don't you bring your things and have a seat right up here by me?" I nudge an empty desk in the first row with my foot.

Someone snickers and a few others join in hesitantly, testing the waters to see if I'll call them on it. I don't. Without further comment, she picks up her backpack and wiggles her way through the rows of desks to take the seat that I have indicated. Once she's seated and I have a good look at her, I notice immediately that she appears disheveled, as if she's been in a tussle. And pale. Is that blood on her temple? Christ. I'm tempted to ask her what the hell she's gone and done now, but I ignore the impulse, instead reaching for the box of tissues sitting behind me on my desk. I pull out a wad and hand them to her, leaning closer so no one will overhear us.

"You have something on your forehead," I murmur.

"Oh. Thank you," she says in barely a whisper, her cheeks coloring. I watch while she dabs at the cut. After a few seconds, she looks up again and I continue, just as softly.

"I'd like to speak to you when class is over." She gives me the slightest nod of her head.

I'm not supposed to dislike students. Or like them, for that matter. I'm just supposed to teach them to the best of my ability. Yeah. Right. Easier said than done. Temporarily satisfied, I stand up straight again and clap my hands together.

"All right, please pass your homework forward to my desk and let's talk about the midterm projects, shall we?" I brighten up and walk back around to the board on the far wall behind my desk. I write a date at the top in red then underline it for emphasis. "As you all know, they're due at the end of the week. And I've decided to cancel class on Friday so you can take the time for any last-minute preparations."

A soft murmur of excitement ripples across the classroom.

"You can have up until Friday to get your paper in. *But*," I say with emphasis, "I think you all know by now that I leave early on Friday afternoons. So, if you plan to take advantage of that extension and turn it in on Friday, you must deliver it to my home by five p.m. There is a cylinder attached to the bottom of my mailbox, where the newspaper goes. You can leave them there. Please do not put them inside my mailbox, that's against the law and I'd hate to have to sick the Postal Inspector on you."

A soft chuckle from around the room.

"Please don't ring my doorbell," I continue. "Please don't slide it under the door or give it to my neighbor or tie it to a brick and throw it through the window."

Some snickering and a couple of amused faces. Yeah, I know at least one or two of them who'd happily deliver their papers that way.

"I'm serious," I warn, scanning the room and making eye contact with as many of them as possible. "I'm going to walk out of my house on Friday at 5:01 p.m. and if your project isn't where it's supposed to be, then too bad for you. In fact, I *strongly* encourage you to get it in before Friday so you don't have to worry about that."

We spend the next half hour going over the details of the assignment until the clock strikes eight forty-five. I send them on their way. All, that is, except for Katherine Brenner. She's sitting silently, staring down at her hands and waiting for me to finish making notes at my desk. Her hair hangs down on either side of her head like a dark-brown veil.

Finally, I take my glasses off, rub the bridge of my nose, and sigh.

"Miss Brenner," I begin wearily, "you and I have a long history. And not a very good one. You don't have much time left before you graduate. That is, assuming you *do* graduate." She sits up straight, eyes widening.When I slip my glasses back on, I notice the nasty-looking gash on her forehead is bleeding again, a thin trail of sticky crimson wending its way from her hairline to down behind her ear. I hand her more tissues and she gets the idea.

"Ugh," she grunts in frustration.

"You might need a few stitches," I point out.

"Yeah, I know," she mutters in response.

"I want you to be crystal clear on this point," I say, poking the ink blotter on my desk with my index finger for effect. "I expect you to be on time every day between now and the end of the semester. No sneaking in after class has started. In fact, I want you in *that* seat for every class. Do you understand?"

"Yes, Dr. Markham, I understand," she says, keeping her voice soft and even.

I shuffle through the stack of papers on my desk—the assignment that they just turned in. When I come across the one with her name on it, I hand it to her. She looks perplexed. "I'm not accepting your homework assignment," I explain and her eyes widen in disbelief.

"But it's done," she protests, her calm exterior cracking all at once. "The assignment is *done*, Dr. Markham!"

I shrug unsympathetically. "Then you should have made sure it was in on time."

I watch her take a deep breath, close her eyes for an instant, and start again. "Dr. Markham," she grits, "I was three minutes late to class. You hadn't even *asked* for the assignment yet," she reminds me.

I shake my head.

"Miss Brenner, I'm done discussing this. You might as well take those papers and dump them in the trash can, because I won't even consider them at this point. So, I strongly suggest you turn in a spectacular midterm project to help make up for the grade."

I can see the wheels turning. She's furious. I'm sure she wants to tell me off, but she knows how close she is to failing my class. And if she wants to graduate on time, if she doesn't want to spend another year waiting to take this class again, she doesn't dare risk pissing me off any more than she already has. I'm surprised by what she *does* dare do, though. Katherine Brenner leans toward me and locks cold, blue eyes onto mine and, for one disconcerting instant, I feel like she can read my thoughts.

"Why do you have to be like this? What's the point?" she asks with more curiosity than animosity.

"What are you talking about?"

She shrugs.

"I'm a human being, you know? I have a complicated life outside of this classroom." She peers at me for a second before continuing. "What are you? Four, maybe five years older than me? You were in my shoes not so long ago and you know as well as I do that things happen, Dr. Markham. Things that are out of my control."

I feel a wave of irritation wash over me. I don't care how close in age we are. I don't like being lectured, especially not by one of my students. Especially not by this student.

"*Miss* Brenner, you are on extremely thin ice here," I tell her coolly. "I think you'd better go now before one of us says something we'll regret."

She gets up without another word, abandoning her assignment on her desk and walking out the door without so much as a glance back.